I0549611

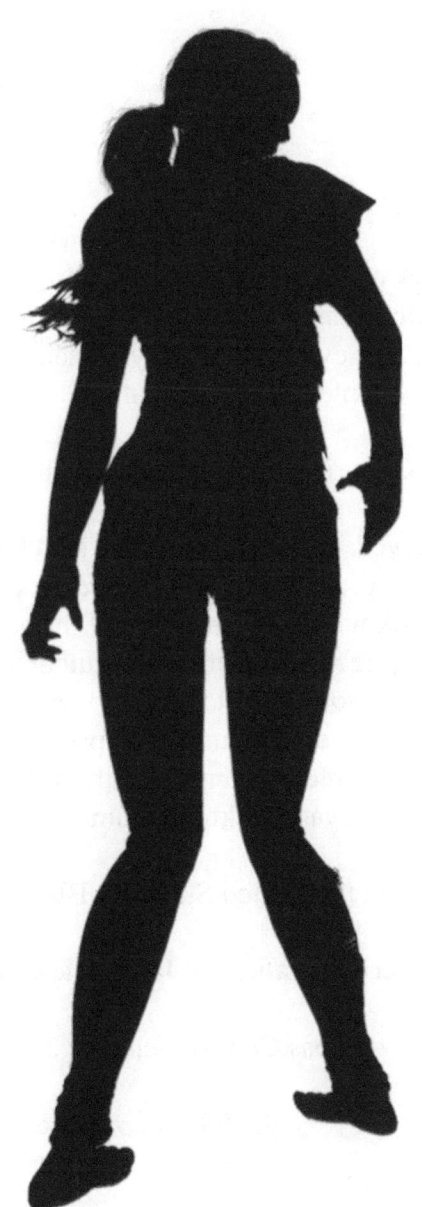

This is a work of fiction. Names, places, characters, and incidents are fictitious. Any resemblance to actual persons, living or dead, or events is entirely coincidental and not intended by the author.

Copyright © 2019 Aya Knight

All rights reserved. In accordance with the U.S. Copyright Act, the uploading, scanning, and electronic sharing of any part of this book without permission of the author constitutes unlawful piracy and theft of the author's intellectual property. If you would like to use any material from the book (other than for review purposes), prior written permission is required by contacting the author at: aya@ayaknight.com

Published in the United States by Black Forge.

Cover illustration by Jarek Madyda

Library of Congress Control Number:2019909356

ISBN 13: 978-1-938083-38-9 (paperback)

THE DAY I DIED

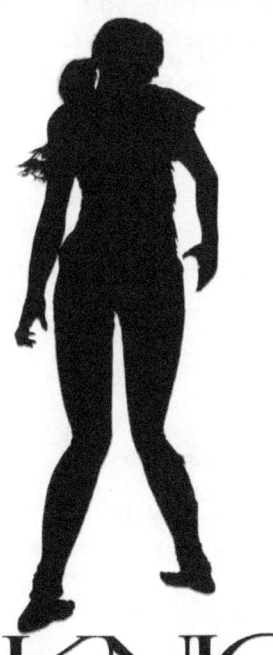

AYA KNIGHT

DEDICATION

To Ryu and Hiro; you inspire me every day. I'm so lucky to have both of you in my life. You are my world, and I love you so much.

To Mom; I wouldn't be where I am in life without you. You're my best friend, beautiful inside and out, and someone I genuinely admire. I'm so thankful to have you as my mom.

To Manon; thank you for your support over the years. You continue to encourage me to chase my dreams, and have contributed immensely with creative ideas.

PROLOGUE

It wasn't easy adapting to my flesh, rotting upon my face. The sun wrapped its fiery heat around me, radiating with an intensity that felt like a cremation chamber. I needed to seek refuge from its blistering rays. Despite the warmth that surrounded me, I didn't break a sweat. My body was changing into something monstrous. The hunger, the desire to feed; it grew harder to control. I was becoming one of *them*—one of the undead.

DAY 1
PART 1

The sirens filled my ears like a sharp needle that pierced my soul. I knew what it meant—someone within the city walls had become contaminated. It wasn't the first time, and wouldn't be the last. The guards would handle it as they always had; with an exploding bullet, filled with a concoction designed to target the nervous system. That one shot would shut down all bodily functions. It was a swift kill—a death *after* death, you could say.

We peeked out from the thick steel bars that covered the windows of my classroom. Dozens of men in black coats known as the 'dark guard regiment,' rushed across the courtyard. This time, there were more than usual. Then, we saw the white coats—scientists who worked to find a cure for the disease. Something was different on this occasion.

The room fell silent as curious eyes looked onward. Moments later, the dark guard regiment returned into view. They huddled around what appeared to be two people at the center. The glint of metal shackles shone in the sunlight. Multiple dark guards held their arms outstretched, creating a barricade. Through a gap between the regiment men, I noticed a long metal pole attached to chains. Though only for a few seconds, I glimpsed what was being guarded in the middle. There were two men, struggling—fighting to be free from their bindings. Thick chains wrapped around their wrists; their arms stretched behind their backs. They both had black sacks over their heads, their identities concealed. *Did I know either of them?*

One of the men jerked his body in a wild fit, the sack upon his head thrown to the ground. A gruesome sight revealed. I cringed and took a step back as a sea of whispers surrounded me. The man had his mouth pried open with a metal device that pulled at his cheeks. Though he stood many yards away, I could see the bloodshot redness in his eyes. Wide and frightened. Dark purple veins ran through his face, and his flesh was void of color. It looked as though he still retained emotion—even had a part of humanity left within.

My mind spiraled with questions. I didn't recognize this person; he wasn't from our city. But, how was this possible if everyone beyond our walls is infected? The undead. Those lost to disease and decay.

The dark guard regiment controlled the situation by sending a jolt of electricity through the metal pole. They concealed the two men with a wall of their bodies and pressed forward. Within seconds, they were out of sight.

I looked to my best friend, Sarah, who shook her head in confusion. Sarah had always been fascinated with the undead, and I knew she'd focus on every detail of the occurrence, trying to analyze what had taken place. My attention diverted to Codah, the most beautiful boy you could ever imagine. We had always been in the same class since young children. And yet, we'd never spoken more than a few words. I watched in silence as he hung an arm around Bethany's shoulders. She reigned supreme as the school's most popular student, and what one might call the meanest. I did, anyway. With her flawless blonde hair and ice-blue eyes, she was the envy of other girls and the quarry for most of the boys. But I was the exception. I never wanted to be someone like her. Beauty only runs so deep, and her rotten insides poured out like a river.

Then, it happened. Codah's emerald eyes met mine. My chest tightened. Heart raced. He smiled, and at that moment, I felt as though I could've taken on the world.

The sirens ceased, and our teacher, Ms. Garmona, called us back to our seats. A loud knock sounded at the door, and Ms. Garmona stepped out. We heard the mumbling of words from behind the steel door before she re-entered, her eyes shifting to avoid contact.

"False alarm," she said while clearing her throat. "Now, back to work, everyone. There will be a test next Friday."

The classroom broke into commotion as students shot off questions about what had just transpired. It seemed as though she was trying to make us pretend our eyes had just deceived us.

"Enough!" Ms. Garmona clapped her palms against the desk as she spoke. "They said it was a false alarm. Let's leave it at that."

I took another glance at Codah, staring at his perfect hair, clean and well-groomed; his perfect body, sculpted from the hours he worked at the butcher's shop. Just the sight of him gave me a sense of comfort in the situation. My breath stopped short in my lungs as he turned, looking back over his shoulder—at me. My stare shifted to my desk, hoping that he hadn't caught my actions. Uncomfortable moments drifted by as though an eternity passed. I let my eyes wander up. In that minute I thought my heart would burst right through my chest. His stare still held upon me in silence, his eyes reading my expression.

A sudden snicker broke my attention, and I found myself the focal point of Bethany and her groupies. She rolled her eyes in contempt before turning to face the teacher.

"It's all right," I heard Codah whisper to me.

I was too nervous to say anything, too intimidated by

his deep, alluring stare.

The loud chime of our school's bell tore into my thoughts. My classmates all rose, slinging their bags over a shoulder. The class ended, but I still felt Codah's lingering gaze.

DAY 1
PART 2

I laid in the grass, staring up into the vast blue sky while pondering thoughts from the day's event. Had my father been alive, I'd hear every detail over dinner. He was a white coat, dedicating his life to finding a cure for what had become of mankind outside of the city walls.

My mind trailed back in time, remembering the stories my father would tell me. He used to say the world wasn't always like this—that we hadn't always confined ourselves within the city walls. We lived in a world without the flesh-rotting undead. I laughed to myself at the thought. My entire existence had been here, in Nialus. The idea of ever leaving terrified me, being out there, with *them*. I saw one once before inside our walls, a young boy. His arm coated in blood so thick I couldn't see his flesh. I can still hear the shouts within my mind, *"He's been bitten!"* I was just a young child, but I'll never forget. The boy had no life left in him. But the worst was yet to come. His body convulsed in sharp, rapid motions. Men scurried to hold his limbs as the boy's eyes fluttered open. Oh, those damned eyes. They're what has burned this memory deep within the darkest corner of my mind, never to escape. The cloudy white glaze removed any trace of a soul as he turned his head, staring at me.

A shrill cry of anguish escaped the boy's dry lips, holding me frozen in place. The next minute of my life was a blur, and before I could comprehend what had happened, they removed me from the room and brought me to my father's office.

Now, as a fluffy white cloud drifted overhead, I couldn't help but smile at how it resembled a heart. My focus returned to the present, and I thought of Codah. A childish giggle rose from my belly as I pictured his alluring stare.

Could he actually be interested me? Nah. Not possible. There's no similarity between me and Bethany. I'd bet he noticed how frightened I was and felt a sense of compassion. It's pity, and nothing more.

A swift jab to my thigh caused me to sit upright, my arms held across my chest. Eyes locked on the girl standing to my right. She pushed her black-rimmed glasses with an index finger and stared down at me with widened blue eyes that revealed her excitement.

"Sarah, what's your problem?" I rubbed my tender thigh.

She stuck up a thumb and gestured to her right. In the shade against the school wall, Codah stood without his usual group of friends. His arms crossed, and he glimpsed in our direction.

Sarah's lips curled. "He's been watching you for a while now."

The air stopped short in my chest, and my jaw dropped.

Sarah stiffened and watched Codah from her peripheral vision. "Oh my god, he's walking this way." She fidgeted and moved a curly blonde lock of hair from her face before taking hold of my arm, helping me to my feet.

"This is your big moment." Sarah shoved my bag against my chest, "You've only waited half of your life for Codah to notice you. I'll meet you by the stairs when you're done. I expect every juicy detail!" She bit at her bottom lip and raised her shoulders. A light giggle rippled from her belly before she left.

I regretted not asking her to stay. How in the hell was I supposed to carry on a conversation with Codah? I couldn't even think straight when he came around, let alone speak.

Maybe he'd planned to meet with someone else. I spun around to see if there were others nearby. The small, grassy opening had no one in sight aside from the two of us. I hugged my bag and stood like an idiot waiting for him to approach.

Those emerald eyes were so piercing and confident. Codah ran a hand through his thick, wavy hair before flashing a toothy grin.

"Hey," he said in his usual calm demeanor.

"Hi?" I replied, awkward as ever.

"Look, I don't want to waste anyone's time here, but I saw you staring at me today. I know it's not the first time, but things were different before. I'll admit, I haven't really said much to you in the past, but Bethany can be jealous. Today, when things went down in class, you looked so calm, and I guess it just made the whole situation easier to get through. You're stronger than most people think."

Who is this guy talking about? I thought. The whole encounter was surreal. And, I'd been anything but brave. Wide-eyed and frozen stiff would be more accurate.

He paused as if waiting for a response. My introverted nature left me tongue-tied and unable to piece together a reply in time before he continued.

"Anyway, after school Bethany decided she didn't want to be with me anymore. She left me for that dumb ass jock, Jake. You know, the one who can't even spell his last name right?" Codah laughed at his remark. It was infectious, and I smiled.

"See? There it is. That look. You should smile more; you're cute when you do." His fingers met with a lock of hair that had fallen loose from my ponytail. He grazed my cheek and tucked it behind an ear.

"Thank you," I said before diverting eye contact.

"Oshin."

The sound of Codah saying my name sent a kaleidoscope of butterflies loose in my belly. I didn't even realize he knew it.

Codah continued, "I'd like to get to know you better. I get it's spontaneous and all, but I've been with Bethany for so many months that I haven't gotten to meet anybody else for a long while." He looked to each side before dropping his voice. "Even though Bethany isn't with me anymore, I have a feeling she'll still be jealous if she sees me getting close with anyone else. I don't want to cause you any trouble. This will sound crazy, but I have somewhere that we can meet up this Sunday to hang out without prying eyes or interruptions. After seeing how you handled today, I'm pretty sure you'll be okay with this, but, it's on the outside."

For a second, I think I stopped breathing altogether—*the outside*. Away from the safety of the city, beyond the wall with undead lurking, and breaking the most enforced law. I'd dreamed of this moment with Codah, but this was risking a lot. My life included.

He set a hand on my shoulder and stepped closer. "I get it, not the ideal meeting place for a first date. But I've

11

been there a lot. There's something incredible I'd like to show you. It's not as dangerous as you might think. I got this," he reached into a pocket and withdrew a small, folded square paper. "My dad might kick my ass a little if he finds out I went through his desk, but you know the old saying, *no guts no glory*." Another laugh.

I could only assume that what he wrote inside held importance. Paper was in short supply, used only by officials within the city. We composed the written word on an erasable board which we all carried in our bags. The white coats manufactured a special ink long before I was born.

"On Sunday, Marty, the guard will leave his post at three. When he does, you'll have a few minutes to plug the door code in and get out. We can meet at the big oak tree. You can't miss it; the thing is huge." Codah handed me the paper.

His hand lingered against mine as I retrieved it from his grip, his index finger rubbing mine.

"It's the code," he tipped his head in the paper's direction. He then leaned in and brought his face to mine, our cheeks touching and his mouth so close to my ear I felt his warm breath. "Tell no one about this. We can't risk anyone else knowing. It has to be just the two of us." Before he pulled back, his lips met my cheek—a soft kiss. "I hope to see you this Sunday. And don't worry, I promise to keep you safe."

My face must've been ten shades of red because I grew dizzy from the high. Codah, the boy I've longed for since I can remember, not only asked me on a date but also kissed me.

"Thank you," I said as I watched him walk away. My fingers trembled over the piece of paper.

Oh god, years of waiting for this moment and the only thing I could muster throughout the entire conversation was 'Thank you'—twice. Why am I such a loser? I'd need to channel my inner confidence before meeting him this weekend—if I met him. This opportunity was huge, but my fear of leaving Nialus left me torn. I'd process the situation more once I arrived home. I needed to get to Sarah. She always had a way of calming me down and distracting my attention.

"Hey lover girl," Sarah said with a mischievous grin as I approached. "Took you long enough. I hope you know that I expect the full report." She draped an arm over my shoulder as we began the path to our housing district. "So?"

"So, what?" I replied—an obvious and lame deflection.

"Did he tell you amazingly romantic things to win your heart?" she exaggerated her actions by curling a fist over her chest as if she were acting out a scripted play, "It is strange though, considering he's never acknowledged our presence before. You never know though! Curiosity's got the best of me."

I loved Sarah. She had been my best friend since I could remember, but she never knew when to close her mouth. The entire walk home had been filled with her one-sided conversation on what she thought the meeting was about. A heavy sigh of relief escaped my lips as we approached my door.

"I'll see you tomorrow," I said, gripping the doorknob.

"Wait . . . what?" Sarah furrowed her brows. "You're joking, right? I came all this way with you to hear what happened! Come on . . ."

I laughed. "You live right down the road and have to pass my house to get home—hardly out of your way." The piece of paper danced within my fingers as I cracked the door open. "Besides, this is something I need to sort out on my own first. I promise I'll tell you everything tomorrow."

"Fine," Sarah huffed in disappointment. "But, if for any reason it's bad and you need someone to talk to, I'm always here for you." She paused. "And if it's good and juicy, I'd better be the first one you tell!" She stuck her tongue out before leaving my porch.

With a final wave to one another, I slipped into my house. Mom was still at work in the greenhouse, so I had the place to myself.

Perfect. I smiled and raced up the narrow staircase to my room. Houses here were built tall, not wide, to help conserve space within the city.

I gripped the paper in my clammy palm and fell back upon the bed. My heart drummed within my chest. I wanted to meet with Codah, yet couldn't keep my worry suppressed. This date wasn't just a picnic in the park. We were putting ourselves in danger.

Sarah's words came back to mind, haunting me. *"But,*

if for any reason it's bad . . ."

What if it *is* bad? If things didn't turn out well on my first date, I wasn't sure if I could show my face again. I'd rather him never speak to me for the rest of our existence than have him tell me I wasn't worth his time. To say I was a fool would be an understatement. All the years I had snuck brief glimpses of him in school. I'd always assumed it had gone unnoticed . . .

I snickered at myself in distaste and pinched my eyes shut. My breathing slowed, and I exhaled. No longer being able to control my curiosity, I unfolded the edge of the paper. My anxiety soared as I read the five-digit code. The weight of the situation bore down on me. There it was, my way out.

DAY 1
PART 3

For the next passing hours, I re-read the code countless times. During dinner, my body was on auto-pilot, going through the motions, while my thoughts focused on what might happen the day after tomorrow.

Sunday. I thought to myself while flicking a pea with my knife. My emotions were in complete disarray, and my stomach fluttered at the thought of Codah wanting me. *Me*, out of all the other beautiful girls in school. And yet, a weight that sat in my gut at the idea of leaving our city. I'd never stepped foot past our perimeter—I'd never even seen what the world looked like out there. Civilians were forbidden. Beyond the massive cement wall was a foreign place. Maybe it wasn't as bad out there as they had led us to believe. Codah's father worked as one of the night-shift guards, so if anyone were to come and go as they pleased without getting caught, it'd be him. He'd have access to all the guard's schedules and security procedures.

I glanced down at the empty spot on the table. My mind was so absorbed with my conversation with Codah that I hadn't noticed my mom taking my plate.

"Get some rest, you seem exhausted," my mom said with a smile as she patted me on the head.

As I pushed visions of Codah out of my mind, I remembered that I hadn't questioned my mom about the earlier alarm. I turned around, but the moment had passed. She was already in the kitchen cleaning up. I headed to bed, making a mental note to ask her in the morning.

"Goodnight, Mom. I'll see you tomorrow," I called down from the stairs.

"Night honey. I love you," she answered.

Sometimes in life, there are those little feelings that tug at our soul—trying to give us a sign. I didn't understand why at the time, but I hesitated with my foot hovering over the next step.

"I love you too, Mom." Each word that left my mouth seemed weighted. An uneasy feeling tugged at me.

I shook my head, forcing my body to continue up the staircase and into my bedroom. After getting ready for bed,

I laid back, hugging my pillow as I gazed upward into the darkness. After all the years of being unnoticed, the thought of Codah wanting to spend time alone with me was still sinking in. It terrified me to picture sneaking out of the city. If caught, I could find myself in the worst trouble of my life. They might lock me up for violating the most important rule of our city. Or, even worse, they might think I'd become infected and bring me into quarantine for testing. And, the risk of *them*— the flesh-tearing undead—the diseased. I'd always imagined outside of our walls crowded with those hungered by the scent of our meaty bodies.

I recalled stories about when it all happened. The virus spread fast and with little warning. Different theories developed at the time; some thought it to be a government plan designed to reduce the population. Others claimed it originated from the military and somehow leaked. Then, there were those who had argued it was a natural phenomenon; something that had evolved and transmitted to people through fleas, birds, or rodents. It occurred long before my time, but the area we lived in was once called Arkansas. A vast world existed out there. After the global tragedy, Nialus had been created to ensure humanity survived. My dad once told me that the virus wasn't the only devastation. Parts of the East Coast had their share of horrors. Millions of people vanished without a trace. The virus showed symptoms around the same time, and we became isolated. I'd often wondered if we were all that remained. The thought of what could be beyond our walls frightened me. Codah said that he had left the city before. *Maybe, just maybe I've been wrong all along.* I considered new scenarios of what it might be like tomorrow. Fields of beautiful flowers, tranquil streams, things I'd only read about in books—the thoughts excited me.

I sighed with a smile, feeling encouraged about what Sunday would bring. Codah said he would keep us safe, and I trusted him. If only I'd known then about the awful events that were about to transpire.

DAY 2
PART 1

I rolled over and groaned from the lack of sleep I'd gotten. My legs rested on the arm of our red, tattered love seat. Just as I'd adjusted against a soft throw pillow, a light drumming on our front door startled me upright. I swung my feet to the floor and wavered as I stood.

"Coming Sarah," I called to the door.

The light hit my eyes like daggers. *Ugh*. I adjusted my shirt to cover my bare belly and stepped outside.

"Did you get attacked by the undead?" Sarah laughed at her cheesy attempt at a joke. "You look just like one of them."

"Nice, Sarah." I rolled my eyes and smoothed the stray hairs that hung from my ponytail. "Did you just get attacked by your grandma?" I added with a smirk.

Sarah punched me on the arm. Her calf-length floral dress looked anything but modern. She'd likely got it as a hand-me-down. Dresses in any color aside from brown or beige were rare. She wore it as though diamonds adorned her body. Slung over her shoulder was a knitted white bag; the one she always brought when we planned to shop in the marketplace.

"Let's get going before I'm left with wilted vegetables again. Mom will kill me if I don't bring home anything good. Pay isn't for another two weeks, and things have been slow at the seamstress'," Sarah said with a pessimistic tone in her voice.

"It'll be okay. Sheriff Banner is doing a speech on the summer relay event. Everyone will be busy gawking over anything he says," I replied as I took hold of an old basket on my porch step.

Sheriff Banner was the judge and jury of Nialus. What he said, went. People seemed to worship the guy; even the mayor agreed with just about everything he desired. I always thought he had a creepy vibe, with his dark eyes and slick mustache. There was just something that never felt right about him.

I hopped down my steps, my basket swinging at my side as we made way down the narrow road to the market. Sarah followed close in my wake as we passed the many tall houses on each side. Their narrow, looming structures gave temporary relief from the sun's blazing rays. Many of the homes we passed appeared on the verge of toppling over. Splintered wood and crumbling stone made up the normal sight you'd expect to see on this side of town. We were commoners, hardworking families that had just enough to get by.

"So?" Sarah broke the silence.

"So?" I replied in bewilderment.

"Did you think I'd just forget about your meeting with Codah?"

I sure hoped she had. She was my best friend, and I hated that I had to lie about it. But I couldn't risk her trying to stop me.

"It wasn't all I had hoped it to be," I forced a sigh as I spoke. "Codah asked if I'd be able to slip him extra tomatoes from the greenhouse next time I visit my mom. Hell, she doesn't even risk bringing extras home to us. There's no way I'll threaten our livelihood by snatching food for a guy who's never even noticed I'm alive. He hasn't said a word to me until he decided he needs something." I rolled my eyes, trying to lay it on thick enough to be believable. Guilt swelled within my stomach, but couldn't turn back now.

Sarah stared at me in silence for a moment, before clearing her throat. "I'm sorry that happened to you. He's not worth it. Really, he's not. There are plenty of other great guys out there. Forget the jerk." She slung an arm around my shoulder and smiled.

Despite her gesture, I still had an uneasy feeling she didn't believe my story. For now, I had to take my mind off of it all. I was already nervous enough about leaving the safety of my city. If I continued to dwell on the whole scenario, she'd pick up on my shift in emotion.

We turned a bend and passed what most of us called the crossover—an invisible dividing line that separated us from the well-off and wealthy. Before my father died, we weren't by any means poor. He earned a substantial pay from his work as a white-coat. But he raised me to live within my means. He had always taught me that just because you have money, doesn't mean you need to spend it on frivolous items and luxury. He showed me that we already had all we needed. We had each other. Who wanted to live near a bunch of snobs anyway? When he passed away, he donated all of his savings to the lab.

I sighed and glanced up at the houses I'd seen so many times before. Despite everything, they sure looked beautiful. Each one made of reddened stone; built much broader than ours. The wealthy were allotted more space than us. They even had solar paneling on their roofs—a luxury most would never experience in a lifetime. Hot baths and lights that could run through the night. In our district, we struggled with a mere 2 hours of electricity per twenty-four-hour period. We had to ration throughout the day for cooking. Or on the rare occasion, lighting for entertainment. Though my dad had spent most of his earnings on the upkeep of our shabby house, I wished that my mom would at least invest in heating for our water. The winters were rough, and those of us living in the gray district rarely bathed during colder months. It was awful being stuffed in a classroom for hours each day with over a dozen dirty teenagers.

"Heads up," Sarah jabbed my arm.

My eyes shot forward just in time to dodge the backside of a stout, older woman.

"You okay?" Sarah raised a brow.

"Yeah, sorry, just got lost in thought," I forced a laugh as the wide-bottomed woman bounced off ahead.

Sarah joined in on the laughter, lightening the mood.

We had arrived at the market, and a sea of bodies soon concealed the woman. We weaved through the crowd, making our way to the food stalls. The market only opened one day each week, which kept things busy. Everyone in the city flocked to the market to get wares and food supplies. If you missed your weekly visit, you'd be out of luck for another six days. This was one way our city rationed food. It ensured everything kept fresh, and nothing went to waste. It also allowed the mayor to keep close tabs on the flow of currency.

I inhaled, puffing my chest out as I took in the sweet smell of baked goods. My palate moistened, and my mouth filled with saliva at the thought of biting down into a soft pastry. There was nothing like treats on the first day they came out of the oven. I couldn't resist as we passed by a small, over-crowded stall. I pulled Sarah by the arm and moved to the back of the line.

As reluctant as she seemed, the line moved fast, and she was more than forgiving when I split one of my berry-filled pastries with her. I slipped the other five into my basket.

We continued past the knocking elbows, colliding arms, and sweaty bodies until arriving at the large vegetable stall. Meat and produce dominated the largest area of the market. A familiar face locked eyes with me; a broad smile formed across the woman's face.

"Hi honey," my mom chirped.

It was her week to manage the stall which she always looked forward to. For her, it provided a break from the humid heat of the greenhouse. As more of an introvert myself, I don't know which I'd prefer. The thought of having to converse with people for endless hours didn't seem appealing—then again, neither did tending to crops while blanketed by unbearable warmth.

She pulled me across the counter, into a tight embrace.

"Okay Mom," I laughed before retracting in embarrassment. "Love you too, but I'll see you at home tonight."

"Sure, sure," she reached down to grab a bunch of vegetables as she spoke, "we wouldn't want anyone to see how much of a Mommy's girl you really are." She stuck her tongue out.

You're killing me here, Mom. I swiped the produce from her hands and shoved them into my basket before tucking my head down to shoulders length in a weak attempt to hide from sight.

"And how are you today, Sarah?" Mom re-directed her attention.

They had exchanged brief conversation before the line piled up at our backs. Sarah wrapped up the visit by filling her bag with a variety of greens. By the time we were on our way to the meat stall, the street had become scarce with bodies. The sheriff had started his speech. Well, at least one good thing came out of it. We wouldn't have to endure the wait to get our beef shanks.

There was no delay in receiving our small shares. We handed over our coins and were about to leave when I saw

Codah out of the corner of my eye. He walked behind the stalls with blood-soaked overalls on. A large slab of meat dangled from over a shoulder. Despite the filth that covered his body, he was still more attractive than anyone I'd ever met. He had a masculine appeal. Before I caught myself staring, he looked at me. I froze, stopping the breath short within my chest. He flashed his perfect white teeth and winked. I looked behind to see if there might be someone else standing nearby. Nope. Only me and Sarah. I swallowed hard. He locked eyes with me for another few seconds—a few awkward seconds as I stood erect and still. Then, he turned, resuming his tasks. A grin crossed my face.

Sarah grunted, knocking me back into reality. I could tell by her tilted eyebrow she suspected something.

"Wow, it's hot as hell today," I tried to play as ignorant as possible. "Let's head out. Once Sheriff Banner's speech is over, hordes will flock back here. I don't want to smell like someone else's sweaty pits, like last time."

"*Hmm*," Sarah hummed aloud. "Sure."

DAY 2
PART 2

We started down our usual back alley path to avoid the crowds. Each step paced as we lugged our heavy haul. As much as I loved Sarah's company, I was eager to get back home and clear my head.

Am I really going to go through with meeting Codah? I pinched my eyes shut. *Yeah; yeah, I am.*

"You're doing it again," Sarah interrupted my thoughts.

"Doing what?" I replied, cursing myself for still not wanting to tell her the truth.

"Look, we grew up together. I can tell something is off with you. I'm just not buying the whole tomato story. Do you want to tell me what's g-" Sarah's words stopped short as I cupped a hand over her mouth.

Her eyes grew wide as her stare aligned with mine. I saw a white coat pushing a wheelbarrow. But it was the contents inside of the wheeled cart that made my stomach churn. A white sheet had fallen to the side. Limbs, a torso, a severed head, and a pile of intestines were exposed. *Human* remains.

Sarah trembled against me. She didn't fear the dead, but the white coats always left her restless.

What in the hell are they doing?

The white coat glanced in both directions before pushing the cart to a nearby door. He spoke into a radio, and within seconds, the door swung open.

We both released a long-winded breath of air as he disappeared.

"W-what was that?" Sarah spoke, her voice shaken.

"I don't know. It looked fresh." I rubbed a hand against my forehead in disbelief of what we just witnessed. "Do you think it has something to do with what we saw yesterday?"

"I'm not sure, but we need to get out of here. Now," Sarah replied as she moved faster toward the gray district.

The rest of the walk remained silent as we both processed what we'd seen. As we approached Sarah's door, she spun around to face me.

"I don't think we should say anything to anyone. It looked like whatever the white coats are doing, is meant to be kept in secret. Who knows what would happen to us, or our families if they knew we'd seen it," Sarah spoke with fear in her tone.

I nodded in agreement. Sarah was right. But I couldn't figure out how to erase the vision from my mind. Despite the horrible encounter, a part of me still wanted to know what was going on. I couldn't ask my mom. She had loose lips, and I didn't trust her not to gossip to the wrong person. She meant well; but her craving for companionship caused her to talk far too much. Sarah and I would have to bear the weight of what we'd discovered on our own.

To avoid the pressing desire to seek answers, I returned my focus upon Codah. After saying goodbye to Sarah, I hurried into the comforts of my home. *Home*, the one place that was reliable, the one place I felt secure—the one place I'd always have.

DAY 3
PART 1

T he sun's rays hit my eyelids, and I moaned before pulling the sheet over my face.

Wait a minute, I thought, *It's morning—Codah!*

I shot upright, hoping I hadn't slept too long. I rubbed my face, slapping my cheeks before throwing my legs over the edge of the bed.

The code! My eyes scanned across the bed. I remembered holding the paper within my grasp as I'd fallen asleep. I had to find it. It wasn't an option to leave any evidence of my plans with Codah. If Mom discovered what I was doing, she'd panic and run to the guards for help. They were the last people I wanted involved. My hands gripped the sheet and tore it back. A gust of breath shot from my mouth as I exhaled at the sight of the paper. It'd gotten stuffed beneath the corner of my pillow. I snatched it into a curled fist and rushed over to my bag, shoving it deep inside.

After rummaging through the few items in my closet, I selected a white, ruffled blouse and jean pants. I completed the outfit with a pair of silver flats that my mom had given me. Fashionable clothing was scarce, and most had inherited it from their family as a hand-me-down. Unless you had enough money to purchase decorative fabrics and hire a seamstress to custom tailor an outfit. I glanced down at my ensemble and straightened my blouse before turning to stare at my reflection in a cracked mirror. I pulled my hair back into a ponytail and flipped it over a shoulder. This was as good as it would get.

I slung my bag over a shoulder and hurried downstairs. My mom had already left, and I knew that it had to be at least eleven o'clock. I bolted to the nearby end table and yanked open the drawer. Inside was our only source of knowing the time—a silver wristwatch that had belonged to my father.

"I can't believe she didn't wake me!" I shouted to myself as I shoved the drawer shut.

One o'clock had crept up fast. I rarely slept so late on the weekend. *It figures, today of all days.*

My stomach growled. I'd need to spare a little time to eat if I would make it through the day. My belly twisted in knots. I made my way to the kitchen and placed a pan on the only working burner of our stove. Mom had promised for months to get someone out to fix it, but such was life when work demanded most of your time. I cracked open two eggs, watching as the whites slid from the shell, followed by a yolk that plopped down into the center. Within minutes, I carried my plate to the table. My palate grew moist with anticipation. I hadn't realized just how hungry I was. Not eating much the night before took its toll. The eggs moved down my throat faster than I chewed. I wiped my mouth, gulped down half a glass of water, and hustled for the door.

I stopped in my tracks while once again contemplating if I should back out—if I should stay home and enjoy the weekend *without* breaking a hundred rules. But I couldn't bring myself to turn away now. No matter how nervous I was, I wouldn't pass on what might be my only chance with Codah. When you have feelings for someone, it overrides your system. Rational thoughts fall void into oblivion.

With a nod of assurance, I turned the doorknob and stepped outside. A beautiful blue sky greeted me; fluffy white clouds scattered in the distance. The sun shined its vibrant warmth down upon my face. I smiled, feeling my first hint of confidence. I had a hunch it would be a day I would never forget. Little did I know just how right I was.

DAY 3
PART 2

I made my way through the city square. My eyes shifted, and fingers fidgeted, but I tried to remain as casual as possible when passing by familiar faces. People were enjoying the day mingling or playing in the large, tree-speckled area. I returned a few friendly waves before quickening my pace. I wasn't cut out for the rebellious life. My hands had become clammy, and I could tell I was acting suspicious. I ducked into the alley between the science and lab towers, making my way toward *the green*—an open, grassy area just before the massive concrete walls that surrounded our city. I paused, hugging against my last form of concealment: a storage unit.

If I didn't plan each step with caution, the guards would spot my presence, so I waited. A teenager roaming around the green would draw suspicion, and that was the last thing I needed. My strong point had never been lying.

What happened next was just as Codah had said. I watched as a guard named Marty left his post. There would only be seconds before the switch occurred and a new guard took his place. My heart hammered in my chest as I dashed forward. I cursed under my breath. My shoes, beautiful as they looked, had been an awful choice. They slid on and off of my heel with every step. The wall closed in fast, and I held my arms up to brace for impact. My body clapped against the concrete, sending a slight jolt to my wrists.

Without delay, I inched my way along the wall, searching for the door. A blinking yellow light caught my attention, and I hurried to investigate. To the far side of the green, I saw movement on the wall—the other guard approached, ready to take watch. My focus returned to the blinking light. Beneath it was a number pad, and I wasted no time in punching in the 5-digit code Codah had given me. A red light flashed, and the door emitted a buzzing sound.

Shh! I smacked the door in frustration before taking a deep breath and trying again. My finger quivered as I press each number. A solid green light appeared, and I heard a clicking sound. *Yes!* I shoved my weight against the door. It was much more substantial than I had expected, but I pushed it open and slipped through, still unnoticed by the guards. After closing the door, I spun around to find a chain-link fence, parallel to the concrete wall.

You have got to be kidding me. I let out a low growl before wedging the tip of my shoe into one of the links. I began to climb, my feet snagging with every tier higher I went. Codah hadn't mentioned this. I bit down on my bottom lip, shifted the weight of my bag, and climbed to the top. From my peripheral vision, I saw movement approaching from the concrete wall. The guard was on active watch, patrolling along the upper walkway. Without regard to the distance below, I leaped from the fence, landing with an audible *thud* in the grass. I winced in pain as the sensation of pins and needles spread through my ankles. I shook the discomfort and raced across the open area. Adrenaline coursed through my veins, distracting my mind from the reality that I was now on the outside with no protection of the city. Ahead, I saw a perimeter of trees. One, in particular, caught my attention: the giant oak.

My focus shot to each side, scanning the area for any sign of Codah. *Nothing.* I made it to the tree and aligned my body with the trunk, concealed from the guard's view. How I got to that point without drawing attention is still a mystery.

My chest heaved, and each heavy breath I took stung. For a moment, I closed my eyes to calm the anxiety that now set in. The reality of my surroundings had sunk in; I had made it outside of the city for the first time in my seventeen years of life. I looked around, staring deep into the depths of the forest. An unnatural silence settled in the area. There were no birds or other indication of life. A shiver rose through my body, and I wrapped my arms around myself in comfort. So many rules broken. Irreversible damage from my stupidity. I stood away from my sanctuary, in *their* territory—the undead. I became scared to move, scared to breathe.

"Codah?" I whispered, terrified of who or *what* might hear.

I mustered every ounce of bravery in my soul and shifted my feet to maneuver around the tree. The guard stood in position, with a gun slung over his shoulder. I tucked back, fearful of being seen. My thoughts raced. *What would be worse: staying out here any longer, or getting caught breaking one of the city's most prominent laws?* Either way, I'd gotten myself into a huge mess.

"Where are you Codah?" I whispered again in frustration.

I feared the worst. Codah might've gotten caught by the guards—or the undead.

The faint sound of laughter stole my attention. My fingers gripped onto the bark of the tree as I once more shifted to investigate.

The sight I saw stole my breath. I felt as though

someone had planted explosives around my heart and set them all off at once, leaving ashy remains and shattered fragments. There, behind the safety of the city's chain-link fence, with an arrogant smirk etched on his face—was Codah.

DAY 3

PART 3

Tears welled in my eyes, vision blurred. Though not enough to conceal the sight of Bethany sliding her arms around Codah's waist. They stood next to three others I recognized from school.

My joints locked as I saw one of the girl's point in my direction. I rubbed an arm across my eyes and watched as Bethany curled her fingers around the chain-link fence, staring out at where I stood. My worst nightmares became a reality. To say I felt mortified would be an understatement. There was never going to be a date. They'd planned it all as one big joke, and *I* was at the center of it.

My anxiety swelled, thoughts raced through my mind. *Maybe this could still be some misunderstanding. Bethany and her flock of groupies might've caught Codah off guard as he was coming to see me.*

My hopes shattered right before my eyes as I saw Bethany's cold stare. Her gaze was sharp and very much intentional. Even at a distance, it pierced into me. Her lips curled to form a callous smile as she reached over to take Codah's hand. My breath stopped short as I watched him turn to face me. The boy who said he would protect me—the boy who I, for a moment in time, thought might share my feelings.

I could no longer contain my emotions; the pain felt alive within me, gnawing at my heart.

"Why?" I whispered and fell to a knee.

Codah continued to stare at me as if I were an exciting attraction for his amusement. Then, Bethany pulled her body closer against his. With a final shrug, he turned to face her. His hand met the back of her head as they embraced one another, leaning into a passionate kiss. It was all a cruel joke. No; *I* was the joke. They wanted to see if the class loser would risk her life for no more than a promise. I'd taken the bait. How did I not know better? Over ten years of being ignored, and then he talks to me. The signs were all there, but I'd been too damned stupid, too wishful to see what was between the lines.

I broke. Heavy sobbing caused me to clutch my gut as I folded over. Each breath harder than the next. My other hand cupped over my eyes as tears streamed down my cheeks. I was embarrassed, filled with complete sorrow, and *alone*. I couldn't fathom how, or why, anyone would be so cruel when I'd done nothing to them. My stomach churned. I tried my best to stifle the noise as I cried, but the emotional pain continued to spill out.

A shrill cry startled me, and I removed a tear-soaked hand to see Bethany's friends huddled together. They stared right at me. I wiped a finger beneath my nose and sniffled before tilting my head in confusion. The tallest girl in the group staggered back before sprinting away. Her two companions followed, and I watched as Bethany threw her arms up in frustration.

My eyes shot up to see the guard leaving his post to investigate the commotion caused by Bethany and her gang.

What's happening? Why did her friends look at me like that? I'd been the subject of their cruel joke, but something seemed wrong. There was no breeze, and yet a chill ran through me.

A sudden *snap* from behind me broke the forest's silence. I twisted my body around. Nothing. Then, I heard the moan—the anguished cry of hunger that could only come from the undead. My eyes widened in horror as I saw a woman appear from behind the trees. Her hair hung in matted clumps against her sunken, decaying face. The flesh of her jaw was torn, revealing yellowed teeth. Her blood-stained clothing swayed in motion with each slow step she took.

I shuffled back to distance myself. My chest tightened and sweat began to bead across my forehead. My breath became short and fast. Though my legs tingled with numbness and shook unsteady, I mustered the ability to stand. As I turned to run, I felt a hard grip tug at my blouse. I yelled aloud as an older male now faced me. His skin looked leathery and clung to his skull like latex. He clawed at me, swiping his thin fingers down. I fought to push his arms away, but his strength was surprising. He snapped his teeth together, like a starving wolf that had just come across a plump rabbit. His breath smelled of rot and made my reflexes gag. I heard the undead woman from behind, closing ground on where I stood.

In a desperate attempt for help, I looked toward Codah and Bethany. I knew that being reckless and running toward the fence would result in getting shot down by the guard. No one would think I was a civilian who had just escaped past the walls without notice. The guards didn't take chances when it came to protecting the city. If you weren't within its walls— you became target practice. Civilians didn't meet criteria for clearance to leave. That was something reserved exclusively for white coats and higher authority.

My eyes widened as I looked toward the two who had betrayed me—the two who had gotten me into this mess.

They were now my only hope for rescue.

"Please. Please help me!" I yelled as loud as I could while continuing to fight against the undead male who closed the space between us.

Bethany looked at me, and for a moment, I thought she showed an ounce of guilt in her blackened heart. Wrong as always. She took Codah by the hand and pulled him away from the fence. They had only one desire, and that was to save themselves from being caught.

A wave of anger rose in my sorrow-filled heart. The brief distraction had caused me to lose my footing, and the undead male pushed his weight into me. I tumbled back, landing hard against the leaf-coated ground. Before I could move, the undead man threw his body on top of mine. I pressed my hands up against his torso, using every remaining bit of my strength to push him to the side. Despite my efforts, he gripped onto me, pulling himself closer to my face. His jaws snapped as he attempted to bite down on my flesh. Tears streamed down my face. Bethany and Codah wouldn't help. It was time to fight for my life.

A deep male voice shouted and I knew that the guard had located Bethany and Codah. My chances for rescue were virtually gone, I had to do something, and fast. At that point, I'd rather have taken a bullet over being eaten alive.

My muscles burned as I pushed against the undead

man. I rolled myself out of his reach and scurried to my feet. A painful sensation spiked at my ankle, and it hurt to bend. I extended an arm and took a step forward just as Bethany and Codah ran through a small door off to the side. The guard approached seconds later, calling out for them to "halt," but the door had already shut. They were likely somewhere hidden by now, free from punishment for their actions.

"Help!" I cried out through the tears and pain.

I kept my eye on the undead man as he struggled to his feet, and took another uncomfortable step forward. My hands waved in the air to draw attention. I hoped that by not running at him, he would see me as the victim I was, and not a mindless corpse in need of a lethal treatment to the brain.

"Please, help me! I'm from the cit—" my words cut short, and I let out a loud gasp.

With my mouth hung wide, and eyes full of fear, my body fell backwards. The undead woman's arms wrapped tight around my neck, causing me to lose any sense of balance. Everything happened so fast, and I'd let my guard down. I watched as the guard turned toward my screams—but it was too late.

She stepped back, and I lost the ground beneath my feet as if I were a puppet at her command. I threw my arms up, swinging them to keep her back. I had to be fast; she repeated attempts to grip hold of my arm. Her mouth fell open, the joint of her jaw at its limit, masseter muscle stretched tight. She was ready to feast.

Why didn't I bring a weapon? I cursed at myself while fighting to break free. *Because I'm an idiot who let loneliness cloud her judgment, that's why.*

To my side, I saw a rock. It looked small enough to lift with a single hand, yet adequate to use against the two undead. My attention shifted, and I saw the undead man dragging his body along the ground. He had given up on his attempt to stand and closed in on me. I continued to shove against the woman with one hand while using the other to reach out for the rock. She had positioned her body on top of mine, and her weight was becoming too much to bear. I needed to make my move.

With an outstretched arm, I extended my fingers and reached for the rock. My fingertips grazed the hard surface, and I cursed out loud. I stretched my arm even farther, leaving it exposed.

"Come on!" I shouted with determination.

I worked my fingers until the rock rolled close enough. My hand clenched down, and without hesitation, I slammed my blunt weapon into the woman's head. It sunk into her flesh, causing her to slump to the side. I rolled over, preparing to strike again before she recovered. As I got to my knees, with my rock-filled hand raised towards the heavens,

I felt it—the tearing of flesh. I turned, dread swelling within my mind. I knew at that moment what had just happened. Emotions exploded. Anger, sorrow, frustration—it all boiled together in an animalistic, violent burst.

The undead man dug into my calf, gnawing his teeth deeper into the muscle. His dry, flaky lips cupped the wound. I cried out in rage as I bashed my rock into his head. His skull caved at the side, and blood sprayed across my face. I was relentless.

A sharp tug pulled me backwards, another set of teeth biting down on my shoulder.

Today was supposed to be the best day of my life. Not my last.

I tried to pull away from the undead woman, but with every tug of my body, her teeth pinched down harder. The pain grew overwhelming.

To my side, I saw two more undead—a young girl who looked to be about seven in age, and a young man. He appeared to be in his late teens. They approached fast. I began to lose my vision as the pain intensified. I could no longer fight, only lay in silence as my body was being eaten alive. The two new undead closed in, the boy's cloudy green eyes locked with mine. That's all I remember before everything went black.

This was the day I died.

DAY 4
PART 1

I heard the pestering hum of flies nearby and laid in silence. My eyelids pressed shut while I took in a deep breath of air.

Am I alive? I wasn't sure I'd want to know the truth.

My body felt strange; numb. I wanted to open my eyes but feared what I might see. I thought about the last things I remembered before blacking out—being eaten alive.

What if I open my eyes and am half-eaten, with only minutes left to live? I struggled to move my body. *No, my arms and legs are still attached.* I gasped. *This must be the afterlife! Oh God, I've passed away. Mom. Sarah.* I wanted to cry, yet no matter how much sadness I'd built up, tears would not fall.

Something lifted my hand, followed by the sudden shuffle of feet. I wasn't alone. My eyes shot open out of instinct, and what I saw before me was unimaginable. At my side, stood the young undead girl I had seen before. She looked down at me, cupping my hand in hers. Dirt and the tinge of blood matted her shoulder-length blonde hair. Her white nightdress looked as though she'd rolled through the mud, and I'm sure it would have smelled terrible, but I had no sense of smell. Across her cheek, a long tear in the flesh ran from the bottom of her eye to her jawline. Coagulated blood appeared to have sealed it from further bleeding. Her skin lacked color, with hints of yellow and purple welts along her arms.

I opened my mouth to yell, but the only sound to escape was a deep moan.

What in the hell was that? I thought to myself. My chest tightened.

I mustered the strength to roll my body in an attempt to distance myself from the girl. I reached the edge of the table and tried to lift my legs to slide down. My limbs wouldn't cooperate. They felt more like heavy bags of sand. The young girl reached her bony fingers in my direction, leaning forward. Without regard to the consequences, I let my body slide down from the table. I hit the floor with a *thud*. Despite my head colliding with the tiles, I didn't feel any pain.

Come on legs!

I strained my lower body, but my limbs barely shifted. All I could do was rock my torso enough to roll again. I felt like a helpless fish out of the water. I looked to the girl's feet, which I saw shuffling in my direction.

She moaned—but not like the undead I'd heard before. It seemed as though she was trying to express herself; trying to communicate. Then, movement sounded from the other room. The undead boy I'd seen before appeared, moving much faster than the young girl.

He looked down at the sight of me, and I watched as he hurried to my side. I tried to yell—to tell him to stay back—but all that came out were indistinguishable sounds. He touched my arm and brought his face down to mine. His hazy, green eyes appeared brighter than I had remembered, contrasting against his brown hair. Though his skin looked discolored, for a moment I almost forgot that he wasn't a living human. He drew closer. The sight of crusted blood at the corners of his lips reminded me he was one of the diseased—a flesh eater.

I needed to get away. Once more, I focused all of my strength, struggling to lift my arm. If I reached the edge of the table, I'd be able to pull myself up.

Why hasn't he bitten me? I wondered. My arm moved at my command for the first time since I'd woken. *Yes!*

I found it odd that the undead duo hadn't attacked me. They only stared in silence. *I can't take any chances. I need to get out of here.*

With an excessive amount of strain and grunting, I lifted my arm. My fingers cupped the edge of the table as I drug myself to my feet. For the first time since I'd awoken, I noticed my surroundings. We were in the kitchen of a house. Shards of glass scattered the counter beneath a broken window above the sink. Sheer, floral curtains danced in the light breeze.

The young man extended an arm, taking a step forward.

Run! I told myself as I turned toward the doorframe.

With a hard clap, my body fell forward against the tile. The boy threw his arms up into the air, releasing a low growl. I watched as the girl shuffled to his side, placing her hand on his arm while shaking her head in disapproval.

He grunted and released a winded sigh, before nodding. His eyes widened, and he turned to the other side of the room. I continued to lay, stricken with fear of what was happening. Seconds later, my bag dropped inches from my side. He dug his hands in, rummaging through my belongings. It didn't matter that he was undead, I still felt violated. Personal items filled my bag—things I didn't want a stranger to see.

Then again, why should I have even cared? I was

already preparing for my demise. The boy snarled, growing frustrated as he shoved the items around. He gripped the base my bag and tipped it upside down. Contents spilled onto the floor. My mind raced in wonder, unsure of what purpose a mindless undead would have with my bag. I had no meat in there; there wasn't anything for his savage feasting.

Then, he did the unexpected. The young man picked up my writing board and scribbled something down. He flipped it over to reveal the words: **We won't hurt you**.

My eyes shot back and forth across the two undead. The young man's expression softened as he pulled the board back to him, using the bottom of his black shirt to wipe it clean. He once again wrote.

I looked forward in horror as he flipped the board over.

You don't need to run. You're already one of us.

DAY 4

PART 2

I laid motionless for a few minutes. Or, it could have been hours. Time seemed to stand still as I stared at the ceiling. Spiders clung to every corner and crevice, spending their day in hopes of prey wandering into their trap. I had trouble accepting the fact that I was now much like them—clinging to this world, unable to move on, and hungry for prey.

The undead boy continued to write: **You'll be able to move soon. This is part of the process. It happened to both of us.**

Us. I snickered to myself in disgust. *He makes it seem as though there's nothing wrong with this situation. Oh, something is wrong all right. I've entered Hell on earth.*

After wiping the ink from my board with the bottom of his shirt, he continued. **My name is Bastion**. He then pointed toward the young girl. **She's Lace. Ridiculous name, I know.**

Short bursts of air escaped his lips, and I could only assume that it was laughter.

Did he just show emotion? Impossible. He's a flesh-eater.

As he wiped the board clean, the pen slipped from his fingers, rolling next to my hand. Out of instinct, I went to pick it up. My trembling fingers rose, then curled around the pen. Bastion grunted as he noticed my movement, then swiped the pen from my grasp. He wrote faster than before, as though agitated. To my dismay, the board flipped to reveal words that left my heart twisted.

Once you can walk, you're on your own. Leave this house.

Although I had only just met Bastion and Lace, I grew comfortable with the notion that they had no intention of eating me alive; if I could even call myself that anymore. *Alive.* My chest heaved as I laughed to myself. My sudden, bizarre behavior caused Bastion to cast a look of confusion at Lace. I couldn't help myself; the irony of everything until this point in my life seemed comical in the worst kind of way.

Not so long ago, I was a warm-blooded, witty teenager who used to self-proclaim that death was better than having to go to school. Now, I'd become a cold, decaying monstrosity who longed to hear the chime of the class bell; or to feel the rough wood of my desk beneath my palms. But here I lay with two of the undead at my side—the very diseased beings I'd been raised to avoid. And they were telling *me* to leave. It just goes to show that there is always a chance in life for the unthinkable to happen.

After my reaction of bitter amusement had worn off, fear settled in. Were all the undead like Bastion and Lace? Impossible. The first two undead I'd encountered tried to have a banquet, with my flesh as the main course. But, could there be others out there who still held onto human emotion? I didn't want to be alone in this new and foreign territory.

As I laid there in self-pity, Lace lowered herself to her knees. She winced in discomfort as she reached the floor. Her eyes met mine, and for a moment, it seemed as though we were peering right into one another's soul. I could tell she was the very essence of innocence in a corrupted world. Her arm reached out, and she began to stroke my hair. The gentle touch of her little hand soothed me.

Bastion glared toward Lace in disapproval. He reached out and took hold of her wrist. He shook his head and pointed toward the far wall.

She huffed and crossed her arms before shuffling her

way to the other side of the room.

I looked to Lace, and then to Bastion. Frustration got the best of me. Never had I felt so much like an unwanted disease—like a *thing* no one, not even the undead, wanted to be near. I mustered my strength and sat upright, snatching the writing board. I pulled it over my lap and grunted aloud. Pain seared in my muscles; something I hadn't expected. With a flick of my wrist, I wrote a single word: **Why?**

Bastion sighed and grabbed the board back into his possession. **Too dangerous. You don't understand what's out there and that puts a huge risk on my sister's safety. I made a promise to her. One I can't let you screw up for us**.

He ran a hand through his dirty brown hair before dropping the board onto the table and walking away.

I brought myself to my feet and examined the room, while still trying to make sense of everything. *How am I a threat to their safety? Ugh.* My eyes scanned the countertops, which had layers of mud, dust, and mold. Traces of blood led to the sink. Flies buzzed like a swarm of vultures.

Lace continued to observe me, watching my every move. Her actions made me uneasy; as though I were a rare specimen under surveillance. I smiled at her. Or at least, I think I did. The muscles around my lips felt stiff and painful to move. Lace's shoulder's relaxed, and she returned the gesture by barring her teeth in a manner that looked ridiculous. I assumed that mine had been just as bad. I huffed air through my dry throat, laughing at the whole scenario. Never could I have imagined finding someone covered in dirt, with decaying flesh so damned adorable.

The warm and fuzzy moment crumbled away as Bastion entered the room. A slab of something pink and coated in blood hung from within his grasp. He approached me, stopping at the tips of my shoes. With his chest inches from mine, I froze in place. Other than Codah, I'd never had a guy so close before. Let alone one who wasn't even alive. Bastion glanced down into my eyes without a sound.

For a moment, I thought he might reconsider his decision to send me off into the wilderness alone. This assumption got a swift dose of rejection as he forced something moist into my hand. I looked down and saw bloody meat between my fingers. For the first time since waking, I could smell. And though it looked revolting, the scent was sweeter than anything I'd ever experienced in my life.

DAY 4
PART 3

Bastion backed away and gestured toward the bloody mess I now held.

Does he expect me to eat this? It looked like an animal, but not one I'd ever seen before. Its skin had been peeled back, exposing its meaty body. The areas still covered in fur had dirt embedded. Entrails dangled on its hind legs.

The dead creature's eyes were still wide open, staring up at me as I held it by its broken neck. I felt a sense of sympathy. Despite my intense hunger, I extended an arm and passed the meat back to Bastion.

He swiped it with a growl and motioned to Lace.

I watched in horror as the young girl I had found to be so gentle dug her fingers into the belly of the carcass without hesitation. She then buried her teeth into the skin and feasted. Lace's head jerked back as she tugged at the intestines.

Bastion dropped my writing board onto the table. My attention pulled away from the bloodbath that covered Lace's face. I glanced down to see the words: **You'll regret not eating. Go now, before dark. And hide.**

DAY 4
PART 4

Angry and confused, I stuffed my belongings into my bag and made way for the door. I paused a moment, glancing back over a shoulder at the two. Still feasting, Lace hadn't noticed my near-departure. Bastion, however, watched my every step. Though his face bore no expression, I saw in his eyes he held a sense of guilt. I stopped in place, looking up into his eyes. I'd hoped he would've changed his mind. The thought of being all alone weighed heavier with each passing second.

Bastion shook his head, breaking our stare. He then exhaled and left from sight. I was on my own.

I pulled the door open and raised a hand to shield the sunlight. My vision had changed, along with my usual response to direct light. I didn't squint as the sun's rays streamed down upon my face, nor did I furrow a brow. It was easy to glance up at the sky, and my eyes seemed unaffected by any alteration of light. I took my first step forward and inspected the area. Every direction looked the same. There were scattered trees and thickets of vines for as far as I could see.

Behind me, the door shut and locked with a click. *Strange*, I thought while wondering why the undead would be concerned with such a formality.

With a heavy sigh, I walked forward. It felt disheartening to have no place to go or any destination. I wandered without cause. So, this was the life of an undead. It sucked. After only a brief time, my body grew weak. Though the canopy of lush pine sheltered the ground from the sun's rays, my skin reacted to the sweltering heat that blanketed the forest. Despite the hot temperature, I never broke a sweat. My flesh had a rough texture; I'd begun to change. This world was mine now—my curse.

I remembered stories that my dad would tell me of a world once filled with beauty. He described the flowers, glistening streams, and green fields. It all seemed like a fable now. The sea of trees appeared to go on forever. I couldn't believe that there was anything else out here. My legs ached, and flies swarmed around my head. I wanted to go home, to wake up and find this all to be a terrible nightmare.

A single moan broke the silence, and I froze in place. I listened. Pine-needles cracked beneath heavy steps. It was heading in my direction. It drew closer—louder. I turned to the right. What I saw sent sheer terror throughout my body. My joints locked, and I found myself unable to move.

Close to where I stood, was not one, but over a dozen undead. They plodded along as though stuck in time. Some appeared to be young adults, while a few at the rear looked elderly. A man, whose arms were missing, led the pack. Shreds of tattered, blackened skin hung from near his shoulders. His left leg drug against the ground, the ankle bent and swollen.

The pack leader approached my side. My thoughts raced. *I'm one of them, so they won't harm me. Right? If I try to run, will it cause them to attack? Maybe I should just continue to stand still.* I chose the latter of the options because I couldn't bring myself to move.

I peered from the corners of my eyes at the armless man. His face moved close to mine, and the pack came to a stop. They were silent—and staring at me.

DAY 4

PART 5

He brought his nose to my cheek and pressed his face into my skin. I felt the leathery graze of his half-sunken cheeks, and gusts of air that escaped from his decayed nostrils. He took in my scent, determining if I was fresh enough to devour. I curled my fingers so tight that the skin on my knuckles hugged every curve of my bone. I prepared to attack, prepared to fight for my life. Or what was left of it anyway. As much as I wanted to run, the distance between us was too short to risk it. With one clamp of his jaw, his teeth would sink deep into my neck. Before I decided how to proceed, the man pulled away. He stepped around me, his eyes fixated on the distance ahead as he continued on his path as though our encounter had never occurred. The group of undead followed, bumping against me as they passed, though never acknowledging my presence again.

What in the hell was that? I exhaled in relief.

All my life, this dark world existed beyond my city, my sanctuary. I missed its simple comforts more than ever.

I continued, wandering farther into the unknown. The forest darkened as the sun crept toward the horizon. My once beautiful surroundings were now eerie and unwelcoming— black in all directions with small gaps through the branches that allowed the glow from starlight. Although I was one of them now, the undead still scared the crap out of me. Sharp pain in my stomach and lingering aches in my legs told me I needed to rest. I found concealment between the trunk of a tree and a thick bush. Although the other undead didn't seem to have much concern for me now, the thought of running into more paralyzed me with fear. There was something about the night that added another layer of terror. My knees tucked against my chest, and I sat in silence. My body felt defeated; exhausted. No matter how hard I tried, I couldn't fall asleep. It was as though something deep within my brain forced me to stay alert; to suffer from the pain of death. The stabbing hunger intensified with each slow-passing minute.

I need food. I need to eat. The thoughts dominated my mind.

As the night carried on, I appreciated the periodic sounds of leaves and pine-needles crunching beneath the feet of other undead as they passed. Though I dared not leave my place of hiding, and still couldn't stand the thought of facing them again, the sound distracted me from my ever-growing desire to feed. A sad realization carried through my thoughts. *The undead seem to have no purpose. They roam the land, hungry and dying.* Fear of the future began to set in. *I'm going to watch my body rot away until there is nothing left of me to move. I'll be alone. Will my mind still realize what's happening? Or will I become crazed and lose who I am?* I almost longed for the latter option. I didn't want to comprehend what happened in the end. It would be a slow, suffering torture until the maggots or vultures came to eat away everything I was.

I hugged my legs. The loneliness of the forest made my heart ache. I sobbed, but no tears fell from my eyes. I'd become a monster, an outcast from the life I'd known. All because of a damned crush. I was such a fool.

Enough is enough. I shook my head to cleanse my mind from all the depressing thoughts. *I'll figure something out tomorrow. It's a new day, and I'm not dead yet.* I plucked at leaves to pass the time.

A flicker of light pierced through the darkness. It came without warning, too close for comfort. It stood out against the night like a beacon, calling me towards it. I peeked out from behind the bush to see a torch waving in the near distance. The torchlight shifted, and I heard the savage growl of an undead. A loud cracking filled my ears before a voice called out: "I've got another!"

I scurried backward, unsure of what to do. My nose picked up on the scent. Fresh meat. *A human—a living human.* I wanted to make contact, to let them know I wouldn't harm them. But how? After what had happened with Codah, I wasn't about to dive into anything without taking time to assess the situation.

I crept out on hand and knee before forcing myself to stand. The pain in my muscles was incredible. My legs were stiff, and each step burned like fire in my joints. I kept my distance and followed the swaying light. A moth to its lure. The shape of a man came into view, his scent strengthened, despite our distance. I smelled the odor of his body, and the blood that rushed through his veins. My hand clamped against my stomach and shook my head. As I continued to creep in his wake, I heard him speaking to himself. He muttered curses and something about saving the earth by ridding it of all the diseased. I stifled a gasp as the torch shed light on the dark mass that drug along the ground within his grasp. It was a body. A shiver ran down my spine, but curiosity kept me moving forward. The man stood tall, with long, tangled dark hair. His overall pants hung from his thin frame. It surprised me to discover that humans were thriving out in the undead's territory. I had always assumed the people of Nialus to be all that's left of humanity. *If this man is out here, alive, then there must be others.* A sense of longing crept over me, and I wished I was like him; alive. Not the creature I had become.

As we weaved around a thicket of trees, a bonfire came into view. Each flicker of flame reached high into the night sky as if trying to escape this cursed place. Another man approached the fire. My stare shifted from the men to the protective barrier around the camp. Branches, shaved into pointed spears protruded in a circle that enclosed where the men stood. Only a narrow path between the spears allowed entry. I ignored the pain in my body and crept closer to watch the men better.

"You finally back?" the second man with a much deeper voice asked.

"What's it look like?" The long-haired man let the body drop at his feet. "Got another. He was wanderin' around. The bastard got too close to camp. Looks like the same one we saw a few nights ago." He pulled a small pocket knife out and knelt at the undead's side. "Maybe we should put this thing out," he gestured to the fire as he spoke. "Seems to be attractin' more of 'em near camp."

The second man stood like a tank at his side. Broad shouldered, brawny, and bald. He rubbed a hand across his smooth head, down to the scruff on his chin. "You know damn well we can't let the fire go out at night. The ravangers will eat us down to the bone before sunrise. Use your brain, idiot." He slapped the long-haired man on the back of the head. "That fire is the only thing keeping them out."

Ravangers? I thought. Does he mean the undead? *No, the long-haired man said the fire attracts us.* I remembered how the light of the fire pulled me in. The flame had some alluring hold on me, and I found myself drawn to it. *But if it's not the undead he's talking about, then what are ravangers?*

I continued to watch in silence, more curious than ever to find out what two humans were doing in the middle of a forest filled with undead.

The long-haired man fidgeted with his pocket knife, opening and closing the sharp edge of the blade. Once he'd finished, he laid out the undead's body and knelt close to its face. Confused, I inched closer to get a better look through the barrier. The steel of his knife glistened in the fire's light. He lowered the weapon to the undead's neck. The tip of the knife traced from one side of the undead's throat to the other. Then, without a hint of emotion, the long-haired man plunged the blade deep into the undead's flesh. I cupped a hand over my mouth. There was a joyous gleam in the man's eyes as he pumped the small blade up and down. Blood oozed from the undead's neck, forming a puddle on the dirt.

With everything happening, I hadn't noticed the brawny man's disappearance into a nearby tent. He emerged with a hand-saw in his grasp.

"Here." He handed it to the long-haired man.

My focus stayed on their actions, unable to turn away, despite the horror. I cringed in utter disgust as the long-haired man began to shift the saw back and forth against the undead's neck. The head hanging on by a thread of skin. It was the look of pure enjoyment on the man's face that scared me the most.

"This one won't be botherin' us anymore," the long-haired man said as he lifted the undead's arm at the wrist. "You think it's still good? I'm starvin'."

The larger man rubbed his chin and shook his head. "I know you ain't the smartest, but keep asking questions like that and I'll smack the teeth from your mouth. You eat that thing and you'll either end up with the shits or filled with disease."

"Damn," the long-haired man sighed. "In it goes then."

He stood up, leaving the saw on the ground. With a violent thrust, he shoved the toe of his boot against the undead's torso. The limp body flopped closer to the fire. Flames reached out, catching on the undead's tattered clothing.

Laughter erupted from the two men as they leaped back from the body. The undead's dry skin emitted a strange green flame, lighting the two men's faces. Both bore a devilish, toothy grin.

I'd seen enough. I needed to get far from the camp

before meeting the same fate. My worst nightmares couldn't conjure up what I'd seen tonight. My feet inched backward, my eyes fixated on the two men.

The loud *snap* of an object beneath my foot startled me upright. I cupped my mouth in sheer terror and lifted my foot from the thin fallen branch. *Maybe they didn't hear me.*

"What was that?" The long-haired man shot his attention in the area where I stood.

No. Please, no.

"That's just the fire settling, fool," the large, bald man replied.

My body remained frozen in place, and I hoped that the vibrant glow from the fire was impairing their sight. I held my breath until watching the long-haired man look away.

Relief washed over me. I took another step back, this time careful.

"I dunno, Judd, I'm pretty sure I heard it out there. I'm not gonna take a chance on one of them bastards getting in here while we got our backs turned," the long-haired man said while cupping a hand over his eyebrows. He squinted his eyes and peered back out into the darkness.

"Better hope it's not the ravangers. I'm not coming to save your hide this time." The large man shook his head and left for his tent.

No. Oh, no, no, no. I watched as the long-haired man pocketed his knife and retrieved a machete from a nearby box. *What do I do? If I run, they'll hear me. I don't want to die. Again.* I looked around in panic. *I need to hide.*

At my side was a thicket of vines. I parted the thick, green drapery at the middle. The cascading vines and broad trunk of a tree had just enough space for me to squeeze in. I hurried to adjust the foliage, my body concealed.

I clenched my muscles to fight back the natural urge to tremble in fear. The air in my lungs burned as I fought to not let any escape through my nose. One slip-up, one hint of where I was hiding, and I'd end up their next target.

Through the small gap in the vines, I saw the long-haired man waving a torch as he strode past the barrier of wooden stakes.

"Can't see a damn thing," the long-haired man muttered.

He extended his arm, allowing the torchlight to shine ahead. A warm glow filled the area, and he crept forward in my direction.

Please, no. I remained as still as the tree pressed to my back. My fingers curled around the base of my shirt. Fear consumed me. Every part of my body struggled not to move. The man was a hunter, and I his prey.

Though I had limited visibility, I saw him. He paced

around my direct vicinity, pausing every few seconds as if to listen for any hint of sound. I let air slip from my nose, scared to breathe. The man then turned and strode off in the opposite direction before coming to an abrupt halt. I heard him laughing at himself.

He spun around, now facing where I hid. My jaw dropped in surprise as a wave of intense worry swept over me. Every joint in my body locked tight as I looked through the small gap. The man drew closer, the light of his torch shining into my eye.

He paused, peering at the vines. His stare felt like daggers to my chest—it seemed like time itself had stopped moving.

I pinched my eyes shut, fearful that he would see a reflective glow from the fire's vibrancy. Aside from the crackle of flame feeding on the torch, it was silent. I swore I heard my heart drumming within my chest. Then, nothing but darkness. I no longer saw the faint glow of light through my eyelids. After many seconds of silence passed, I opened my eyes. The man was gone.

My pupils shifted to each side, scanning every inch of ground I could see—*all clear*. My breath shook as I exhaled. Once the tension in my arms relaxed, I reached up and parted the vines.

Close call. Too close. I readjusted my bag on my

shoulder and prepared to make my way far from the camp of horror.

As I took my first step out of concealment, a sharp tug pulled me back.

"Where do ya' think you're goin'?" a man's voice broke the silence.

His thin fingers held onto my ponytail. My feet staggered back, and I threw my arms in the air to catch my balance. A groan erupted from my throat as his foot struck hard behind my knee. My leg buckled and I fell to the ground. A final moan slipped past my dry lips as I looked up into the face of evil.

There, glaring down at me with the most sinister expression upon his face, was the long-haired man. His eyes held wide and crazed as if he were more inhuman than I. From my peripheral vision I saw the torch wedged between two branches. The light cast down on us. The machete, now raised at his side, gleamed on contact with the fire's glow.

"Caught ya'," he said with a grin.

DAY 4
PART 6

Rocks and twigs scraped against my body as the long-haired man drug me by my ponytail. I grunted and called out, pleading for him to stop, yet no words were distinguishable.

"Told ya' I heard another one of 'em outside of camp," the long-haired man spoke with pride.

I swung my arms in wild circles, trying my damnedest to claw at him and free myself. Despite digging my fingers in as hard as possible, I couldn't break through the thick cloth of his sleeves.

"She's a feisty one. Where's the rope?" The long-haired man wrestled my body over and shoved my face against the dirt.

"Why in the hell did you bring it back alive?" the bald man said as he pressed the tip of his boot against my side. He dropped a coil of rope on the back of my head.

The long-haired man squeezed my wrists and held them in place. He wrapped the rope around, binding my hands together. My legs kicked out in an attempt to avoid his grip, but he was too strong and with little effort, he bound my ankles.

"She looks freshly turned, Judd. Bet she still has a nice little body. Warm on the inside. I wanna see it before we burn her in the pit," the long-haired man rubbed his groin as he spoke.

"Do what you want, but it's on you if something goes wrong. I'll have you in the fire right next to her if you get bit." The bald man walked beneath a tarp and sat on a wood stump. He withdrew a small knife from his pocket, then reached at his side to retrieve an animal carcass. Without concern for what was happening mere feet in front of him, he skinned the animal.

Before I could pay any more mind to my surroundings, the long-haired man gripped my shoulders. He rolled me onto my back. His narrow tongue shot out and licked his thin lips; his eyes scanned over my body. I'd rather have had a bullet through my skull than endure what he had planned for me.

He pulled his pocket knife out and pressed the tip against my cheek. It pierced into my skin, and the light secretion of blood rolled down toward the back of my neck.

"Try to bite me, and I'll take that pretty little head right off," he warned while grazing the blade over to my lips. The weapon caressed my mouth with the sharpened edge.

Struck with fear, I wiggled my arms to try and loosen the rope. My wrists remained pressed together, unable to move. Between the weight of my body and the bindings that left me stuck in place, I couldn't escape.

It can't end like this.

I shook my head and whimpered, attempting to plead with the man in the only way I knew how.

He ignored my gestures and brought his blade to the bottom of my blouse.

"Let's see what you got under there."

My eyes widened as I heard the soft popping sound and felt my blouse loosen at the base.

He bore an expression of pure delight as he clicked his tongue. I could no longer bear to look at the face of such a monster. My cheek turned. His fingers traced along my belly, and soon after, the warmth of his breath met my skin. His thin, dry lips pressed against me, kissing in rows.

No, please stop.

I yelled, pushing the air hard from my lungs.

A loud *crack* broke through the sound of my cries. The man's movement came to an abrupt stop. His weight dropped on top of me. I turned my face to see salvation. There, towering above, was Bastion.

DAY 4
PART 7

Bastion glared down at me and shook his head. A tree branch rest snug within his gripped fingers. I'd never been so relieved to see someone until this moment. I struggled to move from beneath the limp man, squirming my bound legs like an inchworm.

Bastion sighed. He kicked the man in the cup of his armpit and forced the motionless body to roll over on the ground. Bastion's free hand shot out, taking hold of the man's knife. He wasted no time in using the weapon to slice me free of the tight bindings. The area where they had chaffed my skin burned—but not as painful as I'd expected it to be. I flexed my wrists and ankles before taking hold of Bastion's extended arm. His firm tug caused me to stumble forward into his chest. For a moment, our bodies pressed against one another. I looked in the other direction, stifling my embarrassment. Now was not the time to get caught up in emotions. My appreciation for his arrival would have to wait. At that moment, our focus needed to be reaching as far as possible from the camp.

Bastion took my hand in his and led me toward the small gap between the barrier of wood stakes. Just ahead, I made out the white shape of Lace's dress. It stood out like a pale moon against the darkness.

We made it!

Before relief could set in, an intense pressure struck my back.

"Where in the hell do you think you're goin'? It looks like I got a two-for-one," the long-haired man spoke from behind me.

My eye's widened, and I squeezed down on Bastion's hand. I felt a sharp pull, and the pressure subsided. I turned to see a knife, the first two inches of the blade stained in my blood. The long-haired man waved the weapon as though to taunt us.

"I wasn't done with you yet." He looked into my eyes

with a wild madness in his stare. "This ugly thing can roast in flames." He gestured toward Bastion.

Bastion shot his arm out across my chest. He urged me back behind him.

Before either of us reacted, the long-haired man jabbed his blade forward. The tip dug into Bastion's forearm. Blood trickled from Bastion's wound, onto my blouse. At the moment that Bastion withdrew his arm, the long-haired man reached out and took hold of my hair. He pulled me toward him with a single, violent tug. His dirt-crusted fingers pinched down on my jaw, my face forced to the sky as he exposed my neck.

"*Mmm*, still tender," he said before pressing his tongue against my skin.

Bastion's stare burned with rage.

"I wouldn't make any sudden moves," the long-haired man flashed his knife. "Ya' know, it's pretty funny." He laughed. "Two dead bastards tryin' to save each other. I never saw anything like this before. You creatures ain't got feelings." His grip tightened on my jaw. "Sorry to tell ya', but you won't be getting' her back, lover boy. I'm gonna' do things to this body you couldn't imagine in your wildest dreams. Then, when I'm done, I'll cut her pretty little head clean off to keep as a warning for the rest." He leaned in over my shoulder. "Would you like that?" He forced my head to nod.

My body moved like a rag doll in his grip. There was no way I'd remain helpless while he continued to violate me, not after Bastion had risked his life to help. With a sudden jolt, I swung my arms and twisted my body to break free. Despite my outburst, he held firm.

A sharp pressure struck my back, followed by a series of more jabs. I looked to the ground to see blood splattered near my heels and knew that the long-haired man had stabbed me again. Though the pain wasn't as unbearable in my current state, adrenaline kicked in, and I panicked. *Can I lose blood and remain conscious? Did I just drag Bastion to his death? I won't accept this!*

I wailed out and kicked a foot back, hoping to land a blow. My heel struck his shin, hitting hard against the bone. He stumbled back a step, loosening his grip—an opportunity we needed to take.

Bastion moved swift and steady, despite the difficulty he endured while trying to keep up with such a pace. He seized the long-haired man's moment of vulnerability and dove forward. With a single motion, he pushed his weight against our assailant. The long-haired man's fingers slipped from my face as they both tumbled to the ground.

Bastion mounted himself on top, hammering his fists down against the long-haired man's face. The man's head jerked to the side, struck many times more. Blood spouted first from his nose, then from his mouth. His skin became swollen and red.

I watched as the long-haired man's right arm rose. The knife gripped within curled fingers; the tip pointed at Bastion's rib cage.

Watch out! I tried to yell, but all that emerged was ghoulish sounds. *Damn this body.*

Too late. The long-haired man dug the blade deep into Bastion's side, twisting the handle. I saw the glistening of blood as it reflected in the fire's glow. My mind swirled; I didn't want to wait and test our limits as undead. We still had functioning organs, and who knows what would happen if he punctured a lung. All of this started because I was weak—because I couldn't handle myself out here in the *real* world.

I had to do something. My eyes scanned over the man, and I drew my foot back to deliver a swift blow to his groin. Before my leg unfolded, a deafening bang sounded. My balance wavered, and I stumbled forward. My footing steadied, and I froze in place.

There, storming out from beneath the flap of his tent, was the bald man. He furrowed his brows, though his gaping mouth and heavy breathing revealed the frightened tension he felt.

"Dammit! Shoot 'em in the head, you moron!" the

long-haired man yelled.

The bald man raised his gun, his hands clenching down to steady the aim. He held the barrel forward.

"Hurry the hell up! More of the walking corpses will come from all this noise. What are you wai-" Gurgled noises filled the air as the long-haired man's words cut short.

Bastion hunched over him, tearing into his throat with barred teeth. Blood sprayed like a fan across Bastion's face as he pulled a thick chunk of meat.

My mind became clear and focused. Bastion risked it all to protect me—I had to fight too. Death for us crept all too near, but it would not be tonight. Without hesitation, I ducked down and hurried toward the second tent. Adrenaline coursed through my veins. I entered the make-shift shelter. I assumed that their ammo was in minimal supply. Otherwise, I couldn't understand why my head still rest upon my shoulders. Just then, a bullet shot through the fabric of the tent, missing my cheek by inches.

He's coming! I ducked down even lower. Maybe I was wrong about the ammo. *Come on. Come on!*

I reached out, scavenging through cluttered junk across the floor. My eyes darted in all directions.

There has to be something.

My finger bumped against something with a light sheen that stood out against all the other useless garbage. I pulled it up to my face for further inspection. *A pocket knife!* I pinched my fingers to each side of the blade, flipping it open. The odds were not in my favor to step into a gunfight with only a pocket knife. I'd have to muster every ounce of my strength to hurry. My body was overexerted and feeling the extreme effects of muscle cramping.

Focus! I said to myself.

I crouched low, and inched my way toward the front of the tent. Another gunshot fired, but this time in another direction.

Bastion! My heart thumped against my chest.

Without considering the consequences, I pushed my way out of the shelter. The bald man stood with his weapon aimed at Bastion's back.

"You killed him! Y-you bastard, I'm gonna' fry you good!" the bald man yelled with such power that the veins on his slick head bulged.

My focus moved to Bastion. Relief swept over me. The bald man's aim was so poor that no bullet had met its mark. It'd be impossible to close the space between the man and myself, so I did the only logical thing in my mind. I threw the knife as hard as I could in the man's direction. Time seemed to freeze as the blade spiraled through the air. I watched as it descended toward the man's thigh, sticking deep into the muscle. *I did it!* All the months playing darts at

Sarah's house paid off.

"Dammit!" the bald man shouted, along with other profanities as he clamped his hand across his thigh. His fingers parted just enough to allow room for the weapon that still stuck out from his flesh.

He lifted his head; his lips curled, mouth snarled.

"Time to die, bitch."

His other arm rose, gun pointed at my head.

In the time I took to throw my arms up in front of my face, a low growl rumbled. Lace emerged from the shadows and threw herself onto the bald man's back. Her lips tucked back and teeth bared in the same animalistic manner as when she devoured the animal back at the house. She bit into the man's shoulder, sinking her teeth deep beneath his skin. Maybe it was my hatred for this man, but my mouth watered at the sight of blood gushing down his arm. Lace had become captive to the desire to kill—to feast.

The man buckled down onto a knee. He bellowed loud enough to make my ears ring. His torso collided with the floor and he reached and scraped to free himself from the tiny girl's wrath. Lace, despite her size, held her grip. He bent his arm and shoved his elbow into Lace's side with immense force. Why couldn't I move? Why didn't I rush to her aid? I think because, at that moment, I knew there was no stopping Lace. Or, maybe I was just a coward. This man had signed

84

his death wish the moment he attempted to attack her brother. Lace's body rolled across the dirt by the force of the man's blow. Her face bore no reaction as she returned to her feet. She dove at the man while he pulled himself up onto a knee. His body flung back. Lace positioned herself on top of him before he responded to her movement. Her milky eyes held wide, wild, and consumed by the desire to eat. I wanted to shut the whole situation out, to imagine I was in a dream; but my eyelids no longer functioned. I couldn't close my eyes and drown out the sight. I'd become trapped in this harsh reality. If the situation were any different, I'd be in a panic by this sudden realization. But the sight before me consumed all other thoughts. It filled my mind and struck me still in place. Turning away wasn't an option. It's one of those things you know you'll regret watching, but don't have the will-power to look in another direction. *Oh, how I wish I could un-see what tonight brought upon me.* A part of me would never be the same.

Lace brought her face down to the man's gut. It all happened so fast that his brain hadn't processed the next move to retaliate. His arms held frozen at his sides. She once again bared her teeth, and bit right through his shirt. Her jaw opened and shut like a rabid animal attacking its prey. The man no longer screamed—no longer cried in pain. He now experienced a feeling beyond that, a numbness that comes when you have lost all hope for survival. Blood bubbled at his lips. He coughed with his head to the side. If I hadn't known how cruel this man was, I might've held the weighted burden of guilt. But no—he fit the true definition of a monster. As horrid as the sight before me looked, a part of me felt a sense of justice served. But even still, I had a hard time processing such a sweet little girl, now dining on a grown man's intestines.

I looked over at Bastion, who staggered to his feet. Blood masked his chin, and he glared in my direction. His wounds looked terrible.

Carnage surrounded us. Bastion was injured, and Lace had her body embellished with human entrails.

They had *murdered* two people—because of me.

DAY 4

PART 8

Bastion walked forward with heavy steps, his arms stiff at his sides and fingers curled.

Here it comes.

I braced myself for hell's fury to unleash. I'd placed both he and Lace in the heart of a snake pit. It seemed like they'd been dying in relative peace until I came along.

I winced, even though he stood a short distance away. Just as I was about to take another step back to keep the space between us, he turned to the side. Instead of coming for me, he approached Lace. She remained hunched over, with fists dug deep into the man's torso. Her little fingers tore at his innards. Her eyes lost from humanity.

Bastion reached out and gripped onto the back of her nightgown, pulling her away from the feast. My jaw dropped; I'd never seen such a change of character before. Lace hissed and flailed her limbs as though she didn't recognize her brother standing at her side. She snapped her teeth together with white eyes that remained wide and crazed. Bits of the man's insides stuck to her chin and her blood-drenched gown hugged her tiny frame. It was horrific to witness such a sight—she was just a child.

Bastion forced Lace to the ground, pinning her wrists above her head as he mounted her from the top. He pulled an arm back, and for a moment, I thought he would strike her across the face. His hand froze in place; his chest heaving as he grunted aloud. Despite his angered demeanor, I sensed that a part of him pleaded for her to calm. His eyes remained fixated on Lace until her breathing slowed and her body relaxed. A tiny whimper escaped as she stared at her brother.

He lowered his arm, hanging his head as a burst of air pushed past his lips. He then stood, lifted Lace into his arms and cradled her like a father to his child. She buried her face against his chest, Bastion's shirt muffling her steady whimpering.

His focus redirected toward me. If a stare could cast death, his would do the trick. Though a white film eclipsed the green hues in his eyes, I saw they held so much pain.

The moment felt so intense that struck me in the heart. His expression said it all. He was losing Lace, the only family he still had in this forsaken world. It scared him. She was abandoning the young, loving girl she'd once been, becoming something inhuman—something abominable. I couldn't even imagine having to stand by and watch someone I loved go through that. I stood and returned his stare as the minutes passed, unsure of how to react to the situation. Then, as if on cue, my doubts subsided. I shook my worries and knew without a doubt, that I wanted to be there for him—for both of them.

There were no second thoughts. I approached where they stood and slid my arms around them both. To my surprise, the weight of Bastion's head pressed down on my own. Time ticked by as we remained huddled against one another. The glow of the fire gave a sense of comfort in contrast to the surrounding darkness. It was a symbolic moment. Darkness surrounded us in life. With each day, the future remained uncertain. We didn't know how much time was left, or what dangers we'd meet. But I wanted to face it together. We were the light in the center of it all.

DAY 4

PART 9

The fire snapped and crackled. Logs settled into the hot embers. In Nialus, fire symbolized death. It was mandatory to burn those who passed. They said it helped cleanse their souls, and ensured they wouldn't return as one of the undead. For every passing, we would gather near the east square to watch as a shell of one's former self, ignited into flame. Here we sat, just the three of us before the fire's glow. The light soothed my mind and distracted my thoughts. People had died, but I didn't mourn.

Lace slid to my side, tired from the night's events. She allowed her body to fall to the side, her head now laying on my lap. How scary it must be as a child stuck in this land of the dead. I sympathized over the hardships she must have endured at such a young age. She was dying before she ever had a chance to live. The disease stripped away her childhood. It all seemed so cruel and unfair. I overlooked the crusted blood on her face and stroked her matted hair. She hummed in comfort. It was a moment of peace in this twisted world.

To my other side, Bastion pressed against me. He tightened his lips together and grunted, pulling his legs up against his chest. His arms wrapped around both knees. He stared ahead. The orange hues from the fire reflected off of his eyes, making it difficult to read his emotion. I couldn't imagine what must run through his tormented mind.

His simple gesture of affection made my throat dryer than usual. I swallowed hard while trying to maintain the rhythm of each breath. Before I filled my head with hesitation, I tilted my neck and rested my head against his shoulder. Though everything in the world was wrong, being with Bastion and Lace felt right.

I enjoyed their comfort for what seemed like hours until Bastion's sudden movement startled me upright. He stood, scanning the area at full attention. Something to our right caused his jaw to tighten. His hand shot out, signaling Lace and me to remain in place. My pulse raced so fast that I could feel it throbbing in my head. I watched on with uncertainty.

The reason for his sudden alertness became clear. The crunch of dry pine-needles drew near from outside of our camp. Whatever had caused the noise, now moved through the darkness. I heard the rhythmic sound of steps. It circled around the makeshift walls, just beyond lights reach.

Curiosity got the best of me. I couldn't remain sitting, waiting for something to attack us. My arms nudged Lace from my lap, and I pulled myself onto my feet. I pressed a finger against my lips, letting Lace know that she needed to remain silent until we figured out what was happening.

Her small hand shot up, taking hold of my pant leg. Her eyes were wide with fear. My stomach fluttered, and I had a grim feeling that she already knew what crept beyond our sight. Without wanting to frighten her any more, I patted her head in an attempt to provide reassurance. With a light tug, I pulled free from her grip. I approached behind where Bastion stood and strained to see into the forest, draped in black. My vision only reached as far as the fire's glow. *Dammit*. I felt like a prisoner inside the fragile barrier of shaved wooden spikes. Another sound amplified above the crackling fire. Steps on the opposite side. There was more than one. Whatever stalked out there, hadn't come alone.

Bastion's jaw tightened, and his fists curled. My intuition continued to tell me that both he and Lace knew what lurked in the darkness.

A loud snapping startled us. I turned to see the largest log in the fire pit implode at the center. Small flakes of ash drifted into the air. The log now consumed with fiery embers that crackled. Within moments, the flames that had once licked at the wood's side, now dimmed. Before I returned my focus on the forest, two arms shoved me back. I locked eyes with Bastion, who now appeared frantic. My back leg shot out, stopping me from stumbling onto the ground. *What in the hell was that for?* I wanted to shout in frustration.

He answered my question, without an exchange of words. His hand reached to take hold of the long-haired man's knife. He then dug it into the dirt, spelling out the words: FIRE. LIGHT.

I looked to the fire, which was dwindling into a bed of ember. Our circumference of light had almost diminished. The outside darkness crept inward. My mind triggered back to the two men. They had spoken about the fire keeping *something* out. *"The ravangers will eat us down to the bone…".* I heard the man's voice play within my mind.

Ravangers. I swallowed hard, not understanding what they were. But, if two men who had no fear of slaughtering the undead seemed worried, it must be trouble.

Bastion staggered over to two small logs and a scarce pile of twigs. He lifted them with struggle and made way back to the fire.

I've got to help. I'll prove that I'm not useless. I won't let it end here tonight.

I glimpsed upon Lace, who now buried her face

between her knees and chest. Her little body rocked to each side as if to pull her mind from the grim predicament.

What could be more frightening than what we'd already become?

I wasted no more time pondering the unknown. My mind was made up, and I felt ready to confront my uncertainties. I looked across the area for anything to contribute to the fire. Dirt in all directions. Useless objects that would take more time than we had to catch fire. It wasn't an option to lose hope, I'd keep trying. A colorful pile caught my eye, and I hurried back in Lace's direction. There, on the ground was a small pile of clothing they must've set to dry. They didn't appear damp.

It might not burn for long, but it'll help the wood catch flame. I remembered the many nights helping my mom to light our stove. On some occasions, we had forgotten to stock wood, leaving us to improvise ways to start the fire. This was one of those times I'd have to make do.

The flames took to the cloth fibers, feeding on each piece. A burst of brightness shot toward the sky before the fire once again settled. Within minutes the vibrancy dulled. The limited amount of wood Bastion had brought remained lit, but it wasn't enough.

I turned to the side and looked over every inch for anything else I could use. The two men had a lot of cluttered junk, though nothing of use to add in fueling the fire. A faint pop drew my attention to the outer perimeter. Small scattered branches lay close to one another within the light's reach. The fire settled into a dim glow; there wasn't much time left. Darkness would soon conceal us. I puffed my chest and curled my fingers—I wouldn't let the fire die on us.

My feet shuffled forward, and dirt parted to each side of my shoes as I inched closer. A steady hissing from just beyond the camp perimeter left me shaken and afraid. But I wasn't about to let Bastion or Lace down. Multiple low moans filled the night. Whatever lurked out there knew where I was. It, no, *they* were waiting. With trembling fingers, I reached down to retrieve the sticks. I pinched each one within the bend of my elbow, and stacked them into a bundle. Another loud hiss set my spine upright. This one was closer. For a moment, I paused as a wave of unease swept over me. How could nothing more than light protect me from the threat out there? It made sense when I lived behind walls. But here, there was nothing between us but empty air and some carved sticks. Not enough to keep an animal out, let alone whatever lurked in the darkness. A shiver raced up my back. I realized that I'd allowed my mind to wander. My arms readjusted in position, causing a few small sticks to slip from my grasp.

They're too important to leave on the floor; we need all the fuel we can find.

I clamped down with my left arm, reached out with

my right. Fingers extended toward the ground.

Got ya, I thought in relief; the wood now back in my possession.

As my pupils rose, the breath within my lungs remained. My sides burned from the inability to release the air from inside. There, standing only a few feet away was the most repulsive sight I'd ever seen. A human—or at least, it once was. It stood without clothing but bore no genitals. Its flesh had taken a leathery texture, thin and stretched tight. And yet, there it stood, as steady as the surrounding trees. Most menacing of all were the dark sunken holes where eyes once rest. The creature's lips had long deteriorated, leaving its teeth exposed. It snapped its jaws like a starved animal, inhaling with two holes where a nose used to be.

With a sudden *pop*, the remaining wood collapsed into the bed of coals. The light that had once surrounded me with protection withdrew. Darkness veiled over my body, and I turned to seek Bastion's guidance. Before the ball of my foot rotated, bone-thin fingers wrapped around my arm. It clamped down with inhuman strength that caused my muscle to spasm. There wasn't time to move before its teeth bit down with incredible power and dug into my shoulder. I dropped the bundle of sticks and reached out to ward off the attack. It didn't move sluggish like most of the undead who bore the onset of decay. This thing moved fast and was far stronger than me.

A radiant glow approached from my peripheral vision, and I bent my neck just as a sphere of flame zipped past. It struck the ravanger in its face, casting tiny embers and ash into the surrounding air. The ravanger released a sharp hiss, before scurrying back into the darkness. The smell of burnt hair filled my nose, and I pat at my head in a wild frenzy. I felt where the fire had singed many strands of my hair. My ear now exposed. My eyes met with Bastion's, and I read his *'Don't you dare complain when I've just saved you, yet again'* stare.

He tossed an armful of pine needles into the embers. I sighed in relief as they took to the fire's intensity. Bastion wasted no time in nurturing the flames with sticks, clothing, and anything else he had come across that could burn. As the fire rose toward the sky, our circumference of safety returned. With a loud grunt, Bastion prodded the fire with a sock at the end of a sharpened stick. The flame fed on the cloth fibers. He lifted the makeshift torch to eye level and approached where I stood. With the tip of his chin, he gestured out to the forest. He tossed the torch with little effort, sending it just beyond our circle of light.

A symphony of low growls broke through the silence, and I cupped my mouth at the sight. For the moment that the sock remained lit, dozens of ravangers came into view. Though their browned skin looked dry and sunken, the scent of rot didn't permeate the night air. It differed from ours. They stood like statues in place, waiting for the chance that our light would cease and they could feast.

After retrieving all the wood I'd dropped, Bastion curled his fingers around my wrist and tugged me toward the fire. He held his eyes on mine, and I knew he was attempting to force my focus off of the surrounding threat. We were stuck until morning—prisoners at the mercy of flame.

Lace watched my expression as we approached. Her thin arm extended up, and she pulled on the bottom of my blouse. With great discomfort, I lowered my body to the ground. Despite the horrific behavior I'd seen before, she still seemed so loving. Her presence had a way of soothing me. Her head rested on my shoulder, and for the first time that night, I smiled. I draped an arm around her small frame as we sat and watched the fire. Time moved slow.

There's nothing we can do now but hope the fire stays lit until dawn.

I remember how I used to dread bedtime. Now, as my fatigued body was forced to remain awake, I realized just how much I longed for a soft pillow and the ability to dream. A luxury to escape all the horrors of this world. Even if for just a little while.

A flash of flame and scattered ember put us back at alert. Bastion tossed another small branch into the fire. I'd drifted so far in thought I didn't have the vaguest idea how long he'd been standing at my side. Without acknowledging me, he sat to my right.

The sound of snarling started up again in our surroundings. We turned our attention to the far side of the camp in time to see several hands stretched into the perimeter of light. Their fingers dug into the dirt. They fought to extend their reach.

The dead body. The ravangers are trying to get it.

One of the ravangers latched their grip onto the long-haired man's corpse. I'd never seen something move so fast. The body almost appeared to be hovering above the ground as they pulled it into the darkness. I heard the wetness of his innards as their teeth tore into his flesh. Their growls became loud, ringing with intensity deep into my mind. The fear inside me struck my core like a living force, holding me in place.

There was a minute of stillness before Bastion slid his hand across my back. I arched in surprise as he pulled Lace and me closer. He rested his head down against mine. I felt safe within his arms and buried my face against his side. We let our guards down, allowing ourselves to be emotionally vulnerable after the long night we'd had. I thought about Nialus to ease my worry. He squeezed us in comfort. We each fought to drown out the cries of hunger that wailed through the night. A night I'll never forget.

DAY 5
PART 1

Time ticked by; each moment, every breath like an eternity had passed. The surrounding ambiance subsided to an occasional chirp from distant birds. Dawn approached. Relief swept through me at the thought of no longer enduring the tension of night. Darkness was a torturous reminder of what I'd become. My body forced me to remain awake, with no escape into the subconscious of my dreams. I had to face every passing minute with no relief from the overwhelming fatigue my body felt.

The first sight of daybreak washed through the sky.

Pink and orange hues painted above. As the light fell over our camp, I saw the destruction the ravangers left behind. Torn bark where their fingers had dug into the tree trunks marked their visit. Turned dirt and debris encircled the camp. And, most horrific of all was the remains from one of the men. Bare bones, cleaned without a morsel of flesh left.

Bastion stood and stretched his arms at his sides. Without even a glance in my direction, he walked the camp's perimeter. Our warm and comforting moment together was over. He returned to his usual cold and calculated mannerisms. I pursed my lips before shrugging to myself. It proved difficult to stand. My legs ached worse than the most intense charley horse I'd ever experienced. How Bastion rose with such grace was beyond me. I could only assume that one adapts to the pain over time.

I extended an arm to help Lace to her onto her feet. Just as with Bastion, she rose with no hesitation, despite being undead for longer than myself. It seemed ideal to have an inability to register pain, though I knew that this meant we moved one step closer to decay. The thoughts made me curious about just how long Lace and Bastion had endured being undead. I understood little about the whole *being between life and death process*. The white coats, my father included, were very selective about what they shared to the public. Commoners knew the undead were once alive, and that they contracted the disease through things like saliva or an open wound, but that was the extent of my knowledge.

My eyes fell to Lace's legs. Through the dirt and dried blood, I saw that the texture of her skin differed from ours. It appeared more leathery and pale. My heart sank at the notion that Lace might not have much longer in this world. Bastion will eventually perish too. I'll be the one to watch it happen. Then, I'll be alone until my demise.

Wait. I paused. *Bastion never said I could join them. I don't want to spend the last of my days out here in solitude.*

With great haste, I moved across the camp. I turned, glancing in each direction. A wave of comfort blanketed me at the sight of my bag. It had dropped just outside of the camp. Somehow, it'd avoided the ravangers destruction. Bastion had picked up on my sudden shift in behavior and followed in my wake as I left the perimeter to retrieve it. I shoved my hand down into my bag, retrieving my writing board.

Thank goodness. I heaved my chest as I discovered everything just as I'd left it.

My fingers curled around the pen and scribbled the words: **Can I stay with you?**

Bastion looked down in thought, then over at Lace. With a sudden swipe, he took the board from my hand. We exchanged no further communication before he turned and moved back into the camp.

He's so damned rude sometimes.

Frustrated, I followed. At the sight of Bastion holding the board before his chest, I tossed my pen at the back of his head.

Pick it up, jerk. I called out within my mind.

As if unbothered by my actions, he reached to the ground and retrieved the pen.

I watched as he penned out the letter '**N**.'

He's not letting me join them.

Bastion paused. He looked to the ground, again to Lace. With a defeated grunt, he shook his head and wiped the *N* clean.

Fine. But keep up, or I'm leaving you behind. We're taking a different path home, so the ravangers don't follow our scent.

The ravangers! I needed to know more about what we were up against. I reached out to reclaim my writing board.

What are they?? Why aren't they only after the living?

He approached my side to respond.

They're us. Bastion looked into my eyes.

Huh? I'm nothing like those things!

He continued to scribble, taking notice to my expression.

There's a rumor that once we turn, we only have

a little while before we wear away. We walk two paths. Some of us will decay until nothing is left. Others seem to evolve. They give in to their hunger and become driven by adrenaline. Their body adapts. It changes. They change. They lose who they once were. Memories are forgotten, and the only thing that drives them forward is the desire to feed.

He flexed his wrist before wiping the board clean to finish.

When I was alive, no one knew why this happened. But, we believed that ravangers will eat just about anything that moves, other than one another. I guess our flesh is still enough to satisfy their cravings. They hunt at night and seem to fear the light. But during the day they're slow. They stay away from any light. I think it somehow affects how fast they'll rot. It's the only theory I've come up with. What they are is a mutation. Something beyond being inhuman. They're numb to emotion, but seem to have a superior ability to hunt. They aren't intelligent, but they're powerful and fast. I think somehow their instincts to survive consumes them. Their hunger is never satisfied. They're always scavenging. Every single night. Your best bet is to hide, and hide well.

My stomach churned. There was no way I'd allow myself to become one of them. Shoot me a hundred times over before delivering such a fate. If what Bastion said proved

true, then either of us could turn.

So, that's why he locked the door after kicking me out. They've been hiding all this time.

Never in my wildest dreams, did I imagine a life like this existed. Each night, I'd lay my head on a soft pillow. My darkest worries were about my next school test or training to work in the greenhouse. Meanwhile, a war raged. The undead and ravangers at constant odds to survive as long as possible. A terrifying new world I'd known nothing about.

I wondered if my father had known about any of this. *No, there's no way he would've kept something like that from Mom and me.* We'd always heard that the human population didn't exist beyond Nialus. My father was a good, noble man and would never have stood for us doing nothing while survivors fought for their life on the outside.

Bastion had opened my eyes to so many new things out here. I almost felt overburdened by the amount of insight I'd learned within only a couple of days. If not for Bastion, I wouldn't have known about the ravangers. I'd have wandered into their flesh-craving grasp. Hell, I wouldn't have even made it through my first night alone if he hadn't come to save me. I was grateful that he'd let me stay with them. If nothing else, it'd give me the time I needed to adjust to this world. Everyone is on borrowed time—ours just happened to be running out faster. I knew at some point, he and Lace would pass on, and I'd be left to myself once again.

A chill ran down my spine. I'd like to think of myself as a strong-willed person; one who can accomplish what I put my mind to. But the thought of enduring life in solitude out here was more than I wanted to process. I shook my head and wrote.

I'm ready.

DAY 5
PART 2

We walked along a bed of pine needles and oak leaves, a loud crunch beneath each step. I hoped there wasn't anyone else nearby. With as noisy as we moved, I'm sure the whole forest heard us tromping around. Time passed, and we continued weaving through tall, lush trees. They stretched and bent as far as my vision could see. I wondered if Bastion had any idea where we were heading, or if he'd gotten us lost. Every direction looked identical.

A disgruntled snarl overpowered the noise we made. I stiffened my posture and held my head upright. My first instinct was to investigate the area for motion. I still hadn't gotten used to living among the undead, and the noises that came when they were near made my anxiety sky-rocket. I glanced over to Bastion, who stood with Lace behind him. He seemed on-edge; alert. It looked as though he knew something I didn't.

As if to prepare for a fight, Bastion tore off a smaller limb from a tree at his side. He held the branch like a batter waiting for the pitch and took a step forward.

I thought the undead don't harm one another. Why is Bastion being so defensive?

I remained alert and followed behind, unsure of what was to come. Soft breaths slipped past my lips, and I took careful steps to make as little noise as possible.

We rounded the flaky trunk of a thick tree. What I saw on the other side left me stricken with fear. My feet shuffled back; my hand took hold of Lace's. Before us, a ravanger laid across the ground. Its distinct hollow eyes and sunken face left no doubt in my mind. I think it was a male, judging by the lack of breast tissue, though ravangers didn't appear to have a distinguishable gender. Short brown hair, thin and in patches covered its skull.

It clawed at the dirt, and I cringed as I watched one of its fingernails peel back. The ravanger scraped harder and more frantic with each step that Bastion took in its direction. Its legs were immobile, trapped within a device that looked like metal teeth. The device clamped down on its mummified-looking skin that clung to the bone.

Bastion took another step closer, now only feet away.

The ravanger didn't seem to be driven by a will to survive, but the urge to feed. And it was starving. It curled its bone-like fingers into the ground and pulled. The metal trap drug down against its lower leg, tearing into his discolored muscle and tendons.

Bastion approached the ravanger. He needed to strike fast. It's a kill first, or be eaten kind of world. You didn't have the luxury of moral conscience. I still struggled to accept that fact; I wasn't sure if I ever would. There seemed to be exceptions, but I was a terrible judge of character. Codah's name screamed in the back of my mind at the thought. I returned focus to watch Bastion lift his arms above his head; the branch still gripped tight within his fingers.

The ravanger swiped an arm out, scraping the tips of his fingers against Bastion's ankle. This was the first time I got a good look at the ravanger's hand. It looked odd. Some fingers had bone protrusions that made them look like claws; others still had remnants of nails and resembled our own.

With no expression of remorse, Bastion brought the branch down with tremendous force. It sunk with little effort into the ravangers skull. A mess of brain and bone fragments seeped onto the ground. As he withdrew the weapon, bits of skin remained glued on by thick, blackened blood.

Bastion turned to face me, his stare cold and serious. He pointed to the ravanger—or rather the heap of meat and bones that remained. I knew his intent. He wanted to caution me, to show me that you can't let your guard down out here. To make me aware that we'd *never* be safe. The undead were cursed and left to walk the fine line between life and death, forced to spend each day in torment, losing a little piece of their humanity.

I felt my body rotting. My muscles burned as though on fire, and my skin was becoming like rough leather.

A light tug on my index finger turned my attention to Lace. She pointed ahead at Bastion, who gestured for us to follow. I stepped past the remains of the ravanger and continued onward. The forest grew dense and difficult to manage. The overwhelming sting of hunger pulled at my insides. I'd never dealt with such a feeling in my entire life. My whole body ached and my stomach cramped. I placed a hand over my belly, hoping that with time, it'd ease. I wasn't stupid though, and knew the undead had untamed appetites; mine would only grow worse.

We came to a dirt trail that looked well used. I remained unsure if this distraction from my hunger was a good thing, or if I should've listened to that little sound in my mind that screamed, "Turn around while you still can!" I wondered if the path was a common walking area for the undead—or something else.

The story of Pinocchio came to mind. My mom used to tell it to me as a child. I certainly wasn't listening to my own Jiminy Cricket. Here's to hoping that if *Pleasure Island* was ahead, we weren't walking into a trap.

As we continued, Lace fidgeted and quickened her sluggish steps. I heard the faint sound of rushing water. Intrigued, I drew closer, following the noise like a sailor to the sweet music of a siren's song.

Just ahead, Bastion peered over a thicket of bushes. With a silent nod, he pushed the cluster of leaves to the side and continued.

I moved past the bushes and the most majestic sight I'd ever seen captivated me. For a few minutes, I couldn't walk—only stare ahead. It was so much more beautiful than what I'd imagined and seen in old books. Water rushed over smoothed stones and cascaded from rocks. The river went on farther than I could see. I needed to get closer, I'd dreamed about the beauty of the outside world for so long. A little glimmer of light in this shrouded world of darkness had crossed my path. I moved to the water's edge, to a spot where the current slowed from a large rock in its way. My throat rumbled as I fought the pain to lower myself to a knee. My hands fell to the damp earth that resisted beneath my palms. I leaned forward, looking down. Rays of sunlight reflected through the leaves, just enough to allow me to glimpse upon myself for the first time since I'd changed. My jaw dropped in disbelief. I didn't recognize myself anymore. My fingers rose to graze against my cheek; my skin lacked any color. Pale, with gray hues that made my once round cheeks appear sunken. My lips were dry and cracked. From within my throat, I growled and slapped a hand against the water's surface.

No! I won't accept this!

As I pulled my arm back to prepare for another blow to the water, a hand clamped down on my shoulder. Lace had arrived by my side. Her teeth were bared in another comical attempt at a smile. I laughed to myself. Her arms slid around my neck, and she hugged as tight as her little body could muster. Despite not having known her for long, our time out here was short. Days seemed like weeks. I felt the love radiating from her heart. She had grown to care for me. Most likely, I'd been the first female to enter her life since whatever had happened to her mother. The thought chilled me. At that moment, I realized that I cared for her too. I'd never had a sibling, just Mom and me. I wrapped my arms around her, embracing her in return as I stroked her tangled blonde locks. Words weren't necessary to show her how grateful I was for her simple gestures of kindness. She resembled warmth in our cold, desolate world.

A rustle in the brush. A snap of a twig. Our minds shot alert at the sudden sound; cautious. In this new life, the good moments seemed short-lived. Around every corner lurked potential danger. Death was breathing over my shoulder, just waiting for the right moment to finish me. A hand gripped down on my arm. Bastion stood at attention, his jaw tight and his eyes locked across the river. I focused in on where he watched. Movement—rustling in the foliage. I saw it. He released his grip and put a finger to his lips. I fell silent and rose to my feet, following close. Though I didn't have any idea what dwelled on the other side, I knew not to second-guess Bastion's motives. Out here was his land, and he understood it better than I ever would. The thought made me wonder about Bastion's past.

What was it like growing up outside of the city? What happened to his parents? Did he live around here? How long had he been undead?

My curiosity stirred, but right then we had other concerns. My feet stumbled forward as Bastion bumped into my backside. There was no warning before he slid his arm across my belly, backing me up into the concealment of the forest. He watched across the river without a sound. I saw movement. A man and a woman emerged to the river's bank— alive. I peeked out from hiding, my previous encounter with the two men still fresh in my mind. I hadn't realized that I held my breath until my mind spun from the lack of oxygen. The living seemed alien to me, and I dreaded being so close to them. It's a crazy thing to be fearful of what you once were— the very being you still longed to be.

I held watch as the woman knelt at the river bed. She dipped a bucket into the pristine water. The man at her side had a gun slung over his shoulder. He shifted his stare in all directions. After filling the bucket, the woman leaned forward and splashed her face, rubbing at the blackened mess that covered her skin. I was envious that she still felt the cold touch of water. There were so many simple pleasures I'd taken for granted.

The woman dried her hands on the front of her simple, blue shirt, and tucked a lock of hair behind an ear. She flashed a smile to the man and nodded before grabbing the bucket and rising to her feet.

Though I knew nothing of the woman, something was comforting about her. A sense of familiarity as though I'd known her—what a silly thought. Even still, I wanted to stay in that moment just a little longer. I wanted to observe her—a woman out in the wild. Brave. Fearless. Alive. She fascinated me. But the man—something about him that I couldn't put my finger on made me uneasy.

The two didn't stay much longer, and we watched as they returned to the forest. I turned to Bastion, who held a hard stare on the path they'd taken. A nudge from Lace diverted my focus. Her mouth hung open and her eyes fixated in delight. The sight of humans seemed to excite her. It looked as if she tried to hold on to that last bit of humanity inside herself. A relatable reminder of how she once was. Though, I couldn't help but wonder if there was also another side to her intrigue—a desire to satisfy the growing hunger.

Bastion relaxed his shoulders and turned to face me. His eyes fixated on my own. He pressed his brows together and nodded. He seemed proud of me for not being as ignorant as I'd been just the other night. In this world, there were few you could trust. I nodded in return.

My arm reached out, searching for Lace. *Nothing but air.* Bastion and I turned. *No!* Where Lace had stood only moments ago was now an open space. In a state of panic, Bastion trudged through the nearby foliage. By the look of the sun's placement, it was just after mid-day. The heat had become intolerable. You'd think without the ability to feel warmth on my flesh, it wouldn't bother me. But when the sun rose near its peak, my joints stiffened, and my body wore down. I had to avoid direct light when at all possible, or I'd end up decayed and rotted in no time. We had to find Lace. Fast. Our bodies drifted because of the elements; we were vulnerable.

I pressed against branches and brush, forcing my way through a dense section of forest. With all the leaves and pine needles on the ground, it was impossible to track where Lace went. The flowing current made too much noise to hear her. We pressed forward on a blind hunt; a slave to the sands of an hourglass. Time was of the essence and we needed to find Lace before dusk—before the ravangers crawled out of hiding to feast.

DAY 5

PART 3

Bastion looked to the river with gritted teeth. He shuffled along the edge, weaving through the trees which had sunken their roots into the eroded shoreline. I made it to the sandy bank and looked down in his direction. A long, unsteady breath escaped as I spotted Lace. Her little feet scooted across a fallen tree that stretched to each side of the river's edge. Her body wavered, and she held her arms outstretched to keep balance. The tree trunk rocked back and forth with every step she took. It looked as though it could give way at any moment.

Is she driven mad by hunger? There's no way this is just her fascination with the living. Can she no longer resist the call to feed? This whole situation is terrible.

I'd never seen Bastion so unraveled. He tore through the bushes like a wild animal. Adrenaline must have coursed through every inch of his veins because the pace he moved had tripled in speed. His mind was so focused on Lace he remained oblivious to the path within a few feet to his right. Without obstacles in my way, I covered ground fast enough to reach him. Each step I took felt like trying to bend a leg while wearing a rubber knee brace. It proved challenging and took a considerable amount of energy. We approached the shore together to see Lace taking her final steps to the other side. The trunk rocked, unstable and ready to fall as it pressed down against the eroded bank. The water's current rolled over the bark.

Lace folded over to her right, moving her arms in circles to regain balance. No sooner had Bastion stuck his foot out to steady the trunk, his sister leaped the remaining distance to land. Her body landed flat on the ground. Only seconds passed before the trunk lost its grip on the bank. It bobbed once before turning parallel to the river's current.

There it goes.

My heart sank.

Bastion stepped back. His balance teetered as his heel sunk into the spongy ground. He watched in dismay as our bridge floated away.

On the other side, Lace stood, patting at her filthy nightgown. She then crossed her arms, hugging herself as if shaken by the event. She turned to face us and, for just a minute, I thought she reconsidered her actions. Wrong. Her body shifted, and we looked ahead as she disappeared into the forest.

Bastion growled in anger and pounded his fist against a nearby tree. On impact, the skin from his knuckles tore. A splatter of blood remained, marking the pain that swelled within him.

We both knew the hard truth. Alone, Lace would have little hope for survival.

DAY 5
PART 4

B astion took hold of my wrist, his stare piercing through to my soul, pleading for help. I glanced down, taking notice once again to the torn skin on his knuckles. He'd stop at nothing to get her back, with or without me. A dried trail of blood coated his fingers. A reminder of just how fragile our bodies were becoming. My pain grew more numb by the hour as my nervous system deteriorated. I couldn't let him do this alone. We were friends now, and I wasn't about to abandon him when he needed me the most.

He curled his fists, and I noticed the faint glimmer of fresh blood. The wound must've been worse than I thought.

How much longer until his mind is numb to feeling anything? At some point, we'll both fade away.

Bastion replied with a nod that said, "thank you." We continued along the edge of the water, making as little noise as possible. The sun had shifted in the sky before we came to a halt. Shadows now stretched over us. Bastion pointed toward the river.

I saw the sandy bottom; it wasn't as deep as other areas. Large rocks dotted the ground beneath the current; our only hope of crossing before dusk fell.

Bastion took the first step forward, his foot plunging on top of a sizable stone. Water rushed against his pant leg, and he steadied his stance, placing his other foot parallel to the first. His determination motivated me, and I followed behind. My calves tightened. The rocks were slick. I'd almost slipped before securing my footing. Every muscle in my legs burned as I fought against the current. Each step felt as though concrete blocks were tied to my feet.

We inched our way across, keeping alert to the surrounding area in fear that the living humans might return. Bastion paused his movement, and I steadied my footing, forced to a halt. A tingle ran up the back of my neck and I scanned the forest.

Nothing.

He stared down into the water.

You've got to be kidding me.

The next rock was spread so far from where Bastion stood that he'd have to swim.

Hell, I don't even know how to swim. Good luck to us; this is going to suck.

He rocked his body, prepared to jump. Before my next breath left my lungs, Bastion pushed himself forward. Then, the guy who seemed so skillful and coordinated, swung his arms above his head in distress. The current had fought against him, and he'd missed the rock. His body plunged neck deep into the river.

Before he drifted out of reach, I shot a hand out and took hold of his arm. He looked up at me with eyes that confirmed he'd never swam a day in his life. The wetness of his arm made it impossible to gain traction, and he slipped from my grasp. My fingers moved from his forearm, down to his hand. I clamped down, pulling my weight back the best I could while trying to remain steady on the slimy rock. I grunted, struggling to hold on. His hand slid against the tips of my fingers—I was losing him. As our hands brushed past one another, I cried out. Horrified, I watched as he dipped beneath the turbulent surface. There was no reason to weigh my odds. Nothing would stop me from going after him. Without a moment of hesitation, I leaped from my rock. I dipped beneath the surface, holding my arms out to brace for any objects.

A hard surface collided with my bicep, but I didn't feel any discomfort. I'm not sure if it was because of the adrenaline, or the lack of sensory input in my body.

He needs me. I repeated it over again in my mind as I pushed ahead.

My head emerged from the surface just in time to see Bastion thrashing his limbs to reach the shore. I'd almost made it within arm's reach when a shifting current pulled him under. His head brushed my leg, forced down to the river bottom.

Another crushing sensation. We'd hit more rocks and blood washed from my shoulder. I was fine, but I worried that Bastion might've hit his head. My arms splashed around in a panic, desperate to take hold of his body—but he had vanished. I saw him reappear a few feet ahead of me, his forehead oozing with fresh blood. Before I got a good look at the damage, his limp body rolled face-down. He was going to die.

DAY 5
PART 5

I didn't understand what to do. The deepest pool of water I'd ever been in was our bathtub. Even then, we had to conserve water and only fill it halfway. I wouldn't let that consume my mind with fear. This time, Bastion needed me. I pushed forward with every fiber of my being. I closed in— closer. Closer. Like a copperhead snake to its prey, my arm shot out.

My fingers reached until my shoulder felt as though it'd snap out of my socket at any moment. The wet cloth of Bastion's shirt met my touch, and I gripped down with speed I never realized I had. It took a significant amount of energy for me to pull my body near his and kick as I'd never kicked before. The water rolled over my head, and I knew that the moment I stopped, we'd both be dead. The current fought to keep us apart, but I wouldn't let it take him. At that moment, I found inner strength. I wasn't about to lose him. I couldn't.

My arms hooked around his shoulders, locking our bodies together. My back bent, and I rolled him on top of me as I continued to kick my feet. I moved my legs hard and fast, propelling us toward a pebble-covered bank. I was doing it. The water became shallow enough for me to stand. Each breath stung as though needles were injected into my side. I didn't have much left in me. I gripped Bastion beneath his arms and drug him to dry ground. My body could no longer bear his weight. I needed to make sure he was okay before thinking of my own needs. I lowered him to the ground in an area concealed by trees and shade.

His skin looked paler than before, and his lips bore a purple tint. I remembered a technique my mom had taught me. It was part of the adult safety training that all citizens had to pass. The method should aid breathing. I hoped it'd remove fluids from the lungs too. I dove into action and placed a hand on his chest, pressing in a set of three swift pulses. My heart felt five sizes too big for my chest as it pounded. I knew what came next. Focusing on his full lips, I leaned down. I didn't have time to let my nerves distract me. My mouth pressed into his as I released all the air from my lungs. I pulled back and repeated the process. As time passed my anxiety increased—he wasn't waking.

I folded over his chest, resting my head on his collar bone. My fist pounded the dirt.

Wake up. Please, wake up! Dammit Bastion, don't leave me.

A sudden convulsion startled me upright. Water erupted from Bastion's mouth. Within seconds, he coughed. Though my eyes bore no tears, my emotions swelled with joy. I pulled him up against me, cradling his body in my arms. The firm grip around my back caused me to pause my breathing. Bastion held me in return. He rested his head on my shoulder as we took a moment to recover from what we'd gone through. It was a moment of silence where we both understood the gratitude shared between us—we were thankful to have each other.

Once his breathing calmed, he pulled back. He placed his hand against the nearby tree and tried to stand. His body wavered, and he struggled to regain his footing, but he was determined to rise.

Lace.

We had to find her. I rose and placed a hand on Bastion's shoulder, nodding to let him know that I understood. We wasted no further time and backtracked along the river. The sound of the river grew louder as we approached the area where we'd seen the living humans. Bastion shifted to look in all directions, searching for a glimmer of hope that Lace had passed through. Our eyes met the sandy bank, inspecting every inch for tiny footprints. The moisture from the river saturated the bank so much, that only vague imprints of shoe soles, far too large to be Lace's, remained.

Sudden dizziness spiraled in my head. A wave of pure dread, something screaming within me to listen. A feeling you get when your subconscious is trying to warn you—the sense you generally want to pay attention to. I'd had it before, and now again. It was the sort of intuition I always disregard and later regret. My instinct told me to turn around, to find a way back to the quaint little house I'd first met Bastion and Lace in. I could live out my remaining days there in peace.

Bastion grunted, waving for me to follow. And you know what? I did just that.

Dammit. Off I go, shutting out my better judgment yet again. Here's to hoping this time turns out better than the last.

I hated how double-sided my situation seemed. It was as though the hand of fate held a sword above my head, giving me the choice of which side I wanted to be on when he swung. I heard him taunting me with his words, "On this side, you die . . . on that side, you die." There was no winning. In all truthfulness, on my own, I'd probably never make it back to the house without becoming dinner for the ravangers. And I couldn't just turn my back on Lace. She was only a child.

This whole thing was shit. Damned if I do, damned if I don't.

I followed each of Bastion's steps as we moved down a narrow path. There was no overgrowth, only packed dirt. I didn't need to be an expert of the outside world to know it had been well-used. While it seemed like good starting point to find Lace, it wasn't the safest. I pondered the outcome if more living humans came upon us. I swallowed hard, despite my palate being dry.

Bastion must have been thinking the same, and bent down to take hold of a large stone. He then continued down the trail. Rock versus guns—we hadn't thought this through. Then again, there had been no time for a plan. The forest grew darker by the minute, and the sun was soon to descend beyond the horizon.

As we continued to follow the path, it widened. The thick foliage which had pressed at our sides now grew scarce. While I was glad to be free from branches scraping at my arms, we had lost our only concealment. Darkness arrived, and the forest held an eerie silence. The sound of our footsteps made my stomach flutter with unease. No matter how hard we tried, it was nearly impossible to move with stealth.

A sudden flicker caused me to stop in my tracks. Though Bastion blocked most of my view, I could've sworn that I'd seen a light up ahead. I gripped a handful of Bastion's shirt and waited for any indication it hadn't just been my imagination. I took a deep, burning breath.

Stop being so paranoid.

Since leaving Nialus, there hadn't been a moment where I wasn't on edge.

If my deteriorating body doesn't do me in, the constant stress will.

The forest was now so dark we had to feel our way down the path. I held onto Bastion, unsure of what I'd do if we lost one another. In my mind, I saw the sunken, skeletal faces of the ravangers. Torn, leathery skin; cheeks that scooped in to hug against their skull; and eyes that bore no sole—if they had any eyes at all. Most had two hollowed holes where the gift of sight used to be.

I hope Lace is safe.

My body drew to attention as a flash of light shone in contrast to the darkness.

There it is again! I'm not losing my mind.

I had no doubts. There was something ahead and Bastion saw it too. He stopped, placing a hand against my chest to caution me to wait. Then, just as fast as it had shone its luminous rays, nothing but the starless night sky blanketed us. Though our vision was limited, we still made out the white sand that now coated the path. Behind us, a void of pure blackness.

The light flashed again. It was like a lighthouse, luring us in from the storm—or possibly *to* the storm. Whether we were walking toward salvation or death, that was still to be decided.

Instead of moving forward on the trail, he shifted his course and started to our left. He ducked and weaved through the trees, his arms outstretched, always searching for the next obstacle. He was uneasy about the mysterious beacon and used the forest as concealment.

Only seconds had passed before Bastion's hand clamped down on mine. He shoved me against the tree to my side and cupped my mouth. His body pressed into mine, so close I felt his every curve and contour.

But, why?

We remained motionless for a few minutes before I heard what he must've already discovered. Distant wailing from ravangers pierced through the calm of the forest. A rustling to our right made my body tighten. No sooner had I turned my shoulders to investigate, leaves cracked beneath slow and steady steps. The sound approached closer at our left.

They're hunting us.

Bastion nestled the back of my head within his palm. He pulled me so hard against his chest I heard the dulling beat of his heart. As the ravangers drew closer, we determined that there weren't just a couple, but a whole horde. Twigs snapped beneath their heavy steps and foliage rustled. Loud nasal breathing hissed as they traced our scent.

It's over. We tried. I'm so sorry, Lace. I hope you made it to safety. You must be so scared out there, so alone.

I focused on the slow, rhythmic thumping within Bastion's chest. My mind filled with dread. I wanted to drown my fears, drown the daunting noises that closed ground on us.

A low croaking rattled nearby. The steady increase in its audible level moving closer. I couldn't help myself from turning just enough to see the hand that emerged from around the tree next to us. It wrapped its arm around the trunk, digging fingers, so thin that they looked skeletal, into the bark. Their bones popped with each bend of a joint. Then, its face emerged. Even through the darkness, it was so close I made out the sunken features. Long, black hair fell across its face, its teeth exposed and clamped together as it twisted its neck outward. The smell of blood was so strong—they'd already fed at least once that night. It stood less than ten feet from us, shifting its focus from left to right; searching. It stuck its hollowed nose to the sky and inhaled. They didn't seem to have good vision, if any at all, but their sense of smell was incredible. The ravanger hissed before dashing out from behind the tree. It closed the ground between us in a matter of seconds.

Time's up. Please don't be a painful death. I pleaded

to the heavens.

I watched the wide, open jaws nearing my shoulder.

A stream of light beamed across the forest floor, illuminating our surroundings. Though many of the trees stretched shadows around us, the glow was bright enough to buy us time. The ravangers at our side squealed before withdrawing beyond the light's reach. They were gone, just as fast as they'd appeared. At least a dozen of the monstrosities surrounded us, standing in wait behind the brush. They held their ground where the light didn't touch. The night embraced them once again.

Bastion and I looked down the path, in the spotlight's direction. Someone had saved us. Someone was there— waiting.

DAY 5
PART 6

We both knew that the direction of the light was our only chance. Once the darkness returned, the ravangers would stake their claim. There were too many for us to fight. I had to put all faith in my assumption that whoever stood behind the light had the intention of helping. Why else would they risk themselves out here at night? Still, after my encounter with the two men at camp, doubts remained. We were about to find out if salvation or damnation awaited our arrival.

Bastion and I weaved around the trees, careful to take long strides, so we didn't stay in the shadows for too long. We reconnected with the path, the light now flooding over us. It blinded my vision, and made it near impossible to see who, or *what* was behind it. As we closed the ground between us and our destination, Bastion reached over and wrapped his fingers around my hand. His squeeze tightened as the silhouette of someone stepped into view.

My eyes had accumulated a haze that impaired my vision. It was awful having no control over my eyelids. We would have to get closer. I returned a light squeeze against Bastion's palm and clamped my fingers down against his.

"Hurry!" a female voice called out.

A young woman stepped forward. She looked to be no older than in her early twenties. She waved an arm; the urgency of the situation clear by how fast she moved.

I think she wants to help us! We're coming! My thoughts screamed within me.

My reckless nature caused my pace to quicken as I hurried toward our savior. We were almost there when a rough tug forced me to a halt. This seemed to be an ongoing routine for Bastion and me. He was calculated and mentally collected. Me on the other hand, I was fool-hearted and careless at times—more than I'd like to admit.

Two light squeezes from his hand told me we needed to be cautious. He had a natural way of bringing my mind back down to reality. I could be so gullible, and he knew it.

"The girl's with me. She's safe. For now," the same voice shouted again. "I've gotta turn the light off before Pa' sees. He's worse than those things out there when he's angry. You can either come with me or deal with them alone. You got 20 seconds to decide."

Just like with what had happened at the river, this was one of the few times I saw Bastion react without concern. He didn't bother to process the situation or fear for his well-being. At the mention of Lace, caution blew into the night sky. It was clear how much he cared for his sister. I don't think he'd second guess putting his own life on the line if it meant her safety. With our hands still locked together, we approached.

The woman nodded upon our arrival; her short raven-black hair hung over her cheeks, parted straight at the center. A small red ribbon intertwined with a thin lock of hair at the front. Her eyes were sapphire, like two round crystals set within her sockets. She remained fixated on me as I neared.

"All right, now listen—I have to turn the light off. When that happens, we'll only have about thirty seconds to make it to the barn before the Phase-Two's are at our heels," she spoke with authority.

Phase-Two, I thought. My dad would use that term. Though, back then I didn't understand what he was referring to. The days I shared with my dad were vague. He often withheld information from mom and me about happenings at the lab.

"Hey, pay attention," she snapped.

I nodded, preparing my stiff legs to move as fast as they could.

3 . . . 2 . . . 1.

The light shut off with a loud snap, and the soft buzzing of electricity softened to silence. Darkness encompassed everything. If not for the dull sliver of moonlight that spilled in through a break in the clouds, it would be impossible to see.

"Go!" the woman commanded in a sharp whisper.

She pushed off the ball of her feet and sprinted ahead.

Bastion tugged at my wrist as we raced toward the large, red structure. Behind us, the sea of moans had returned, drawing closer with each stride we took. For a moment, I turned to gauge the distance between us. Dozens of bodies spilled into the open field. Their hunched posture swayed as they stopped to sniff the air.

I broke my stare and returned focus ahead. The ravangers rushed forward in our wake, the sound of their weighted steps amplifying the amount of anxiety I already felt.

Damn these slow legs!

We'd fallen behind the woman, time was almost up.

Focus. Focus. Focus. I beat the thought into my mind while trying to drown out the noises from behind.

I couldn't comprehend how they surpassed our speed, even though their bodies looked to be mummified versions of their former selves.

Ahead, the woman stood in the opening of the barn door. She gestured hard for us to hurry. Our feet covered the final space between us and our destination, and Bastion dove to pull us both inside before the door slammed shut.

The woman wasted no time in sliding down a large wooden plank, guiding it onto two curved metal bars that secured the door shut.

I barely had the time to step forward, before the steady thump of hands clapped down on the barn walls. The door shook in place but held tight.

"You two almost became jerky for the phase two's." The woman sighed and fell back on a large bale of hay. "You can come out now, it's safe," she called to the open air.

Why isn't this woman running for her life? Why hasn't she tried to kill us? Hell, why was she trying to help us? We're the undead—the flesh eaters—an enemy to the living.

"I said, you can come out now," the woman repeated.

A soft rustle in the corner was heard, and strands of hay shifted.

"We're not goin' anywhere until the phase two's leave, so you might as well stop being afraid and show yourself."

Blonde hair peeked from above the hay, followed by two familiar eyes.

Bastion swept past me, pushing through the hay toward the corner. A weak wail sounded as Lace rose to her feet. For a moment, she wobbled before falling forward, into her brother's arms.

I sighed in relief, though still keeping my guard on high-alert. We still weren't sure of the woman's motives. I watched as she got up and walked over to a large satchel that hung by a wooden stake. My eyes shifted to a steel rod near my leg, and I reached to my side to retrieve it. If she was preparing to make a move against us, I would ensure it'd be her last.

The woman's hand plunged deep into the sack, rummaging around. She looked in my direction, her lips curling into a grin.

"Feisty. I like that. The weak don't make it for long," the woman laughed and withdrew her arm. "It's just a peach." Her hand clamped down on the fruit. "I won't hurt you. Relax a little."

The tone in her voice caused the hair at the back of my neck to stand upright. It didn't sit well with me. I stood in discomfort as we continued to stare at one another.

"You're safe for tonight," she reinforced.

The woman's words didn't reassure me.

"Tomorrow, I'll let you meet Pa'. He'll be glad to have you here with us."

A tall ladder rested against an upper loft. Shredded hay coated the wooden planks above.

"Looks like I'm stuck here until sunrise. I'll be sleeping above." She pointed across all three of us. "Let me warn you though, if I catch any of you tryin' to come up with me, I'll have your head before you can reconsider your actions. So no funny business."

She turned to face me again, her brows furrowed.

"You know, I can't shake the feeling that I've seen you before." Her shoulders shrugged as she lifted a foot to climb the ladder.

DAY 6
PART 1

Dawn's light trickled in through a small window near the top of the barn.

Lace, Bastion, and I had remained huddled in the corner for most of the night. After my previous encounter with the living, I wasn't about to let my guard down. I could tell by Bastion's stiff, upright posture he felt the same uncertainties. His eyes were glued ahead, keeping a careful watch on our surroundings.

I found it odd that the young woman was so comfortable sleeping with the undead below. It didn't sit right with me, and I assumed that this wasn't her first run-in with our kind. Whether she was friend or foe remained unclear.

Hay crunched above; she was waking. Her legs hung over the edge as she rubbed her eyes.

"Morning," she spoke with a yawn.

She climbed halfway down the ladder, before leaping to the ground. In the light, I saw she wore two knives at her sides. Both had ornate handles, secured in a leather sheath.

"Let's get you guys something to eat. I'm betting you're starved by now. Plus, you didn't try to chew me apart, so that alone deserves a reward." She flashed half of a smile.

She removed the lock from the barn door and pushed it ajar.

"Wait here. Can't have anyone seeing you three yet. Not everyone is as welcoming as me."

Without another word, she left. We had no idea what was beyond the barn door. Between the darkness and the ravangers, it'd been impossible to investigate where we were.

Her steps receded until we were confident she had distanced herself. I pressed my ear to the door and listened. The faint lowing of cattle hummed. Curious, I pushed on the wood panel. It creaked open just a sliver, allowing a golden ray of sunlight to pour over my face. I brought my eye closer. A woman escorted a small herd of cows. A burly man pulled a single bull in his wake. Slung over the woman's shoulder, a rifle hung from a strap. Her eyes held ahead, and it was evident that she didn't feel threatened while strolling across the field.

This place must be some sort of haven. I thought while watching in awe.

Soon after, the muffled sound of chatter amplified. Two men walked near a beige, concrete building to the left of the barn. Both were armed. Even with my poor vision, I made out the fuzzy silhouettes of black barrels facing toward the sky.

They continued ahead, now in line with the barn door. Another person approached them from behind. He jabbed one of the men on his bicep with a playful laugh. As the first man turned, I brought my face closer to the opening to get a better view. A duffle bag, hooked on his arm, bore a symbol. Though I couldn't make it out, the shape resembled one the black coats wore on their uniforms. Curiosity was getting the best of me, and I pulled the door wider. The smell of sweet flesh drifted to my nose. It put me in a trance-like state with its delectable aroma. My tongue tapped against the roof of my mouth as I imagined how succulent their meat would taste between my teeth. Before investigating any further, the door slid shut, almost pinching the tip of my nose.

I took a step back, my foot now on top of Bastion's. He must've been investigating our predicament from over my shoulder.

"You on cleaning duty today?"

I heard a man's voice from outside.

Bastion swept Lace and me into his arms and pulled us behind a large bale of hay.

"Yeah, they have me on for the next couple of days."

It was the woman who had rescued us.

"All right, I'm gonna grab my shovel. Got work on the fields," he replied.

"Wait!" the woman's voice wavered. "I'll get it for you. I'm trying to keep the place in order," she responded, her tone now steady.

"Since when have you cared so much about the barn?" he questioned.

From where we hid, I saw the man's hand pushing against the barn door. His fingers curled from between the gap, preventing the woman from closing it.

Before she interjected, he shoved his way inside. With his hands on his wide hips, he scanned the area in silence. His brows squeezed together, and he brought his face forward as if expecting to find something to confirm his suspicions. He scratched at the unkempt stubble on his chin, before wiping a hand across his mud-stained shirt. His large belly peeked out at the bottom, folding over his pant-line.

I tucked down below the hay and brought my breathing

to a slow, soft pace. A delicious, mouth-watering scent wafted to where we hid. There was something about the man—his pudgy, sweaty body smelled incredible. I imagined my teeth, sinking into his fleshy arm as I tore a chunk from his bones. Saliva pooled beneath my tongue; I felt as though I hadn't eaten in an eternity. I was starving. My belly ached to where I wanted to do anything I could to feed. I dug my fingers deep into my arm, attempting to fight the urge. Blood pooled beneath my nails, and I tilted my head to focus on the ceiling.

Don't become consumed by hunger, Oshin! Don't give in!

To my side, Bastion laid his weight on top of Lace. A hand cupped her mouth as she gripped at his arm to break free. Her wide eyes held that same ravenous desire I'd seen before. A low growl sounded from beneath Bastion's palm.

I froze. My urge to feed now suppressed, my will to live regaining control. The man had shifted to face where we hid.

"All right, all right. Move it along, Paul. I have to get my work done too, ya' know. Otherwise, 'Pa will have both of us on phase-two guard duty. Unless you have balls of steel and perfect aim," she patted a hand against the gun slung over his shoulder, "then I suggest you get moving."

The man rubbed his forehead, before swiping the nearby shovel. "Fine, I'll be on my way," he replied with a hint of irritation in his tone.

Before reaching the barn door, he came to an abrupt halt.

"I sure hope you aren't hiding anything from your father. You know what happens when he's upset. Won't be good for anyone," the man said. His voice was low and intense.

He left without prying any further.

The woman sighed in relief and pressed her back against the closed door.

"You're damn lucky," she spoke in the direction where we hid. "I can't believe I'm risking my neck for you . . . I guess I owe it to *him* though," she muttered to herself.

What's she talking about?

Lace emerged from hiding, her teeth barred in another ridiculous smile.

The woman chuckled and shook her head.

"I've never met any rotters like the three of you. I mean, I've come across some that seem to have a sense of awareness. But it never lasts long. And, you guys seem bonded. You must've been family or somethin'." She looked at me again. "Come to think of it, I'm pretty sure I remember where I've seen you before. But it'd be a far stretch. None the less, I've gotta' keep you away from Pa' and the others while I figure this out. If you are who I think I've seen, there's someone who will want to know. You can stay here for now."

Lace took hold of my hand, tugging me in her direction. *It's safe*, the look in her eyes said.

I paused a moment. Not in fear of the woman's words, hell I had no time to think about them, but for the strange feeling where Lace gripped me. My stare dropped to our hands, and I tried to maintain composure at the sight. Two of Lace's small fingers were hard as rocks. Where her nails had been, shone solid bone. She'd somehow tore the skin away and hadn't noticed. It was happening. Little Lace, so tiny and sweet, caught up in this hellish nightmare—a childhood stolen by the wicked hands of fate. She was driven by instinct, becoming something worse than death.

It'll be okay. Somehow. I tried to convince myself while squeezing down on Lace's hand. My mind fought against the reality of our situation.

"I've gotta' go tend to the livestock. Don't do anything stupid; stay put and keep quiet. I'll bring back some food when I'm done," the woman said as she took hold of a metal bucket. "I suggest you stay hidden. If Paul returns, you'd better hope he doesn't find you."

DAY 6
PART 2

O nce the woman left, I led Lace back behind two large bales where loose hay scattered across the ground. I took three pieces, and tied one end in a knot. Despite its brittle texture, it held well and stayed in place. Then, I intertwined the pieces, wrapping each strand over the other until a completed braid dangled from my hand. My fingers ached, and it took a great deal of effort just to bend at the joints. But it was worth every sharp sting of pain. Each minute we still held onto our memories was precious, and I didn't think Lace had many of them left. I tied the braided hay around her wrist and patted her head.

A series of low sounds came from within her throat before she leaned over and hugged my waist.

Bastion sat with his back against the wall, watching with a slight curl to the left side of his mouth. If my skin wasn't so pale, he might've seen my flushed cheeks. To distract myself from my swirling emotions, I pushed a pile of loose hay in front of Lace and gestured for her to try.

Her arm shot out, and I once again noticed her fingers. I swallowed hard and watched as she fumbled with the hay. She didn't seem to have any discomfort or pay any mind to the missing skin and tissue.

Good, she's occupied.

I crossed the barn to Bastion and pressed my back against the wall to ease the pressure on my knees as I lowered my body. Once situated, I reached into my bag and pulled out my writing board.

I'm worried. I took a deep breath; it burned within my chest. **Lace, she**

Bastion clapped a hand down above mine. He shook his head, and I saw by the grim expression he bore, that he already knew. But the pain of seeing it in the written word was too much. He was hurting—helpless. His hand moved to my board, and he pulled it into his lap.

What's it like where you're from? Most people want to find a way into your city, not out.

I took the board and replied: **It's incredible compared to here.**

Then why did you leave? He responded.

Because I'm an idiot. There was this guy back where I'm from. He, well, as I said, I'm an idiot.

Why am I telling him this? How embarrassing.

Despite my mind urging me to stop writing, I continued to tell him what had happened. Could I be any more pathetic? Was it that I wanted someone to have sympathy for the pain I'd endured? Or, perhaps I just needed to release all the feelings I'd kept bottled inside.

He pulled the board back into his possession.

It sounds like he's the fool. One day, he'll get his. Things often have a way of coming full circle for people like that. Anyway, think of the bright side, you have me now to protect you from assholes like that.

Protect me.

Though my skin was numb to the elements, I grew hot.

You're also beautiful, he continued. **Like I said, he's the fool.**

Before my jaw dropped at the sight, he must've second-guessed what he wrote as his arm rubbed the ink away. My mind spun. What was this? Did he mean that? Or was it just an attempt to ease my battered ego?

I couldn't bear the awkward pause any longer and scribbled the first question that came to mind. Hell, I would've written anything to distract myself from the stillness that had settled between us.

Tell me about where you're from.

It was a lame follow-up to what he'd written, but I wanted to know more about him.

His composed demeanor returned, and the mile-thick walls had been rebuilt to shield his emotions from leaking out. Maybe it was for the best. It's not like there would ever be a future between us. The less attachment you have to anyone, the easier it'll be when they—or you—fade from the world. Most people had a lifetime to share. We had only days.

He took the pen. **I'm from a small town. For most of us, the elders or our parents came as refugees who hoped to find sanctuary from the surrounding areas. The forests, the fields, the old ruins of buildings from long ago, none were safe from the undead. They had overrun everything that wasn't protected by walls. Our little village didn't have the best defenses, but we had built walls of red clay and wood. It did the job. We lived in peace for a long time.**

Bastion stared off as though deep in thought. He then stretched his neck to the side, clearing his mind before continuing.

149

As the years passed, people disappeared. We all assumed they had gotten bit while out gathering. But, we began to suspect more. There was no way that they'd all fall to the undead. Some were skilled hunters who could've outrun an undead horde.

I hung onto every word, engrossed in his story.

I doubt I'll ever know what really happened, but the worst was yet to come. A group of men went out to gather water. Four left, two returned. This was three days after they'd departed. We'd thought them to be dead, just like the others. Despite having been gone so long, they didn't seem to be dehydrated or hungry. A wave of relief swept across the town to see the survivors. But, the strange thing was, they had no memory of what'd happened. After leaving town, they remembered making it to the river. Everything from that point on was blank.

As if Bastion had read my mind, he wrote:

It'd be easy to point fingers and assume they may have played a role in the other two men's disappearance. But, one of the people who returned was my uncle, an honest man. After their return, I never thought my entire world would fall apart. A few days later, Lace and I woke to the screams of our people. Our parents moved us to the back room. I'd never seen my mom so frightened of anything. Her eyes were bloodshot and glassy. From the doorframe where I stood, I watched her rush to the living

150

room window where she pulled the blinds shut. We thought the ravangers had gotten past the walls. It wouldn't have been the first time; though an incident like that hadn't happened for around five years. After the ravangers had eaten almost all of our livestock, we re-enforced the walls taller and thicker. I didn't understand how they got in again.

Anyway, as my mom ran through the house, blowing out our candles, we heard something hit the front door. Before my dad could put up a barricade, my uncle forced his way inside. His eyes looked glazed over, and he had thin strips of meat wedged between his teeth. Blood dripped down his chin and stained his clothing. He was no longer the man I admired. Something terrifying had taken over. He wasn't like us, Oshin. It seemed different, like he had no memory of our existence, and he'd turned so fast.

Once my uncle entered our house, he dove at my father and tore into his throat. I'll never forget the sound of my father's voice calling out as he choked on his blood. He told us to run. Even faced with certain death, he cared for our safety.

I'd seen it all. Sometimes I wish I'd stayed in the back room.

Despite my father's wishes, my mom broke. Whether it was from the sight of her brother becoming something we all feared, or because she'd just witnessed her husband being eaten alive, I knew the pain she must've felt in that moment. She grabbed the spear my father had carved and threw it into my uncle's stomach. What happened next still haunts my thoughts. My uncle continued toward her. The spear had gone straight through to his back. It slid deeper with every step he took closer to my mom. Why didn't she just let go of the damned thing and run? Hell, why didn't I help her? I froze. I just froze.

My mom didn't scream. She didn't cry for help. Instead, she stood in place while my uncle bit into her face. She'd given up on life, and us. I'm still trying to find it in me to not hate her for what she did.

He flexed his wrist, but kept writing.

I hadn't seen Lace come into the room, and before I realized it, she stood at my side.

Lace screamed. I tried to cover her mouth, but it was too late. My uncle noticed. He dove at me first and pinned me against the wall. His breath was hot against my cheeks and smelled like decay.

Lace begged him not to hurt me. That's when he lost his attention on me and took Lace by the shoulder. He pulled her into him faster than I could stop it. Then, he leaned down and bit. Her arm bled, and I can still hear her voice crying for Uncle Joe to stop.

Something triggered. A speck of humanity left within my uncle. He pulled back and ran a finger across his lip. He realized what he'd done. Then, just as fast as he'd come to our house, he left. I held Lace. We both mourned through the night. I wasn't stupid. I understood what would happen to her. She'd been infected, and it sealed her fate. All because I was a damned coward at the moment she needed me most. She's braver than me. She'd tried to protect me. I should've helped stop my uncle, but I was afraid.

Never again.

That night, I changed. I had to make it up to Lace somehow. She's just a kid who paid a terrible price for my weakness.

Once Lace had fallen asleep, I killed my parents. It was their second death that night, and the most difficult thing I'd ever done. Especially now that I know there's a chance you still hold on to your memories. Who you were. I hit them both in the head to spare them from becoming stuck like this. Not dead but no longer alive. But I couldn't hurt Lace. She'd passed out and seemed at peace. It was as if everything had just been a bad dream. But I understood the hard truth. I carried Lace to the bedroom and locked her inside. I didn't know what else to do.

The day caught up with me, and I grew too tired to stay awake, despite everything that had happened. I'd slept more than I had in months and didn't wake until the next evening. I was alert and focused with the energy to think, and I needed to find a solution. When I went to stand, my bicep throbbed. I saw a small bruise, and to this day, I'm sure there was a puncture wound. There were more important things to think about at the time, so I didn't dwell on it. I heard Lace on the other side of the door. I called her name, but the only response was strange noises It meant the worst had already happened. My thoughts spun. I needed to clear my head, so I went outside. It was horrible. My friends and neighbors, all dead. There were so many bodies all over the place. I noticed some had been eaten down to the bone, while many others had a bullet hole in their head.

Only two men in our village had guns, and even then, bullets were in short supply. There's no way my people did it. I went to my uncle's house, and the door was already open. On the inside, black coal covered the walls with the words: DON'T TRUST THE ONES IN WHITE.

I ran back to my house to check on Lace. She was clapping her hands against the door, scared. I had no one left. My world had fallen. I spent the next few days staring at the dried blood on our floor, barely eating or drinking. I was guilty for what happened to Lace, and didn't deserve to be the only one untouched.

I did the only thing I thought would be fit for my

actions. I unlocked the door.

There was Lace, standing in her favorite nightgown that Mom had stitched up so many times. The only family I had left. I hugged her tight, my baby sister. I knew my actions would have a consequence, but I had nothing else to live for. Her teeth dug into me like razor blades. And just like that, I joined my sister in our final time between life and death.

DAY 6
PART 3

After reading Bastion's story, I led with my heart and threw my arms around his shoulders. I pulled him tight against my body. I needed him to know that I'd be there for him until our time was over. There's no way I'd abandon him, not after all he'd already endured. Over the past days, as we'd grown closer, it wasn't because I needed him at my side, but because I *wanted* him at my side. Bastion appeared confident and brave, but I saw right through it. Inside, he was hurting, vulnerable.

He pulled back, just enough to turn his head. His chest remained firm against mine, but his face drew closer to the point where our lips brushed. A part of me wanted to give in, to give myself to what might become so much more. The other side of me, the persistent and rational part tried to convince my heart how gross it'd be—considering we were both, well, starting to decay.

Bastion brought his face before mine, and I froze. His calloused hand reached for the back of my head, and he pressed our foreheads together. His other hand took hold of mine, squeezing down.

I felt indestructible. I mean, sure, I'd crushed over Codah for years (the thought of his name made me cringe). But this, it was surreal; an energy that coursed through every part of me. One you can't put into words. But how could this be? We'd only known each other for days. I guess when days are all you have left, time moves at a different pace. There was a massive lump in the pit of my stomach, and butterflies fluttered around my heart.

The soft grunt from Lace startled me, and I shoved Bastion away in embarrassment. She smiled through gritted teeth and extended her arms. Held with pride, were two braided bracelets. The hay was intertwined loose, and she'd used far too many strands, making it extra thick. But to me, it looked perfect. She brought one to my wrist and attempted to tie it with her skeletal-like fingers. She fumbled with it, growing more discouraged by the second.

Bastion placed a hand on her head and took hold of the

bracelet ends. The task appeared difficult, but he eventually secured my bracelet. I then worked my rigid fingers to tie his. We displayed our gifts by holding our arms high above our heads. It was comical, and I think they were most likely laughing inside too—a moment of joy under a grim predicament.

We settled back behind the stacks of hay and Bastion picked up the writing board again. He was enjoying his first form of communication with someone else since the change. It felt nice to have a companion who related to the situation. Though I wished we'd met under different circumstances.

Did you have any siblings? He wrote.

That was random.

No. I replied. **To make sure the city thrives, there are strict laws on population control. Nialus has a form of currency. A system put in place to maintain order, and to keep the elite in authority. When my father died, we lost so much. My mom's pay just got us by. She wouldn't let me work because she wanted me to focus on school. If I scored high enough on my senior year, I wouldn't have to work alongside her at the greenhouse. I could follow in my father's footsteps and become a scientist, or a medical specialist. We called them White Coats. Then, I'd move us both into a better life. One where my mom didn't have to work until her fingers bled. For most of us, our futures were sealed from childhood. Our scores determined whether**

we'd be assigned to work in the footsteps of our mother or father. A lot of my classmates won't have the option of moving into an elite position. For them, the choice will be between things like sewage duty and butchering livestock. My dad worked hard to accomplish all he had. He always seemed so passionate about his position.

Without warning, Bastion tore the board from my grip and wrote.

White coat? What did he do? What did his uniform look like?

He tossed the board back into my lap and awaited a reply.

The sudden shift confused me; my hand remained still as I processed his words. I didn't understand why he was so intrigued by the mention of my father. Not wanting to leave him hanging, I brought the tip of my pen to the board.

He wa- The next letters were too faded to read.

I tried it again. Nothing more than streaks. My pen had run dry. Out of frustration, I threw it to the side. No more discussions, no more long talks about our lives, that was it. Now it'd be just us with our hand gestures and grunts. Great.

He sighed and directed his stare in the opposite direction.

What was that all about? It seemed important for him to know the answer. But why?

My mind had just begun to analyze the bizarre situation, when the barn door creaked open.

The woman who had saved us hurried inside, a flank of beef pinched down beneath her arm.

"Here," she said as she tossed it into the middle of the room.

The smell. Oh, the sweet, sweet scent that traveled through my nostrils and wrapped around my senses like a snug blanket on a cold day. It was so satisfying and desirable. I had to feed to control my cravings, to survive for another day.

Lace made the first move. She pounced on the meat like a ravenous wolf, starved to the brink of death.

The woman took a step back and watched in satisfaction as if proud we were enjoying her gift.

"The little one seems hungry," she said while rubbing a hand across her cheek. "Looks like she'll be turning soon."

Oh no, she must see the mutations.

Bastion looked up at the woman and gritted his teeth, a low rumble rolling to the top of his throat.

"Easy there bad boy, you wouldn't want to end up doing something stupid. I'm sure you're already aware of it; you understand what's happening to her. There will be a time when you're no longer a unified pack. She'll turn on you."

She crossed her arms and leaned back, still standing.

Why doesn't she seem to have any fear of us?

"By the way, my name's Raven," she laughed to herself. "Not like it matters though, I suppose. You won't be using it." A burst of air rushed past her lips. "What have I gotten myself into? This is probably the worst place for you three to be."

Huh?

"You guys need to leave first thing tomorrow. I was hoping for more time to figure things out, but I can't risk it. The longer you're here, the more risk for all of us. I know I said I would introduce you to the others, but there's something about you." Raven pointed to me. "If I'm right about what I think I saw, then I'll be in deep shit if anything happens. I'll make sure my," she cleared her throat as though she'd caught herself about to give important information away, "I mean, if you're someone of interest, I'm sure they'll find you, somehow. It'll be out of my hands at that point. As for the people here, let's just say that they aren't the welcoming committee I made them out to be."

Her words only spawned more questions. There's no way she'd know me. I'd never seen her before in my life, and I'd remember if I had. As for our upcoming departure, I didn't enjoy being confined within the barn, but the thought of returning to the forest was awful. Unease swept through me like a chilling breeze, sending a shiver down my spine. I sighed, recomposing my thoughts. Why worry about such trials, when it wouldn't matter for much longer anyway? Over the past day, Bastion had greater discomfort with his movements. And I was noticing myself growing weaker too. Earlier in the day, I'd rubbed my head, only to feel strands of hair fall loose upon my touch. My vision seemed less clear, and my nails had become brittle and broken. On the bright side, neither Bastion nor I had shown any sign of mutations.

Raven pushed off of the wall and walked across the barn. The blood from where she'd held the meat flank glistened on her arm from the single ray of light.

"Just sit tight until the morning. I'll get you out before barricade maintenance. That'll give you guys enough time to find a new place before dusk." Her one-sided conversation cut short as a small figure lunged across the room.

Raven landed on her back in a matter of seconds, the air forced from her lungs. She extended her arms, pushing against Lace, who held her jaw dropped and tongue flicking. It looked as though Lace was grasping for a taste, driven mad by the thirst for blood.

Bastion took a wide step toward Lace, his eyes screaming for her to stop.

"Shit! Get off of me!" Raven yelled as she tried to roll Lace to the side.

For such a small child, Lace's strength was powerful.

I wanted to scream her name, to snap some sense back into her mind. It looked as though she had no control over herself.

Bastion's hands gripped down on his sister, tearing her with great force away from Raven. He snarled, reinforcing his status as her older sibling.

The commotion had been too much. As Raven scrambled to her feet, the barn door burst open. I didn't have time to turn my body before a wire collar was draped over my head. It tightened and pressed into my throat.

Two men rushed in, restraining Bastion and Lace in the same manner. Bastion reached for his sister as they wrapped a metal guard across her mouth. The man next to Lace shoved her forward with no regard to her age. In their eyes, she was nothing but a monster.

Stop them, Raven. I looked at her in desperation.

Raven ran a hand across her forehead, still regaining composure.

"I came to get my tools, and they were in here. When I walked into the barn, the little one attacked me. They must've wandered in between patrol shifts," Raven spoke between breaths. She stood, avoiding eye contact with us.

How could you do this? You brought us here, and then said you'd help us get out. You're the absolute worst kind of person. Worse than anything we'd ever become.

"Xavion will be glad for the entertainment. It's a good thing you found 'em before they got the cattle." A tall, thin man clapped a hand down on Raven's shoulder. "Glad you made it without losing an arm."

Raven walked out of the barn, only stopping to glance over a shoulder at me. For a moment, we stared at one another in silence—my eyes filled with rage, and hers filled with emptiness. I wondered if she felt guilt over her actions. From what they'd said, she'd condemned us to a fate worse than death.

The collar pulled hard against my neck as a man ushered me to walk. The wire chafed against my skin, breaking through the layers until I bled.

To my side, more people rushed in to help restrain Bastion, who fought with everything in him to break free. Our eyes met, and I read his thoughts: *I'll get us out of this. I won't let them take you from me.* Words weren't needed to understand the look he bore.

Lace. Poor little Lace. They had buried a steel spike through both of her hands and secured them in place behind her back. I couldn't tell which direction her glazed eyes looked, but her raised eyebrows and creased forehead revealed her fear. She fought an internal battle between a frightened little girl and a flesh-craving beast.

DAY 6
PART 4

The small room was so dark I couldn't see my hand before my face. Guttural moans floated by in waves—the sound of the undead, the agony of being hungered and lost within. There must've been at least a dozen. We were all captive here; wherever *here* was. I patted my palms against the stone wall, searching for any escape. My fingers moved from the crevice of one rock to another, and then against wood. It seemed as though the room had no way out until I met with what felt to be the steel bars of a small window.

Bastion . . . Lace! Are you in here too?

"*Uuugggggghh,*" was the only sound to leave my

throat.

Dammit!

I stood in the corner and cupped my hands over my ears. I had to think. The noise, the sound of suffering, it was too much. Their voices echoed against the walls and shot like daggers into my ears. If I could figure my way out of the cell, I might find Bastion and Lace, then get us the hell out.

I moved back to the small opening and reached an arm through the space between two bars. My fingers stretched and inspected every crevice. A puff of air left my nostrils as my hand met with a square object that dangled from the door.

Shit. I'm locked in. I should've figured this wouldn't be easy. These people are humans who've lived out in the beyond—they're not stupid.

A part of me had hoped they'd be a group of simpletons who only had a basic understanding of survival. But, after meeting Raven, I knew that wasn't the case. She was witty and clever. So smart that she'd managed to lie without stumbling over a single word. I hated her.

Wherever we ended up, the people here seemed prepared. They even looked glad to see us in the barn. The cells were made for the undead. My heart sunk.

What are they planning to do with us? Why didn't they just kill us on the spot?

I didn't like the answers that ran through my mind.

My predicament was more worrisome than the thought of a bullet between the eyes. People don't keep the undead around to admire their good looks or excellent conversational skills.

A wave of defeat swept over me, and I backed into a corner. It seemed like hours had passed, and I'd seen no hint of light. Were they planning to keep us locked away until we succumbed to rotting down to the bone? Or worse. What if we gave into our hunger and devoured ourselves to cure the cravings? Nothing made sense anymore.

Through the sea of sounds, I heard a soft jingle. It was the same noise I'd listened to every Thursday night when Mom would come home late after locking up the greenhouse. I patted the walls to direct myself toward the small opening. My line of sight was limited, but I still made out the cone of light that shone between our cells. The faintest glimmer of light reflected from a set of keys gripped within plump hands. The first door cracked open and audible shuffling scratched against the ground. I pressed my cheeks into the bars, eager to know what fate my cell-mate was about to encounter. The plump hand swung a flashlight, and I glimpsed upon the face of the captive.

Bastion!

I was so taken aback by the sight of him I hadn't noticed the woman approaching my cell. Her arms bulged with chiseled muscles that appeared flexed by the way she held her elbows bent at her sides. Her pale hair stood upright at the top, shaved on the sides. The look complemented her sharp jawline and narrow nose. She reminded me of soldiers I'd seen in books; fierce and prepared for battle. A battle is just what she was about to get. If I got close enough, I might be able to infect her, rescue Bastion, find Lace and get us out. The list grew long, and it was wishful thinking, but I had to try. I had nothing else to lose. If that were to fail, at least I'd distract them long enough for Bastion to get his sister and break free.

What is this? Am I seriously considering sacrificing myself for them?

I was.

Here we go.

DAY 6
PART 5

The lock to my cell clicked, and I dropped my hips down to steady my footing.

Ready to join us, bitch?

A sliver of light washed into my cell. The door creaked outward. Without allowing the woman time to react, I dove forward with my fingers curled, ready to pull her into my grasp.

Click, click, click, click.

The rhythmic buzzing of electricity pulsed through every inch of me. My body tremored, and I saw the rapid flicker of light emitting from a device the woman held.

I knew of them from home, we called them shockers. The wave of electricity sent my muscles into a spasm, and before it came to a halt, she'd strapped a leather mask over my face. Restraints on my arms and legs were quick to follow.

Laughter burst from her wide lips.

"Do you think you're the first to pull that crap? All you did was make this so much more enjoyable. Good effort though," she spoke with a rough voice that sounded aged for her appearance. "Ugly bastards, always trying to feed."

She looked at me as if I were a brainless creature who didn't understand a word she'd said. Or maybe, she stared because she knew I might be aware and alert. Damn, she was hard to read.

Ugly bastard. The woman's insult repeated in my mind. That's funny coming from someone who smelled like she'd shit her pants—and she didn't have the excuse of decay.

She pulled me past the door and paraded me down between the cells.

"We've got a hot one," she said in passing to a man who stood guard nearby.

My warm breath blanketed my face beneath the leather mask.

That went far from planned.

Through the square-cut eye holes, I saw the many

faces of the undead. They pressed against the bars; some looked confused and frightened. Others, beyond hope as they snapped their jaws hoping to pinch down on the tender flesh of those passing by. A few squeezed their leathery arms between the bars, reaching to grab onto us as we moved through. One even took hold of my hair, tugging with so much force they kept a good wad in their clutch.

The woman seemed unfazed by the undead. I had to wonder if this was the life she'd grown up knowing.

If any of my classmates had been this close to one of the undead, we'd smell like we'd crapped ourselves too— because we would have.

A heavy door opened into a lit room where many individuals stood around a long chain, secured to cement in the floor. One man and one woman held guns steadied upright, their barrels targeting my head. Another man wore a surgical mask, concealing his nose and mouth. Within his hand shone the steel of a scalpel.

The woman who had restrained me, shoved her knuckles into my back to force me forward. She then tightened a thick cuff around my ankle.

Now I know that the chain is for . . .

They had me bound and cornered. The chain weighed a lot, and it took a great deal of effort to step forward. I wouldn't let them see my fear, though it terrified me. If these people were going to view me as a monster, I'd play the part and fight to the end. I took another step.

"Easy," one of the gun-wielding guards said as he positioned the barrel closer.

I froze. My instinct to survive still dominated. I'd have to obey—for now—and wait for an opportunity, a window where I could retaliate.

"She's an active one. My bets on her," the guard laughed. "Don't let me down." He winked at me.

I looked away in disgust.

"I dunno, the other one is pretty aggressive. From what I hear, this should be one of the best matches we've seen in a while," the woman to my right said.

What?

Pressure on my left arm went straight through to my muscle. An incision the doctor made was about an inch wide, and my skin split in the almond shape of an eye. He pinched at my skin, squeezing the wound. Thick brown-tinted fluid oozed from my arm and into a thin vial.

Is this what my blood has become?

I had a difficult time watching. There's something unsettling about looking down at your skin, split wide by the blade of a scalpel.

Why are they doing this? What purpose could a small

town, hardly equip for proper research, want with blood from the undead? Unless there's more to this place. My thought process evolved with every passing second, each scenario more elaborate than the one before.

"Sample extracted," the doctor stated in a calm tone as he handed off the vial.

He turned to set the scalpel onto a steel tray, lined with an array of medical tools. At that moment, they looked more like torture devices. It was the back of his lab coat though, that left me motionless. A small symbol, but one I knew well. The symbol of my city. A red circle with a hexagon to symbolize the six founding members of Nialus.

Thieves.

Not only were they brutes but also scavengers who most likely killed to get property that belonged my people.

Scum.

The medical supplies they'd just used on me must have been hijacked from white coats during their time scouting the area for samples. I'd never realized just how brave my father was to take on the challenges of his job. There were so many dangers they faced while out here, gathering samples to research. I wondered who—and how many—these people had killed from Nialus. It made me hate them even more.

"It's time," the male guard spoke to the others.

The doctor nodded, his ice-blue eyes staring daggers

173

into my chest. He gestured to the woman who'd restrained me.

Time for what?

Never could I have imagined what was to come.

DAY 6
PART 6

The restraints no longer bound my wrists, and I stood in a dark corridor, alone, starving, and confused. Dust and other particles had settled on my eyes, and though I could still see, it was becoming worse. I recalled the first horde I'd come across, the man leading them had acted blind to my existence, only sniffing his surroundings as they passed. The door at the end of the corridor had a square window that allowed the warm glow of light to spill in. Silence consumed me and sent a chill up my spine.

Think of something happy; don't let them get inside your head. You can't fear them if you want to live. Those who cower, die. You're strong—you can fight. I forced the

175

encouraging words into my mind. *Sarah—think of Sarah. Or Mom.*

With arms hanging at my sides, I stood facing the window.

Sarah. Mom. Sarah. Mom?

My chest throbbed, heart thumped. It felt like forty pounds of coal had been shoveled into my gut, weighing me down like an anchor at the bottom of the sea. My brain was drowning, dying to the disease. No matter how hard I tried, I didn't remember what either of their faces looked like. How could this happen? Small features remained, like the color of their hair. But their eyes; their expressions; their voices, it was all a distant memory.

I can't lose myself.

My legs grew restless, and I approached the door, my mind frantic at the realization of everything happening. I wasn't only battling the brutes of this town. I was fighting against myself—fighting against time. The sides of my curled fists banged against the steel door. Amid my aggression, I heard a man's voice. It crept beneath the small gap in the door and climbed deep within my ears. I listened.

The words weren't clear, but a wave of cheering followed—or, perhaps rioting; I couldn't tell the difference. There were many people on the other side of the door. The window was too high to see through, so I pressed my cheek against the steel. Its thickness created a barrier, blocking out most clarity. But, I still made out the voices that rang out in sync: "Fight, fight, fight!"

A loud *click* sounded, and the skin beneath my cheek slid upward as if it was being pulled from my face. I tore away as the door rose. My teeth pressed together, jaw tight.

Abort, abort! Run and hide! My conscious screamed. *No more putting on the tough-girl persona.* Those who try to play a hero in a world where villains rule, end up with a bullet buried into their eye socket.

But, where does one run when there's nowhere to go? They had expected this, much like the rats White Coats used. They'd inject them with god knows what and send them through a maze where they'd play puppet master. If the rat strayed from the right path, they'd find themselves forced back on track through cruel means. I still remember one of my father's lab partners sprinkling gun-powder at a dead end. When the rat drew close, he struck fire, singeing the poor rat's face and fur—forcing him in the opposite direction. When the rats completed the maze, only one would be victorious. They'd place them into a cage without food, leaving them to kill the other or starve. My father used to tell me that the sacrifice was necessary in the name of science and that they had bred them for the purpose.

This was now my story too. One end of the corridor, dark and blocked. The other option about to be presented—

and that's what left my heart filled with dread. Light flooded my ankles, making its way up to the top of my head. The steel door disappeared into the wall, and dozens of faces stared at me. Silence fell across the spectators who sat on two rows of raised seats. A tall, circular fence separated us. I felt like cattle in a pen. My feet wouldn't move. I didn't want to step forward and leave the corridor. I knew that the moment I abandoned the darkness behind me, whatever entertainment they'd planned at my expense would begin.

Another snap sounded, and a door across from me rose. My stomach churned, and I wondered what horror stood on the opposite side. It might be one of the men, ready to gun me down. Or some mutation they'd come across, prepared to bury its face in my intestines. No scenario seemed to end well. The light spilled into the other corridor, and a young man came to view. His tall, lean body and dirty brown hair were familiar.

Bastion!

He looked at me with a cross of confusion and regret. I assumed that he blamed himself for my predicament. He looked around at the spectators, his expression changing to radiate the rage he felt inside.

A sharp jab to my back sent my feet shuffling forward. Someone was there—but when the hell did they enter the corridor? I hadn't noticed their presence with everything happening around us. They held a lance that threatened my legs to move farther.

Bastion didn't need coaxing. He walked toward me, numb to the howling cheers of the crowd. His arms wrapped around me, squeezing as he tucked down, shielding my body. He roared in defiance, making it known he wasn't interested in their mind games and fear tactics.

There we stood, in the heart of chaos itself. I couldn't help but notice the amount of blood that stained the ground and walls.

This is it, Bastion. It was good while it lasted.

I struggled to keep my emotions from spilling over.

No, that's a lie. It hasn't been good—in fact, it's been awful since the minute I left Nialus. And yet, despite everything, I was glad to have met him and Lace.

His fingers pressed into my sides as he squeezed me tighter. He wasn't a fool. The odds of us finding a way out of the enclosed pit looked pretty much nonexistent.

My arms rose, moving to his hips.

"Greetings everyone!" a voice boomed on a loudspeaker.

I jolted back into a stiffened position with my arms parallel at my sides.

Scattered whispers, loud enough to hear but too low to make out spread across the stands. Bastion and I turned to see an older man with a long, thick mustache that feathered out at the ends. His eyes were dark as coal, but his stare as cold as ice.

"Today, my friends, we have an extraordinary treat. The roamers in this match arrived here together. As you can see, it appears they care for one another." He pushed his bottom lip out and mocked us with the most unsympathetic "*Aww.*"

The audience erupted with laughter.

I'll kill you all, sick bastards. These empty words ran through my mind as I peeked from Bastion's arm.

"I don't think we'll be able to convince this pair with words alone. What do you guys think? Don't let their little facade fool you. We all know how vicious the diseased are. So what do you say, my friends—do they need a little motivation to follow the rules?" The man threw his fist above his head, and cheers from the stands followed.

The people hung on his every word. Men and women watched with a glimmer of excitement in their eyes.

"All right, all right. Quiet down now, folks. Raven has brought us a little surprise," as he spoke, the dark-haired woman who had led us to the barn appeared.

Her eyes were wide, and she avoided looking in our direction. That didn't deter me from holding my hard stare on her. I wanted her to feel my eyes burning into her, feel the anger rising from my core. She was a traitor. She'd lured us in, took our guard down, then betrayed us.

The crowd fell silent, and a series of loud hissing sounds wound around us like coils, paralyzing all movement. A chilling moan pierced the minds of our onlookers; their bodies now stiff and upright. I knew the sound well.

No. No, please.

Bastion broke away from me and rushed to the far side of the fence. He scraped at the sides, trying to climb his way up.

"Now, we have a show," the man chuckled as he spoke into the microphone.

Bound in chains, standing on an elevated platform, was Lace. She jerked her body to each side in an attempt to tear free from the restraints. Her eyes were devoid of humanity—lost to the disease. She bared her teeth and snapped while contorting her back in more failed efforts to remove the chains.

"The rules are simple. And please, spare us from the dumb act, I'm already aware that you understand what I'm saying. I can't say the same about this one," The man prodded at Lace while he spoke. "If you want the girl to survive another day, all you have to do is kill the other." He knelt and pointed in our direction. "I'll elaborate, in case those rotting minds of yours have deteriorated. You kill her first, or she'll kill you."

He flashed a smile at me and winked.

"Though my bet is on Princess here," he said while waving his finger in my direction.

The man disgusted me beyond words.

He stood. "When only one of you remains, we let you and *this*," he shoved the tip of his brown boot into Lace's back, "crawl back into the forest. However, to be sure you're not gonna' fall short of a good show, there will be consequences for not playing by the rules. If you refuse to play, or if you remain idle for too long . . ." his voice trailed, and he looked to his side. He flicked his wrist, and the muscular woman stepped forward, her gun now pressed against the back of Lace's head.

"Well, you get the picture." He grinned.

My eyes scanned the room, hoping to find Raven. I despised her—but what if she still had some empathy left within her soul? Maybe she could stop this all from happening. It was the only thing left I could come up with. I'd looked a dozen times before realizing she wasn't there.

Bastion roared; it held such intense fury I felt it pouring out from within him. He slammed his palm against the wall.

We can't leave here together. The rules floated through my mind. *You know what you need to do, Oshin.*

I wouldn't be around much longer anyway. A couple

more weeks? Days? Maybe even hours. The disease might sweep in and tear through the last of my rational thoughts without warning. I didn't have family out here like he did. Aside from Bastion and Lace, I had nothing to fight for. It's not as though I could stroll back into Nialus and live with Mom. Oh, the irony. I was the girl who would whine if I'd gotten a splinter in my finger. Now, I had accepted death— most likely a brutal one, under the circumstances. I'd only hoped that Bastion would make it quick.

I'm ready.

My feet inched forward before my mind could convince me that this was the wrong answer.

I approached Bastion's back and slid my fingers over his shoulder. He turned to face me, and I nodded—a nod that expressed a mountain of words. It was a firm nod, a proud one. I wouldn't give those barbaric bastards the satisfaction of seeing my weakness, though inside I was terrified.

Bastion looked to Lace, then to me. To Lace, then me. I knew his heart was torn. My hand reached to his cheek, and I once again nodded.

Let me go. Do it Bastion, before it's too late.

I fought through the resistance in my legs and dropped to my knees. My arms hung limp at my sides.

Snap my neck, tear an artery—make it fast. I'm scared; I'm so scared.

"Come on now. Tick tock," the man clicked his tongue like the hands of a clock.

If I could've closed my eyes, I would have. Their stare violated my soul and devoured my courage by the second.

Bastion gritted his teeth.

May we meet again in the afterlife.

I prepared for the blow, waiting for his arm to rise. Time slowed, and I stared ahead. But he never struck.

Bastion fell on his knees before me, his expression filled with defeat. He couldn't do it.

He reached a hand beneath his shirt and into the waist-line of his pants. Within his grip was a triangular piece of plastic, sharpened at the edges. His jaw muscles flexed, and he placed his free hand over my heart.

He changed his mind, he's going to go through with this. They have Lace; he has to.

A hundred thoughts rushed through my head. He could stab me in the heart. Would I die instantly? Would I feel any pain, or is my body so far gone that it'd be numb?

He took my hand and placed it over his heart. He wanted to speak; to say what rested on the tip of his tongue. His fingers took hold of my chin, forcing my stare with his—those green eyes with specks of honey, captivating and entrancing. I wanted to stare forever, watching a dozen

184

lifetimes pass by. I did as he wanted until I felt the burst of pent-up breath pass his lips. His pinch tightened, and I knew something wasn't right.

I pulled from his hold. In the seconds it took to move my eyes from his face to his torso, my heart shattered into a thousand tiny pieces.

Oh, Bastion. No, please, no.

Clamped within his hand, was the triangular weapon, now buried into his abdomen. Blood welled between his fingers, yet he held his stare—a stare that said: "It's okay."

No, this is far from okay. I can't lose you like this.

Bastion pulled the shard out, his shirt saturated where the wound was. He understood what it meant to remove the weapon with such force. He wanted to get it done. His arm rose in height with his forehead, prepared to strike his gut a second time. Before my arm could shoot out and stop him, the large speakers within the room crackled. The man's voice followed, his mouth so close to the microphone that every word hammered through my ears.

"I think our boy here has a *thing* for the princess," he gestured to us. "We know what you really are—infected killers. Your mind never lasts for long. Stop trying to hang onto your humanity, just let it go. It ain't comin' back. You've become the trash of our planet. The ones who failed, dispensable. A plague upon the world. It's Gods way of weedin' out the weak. We're here to better this place; to clean up the filth. There's no harm in a little entertainment along the way. Don't you see? It's you, or us that has to go—and it sure the hell isn't gonna be us." He laughed, and the crowd joined in.

A middle-aged man in the audience stood, his red beard woven into a single braid. Though the whiskers, his lips puckered. He leaned to the edge and released a torpedo of saliva at us. His gesture sent the audience into a frenzy, and others followed suit.

"Settle yourselves," the man at the microphone waved a hand as he spoke. The crowd hushed and he continued. "We have a little problem here." He stared down at us, shaking his head. "The rules were straightforward: one of you must kill the other, or this little shit over here gets it." He approached Lace and took a fistful of her hair between his fingers, pulling her head back.

Bastion stood, blood oozing as he stepped forward.

"Oh, my boy it's too late for that. You lost today's round. Maybe you'll have learned your lesson for tomorrows match." He gave a firm nod to the muscular woman. "Game over."

The butch woman pointed the barrel of her gun to the back of Lace's head.

Bastion howled in pleading sorrow.

Lace, who had seemed lost from this world, froze at the sound of her brother's cries. Her ravenous behavior ceased, and she stared at him with wide eyes. Her thin arm reached out, bearing the weight of the heavy chains.

That was the last memory I have of her.

The bullet exploded from her forehead, shattering her skull from the close-range impact. Bits of her face sprayed out into the arena.

Bastion stood, frozen. His mouth agape and hand wrapped so tight around the triangular weapon it'd pierced his palm. He staggered back, staring at the fragments of his little sister.

The room froze and time stood still. My body numb to pain, yet my heart aching. Lace was just a child, a little girl with so much love. She accepted me in a way that people who'd known me a lifetime hadn't. She was the first to pick me up when I thought all was lost. I hated this world—hated these people, hated what had come of everything. I tore my eyes away. Lace's lifeless body still burned in my mind. The little dress, the one she loved so dearly, now covered in her remains. Her tiny feet, crossed over one another, limp and pale. Her hands that dangled at the wrist from thick chains. And the blood—everywhere.

"Now, let this be a lesson. Tomorrow, if you try to be a savior again, princess gets it too." He pointed at me with another wink. "In fact, I think we'll take one of her hands tonight, just to show we mean business." His chest bounced in laughter as if this were some comedic stand-up routine. And yet, his expression told us he was serious. "All right, all right, you know what? I'm feeling sympathetic today. You can keep your parts for now. I think the message has sunk in." He waved a hand. "Put 'em back in their cells; we got-" His voice cut short as the deep thumping of a drum sounded.

A unit of armed individuals rushed into the arena. They whispered something inaudible before leaving.

"Shit!" the man with the mustache tossed the microphone and ushered everyone out. "Get to the bunker if you can—kill as many as able along the way!"

What's happening? My mind raced faster than my heart. I held so many emotions I thought I might burst at any moment.

Lace, sweet little Lace. It seemed surreal—a nightmare within a nightmare.

The current situation made it hard to mourn; my body couldn't decide which way to proceed. A part of me wanted to collapse to the ground, to weep inside for the child who lost herself to this world. The other side of me didn't want to give up.

A loud bang to our side reminded me of the corridor— it was open! Either this was the next part of their sadistic games, or something big had happened.

I looked to the ceiling and released the full capacity in my lungs. *Rest in peace, sweet Lace. I'm glad I got to know the real you before the sickness of our world stole your innocence. I'll mourn for your loss—but right now, I have to save your brother.*

Other than my father, I'd lost no one I cared about. I felt sick; empty; broken. But I had to push on, to keep fighting. He needed me now more than ever.

DAY 6

PART 7

I clamped my hand around Bastion's arm. My knuckles grew white, and I felt the tightness in my fingers. His feet remained planted in place, his mind lost.

Bastion, let's go!

I grunted loud enough to get my point across.

He tore his arm in the opposite direction until breaking free from my hold. His feet shifted, taking slow, staggered steps forward. A trembling hand reached down, picking up a lock of Lace's hair. It was still attached to a piece of her scalp.

Within just a matter of days, I'd become numb to the sight of blood. But my heart hadn't shielded over to wash away emotional pain. I couldn't imagine what he felt. I hurt; a deep sadness that rooted itself inside of me. If I ached like this, what about him? His reason to go on was now nonexistent. What happened was beyond horrific.

Stay strong, Oshin. He needs you.

I approached him again, this time with a gentle touch to his arm. My fingers applied pressure, a soft squeeze to get his attention. I pointed to the door. We didn't know when they'd be back for us—this might've been our only chance to get out.

He clenched down on a clump of his hair, his chest heaving. If we could shed tears, sorrow would soak his cheeks.

I'm so sorry for what happened, Bastion. But, your grieving will have to wait. I won't let them take you too. Forgive me.

Under the pressure of the situation, I did the only thing that came to mind. Faster than I thought possible, my hand shot out and pulled the triangular weapon from Bastion's grip.

Okay, Bastion. Maybe this'll get you to listen.

I brought the makeshift knife to my throat, my stare burning into his. He stood straight and stiff, caught off-guard. I pressed the sharpened edge harder against my neck until my skin bulged on each side from the pressure.

He released the grip on his hair and swooped out an arm to stop me. But my mind was sharp, focused. I stepped back to avoid his advance.

Please let this work.

One. Two. Three. Four. Only around six more steps to reach the corridor.

I shuffled my feet back until darkness swept over us. At the far end, a spiraling red light warned of danger.

Keep going.

My back hit the door, and I bore my weight against it.

Click.

The door inched open. Halogen bulbs flooded our surroundings with light. It was the same medical room where they'd taken my blood sample. Two white doors were on the opposite side of the room. There'd been so much going on the first time I was there that I couldn't recall which one I'd entered.

Bastion wasn't a dumb man. He'd figured out my intentions. He looked back down the empty corridor before smacking his hand across a nearby drip bag. It flopped to the pristine, waxy floor like a dying fish. His arms lashed out, taking hold of a tray. Medical tools flew against the wall, clanging in every direction.

Shut up, Bastion!

I knew his emotions had erupted. There was a tsunami that swelled within him, releasing in his core and taking out everything around him. He was drawing too much attention. We'd made it this far; I needed to keep him moving—to get him out. My hand clamped down on his forearm, and I brought a finger to my lips—the timid girl I once was had no place in this world. There was no backing down if we were going to survive this hell-hole.

A glimmer on the ground caught my attention, and I noticed two scalpels in the scattered mess of tools. Hell, it had to be better than trying to dig my teeth into someone as my only means of defense. I took one for myself and held onto the other for Bastion. I wanted to trust him but his broken state of mind seemed unstable. My hands moved to his shoulders, and I forced him to face me. His breathing was ragged, but I could see in his eyes he was still with me.

Are you ready to do this with me? We're a team. My eyes shot into him like lasers. I took several heavy breaths to coach him into a calm state—something my mom had done anytime I was upset.

He took a single, heavy breath and nodded.

Don't let me down.

I handed the other scalpel to him.

We stood before the doors as I fought to remember which way to go.

Screw it.

I pointed to the left.

The handle moved without restraint, and it opened outward.

Please let it be clear.

As the light washed into the next room, my head snapped to the side in disgust. It wasn't any place I'd been before. Rows upon rows of fluid-filled jars contained a variety of body parts and organs. I almost stumbled over my own feet at the site of a shelf to my right. There were around a dozen displays, each one showcasing the face of an undead man, woman, or child. There were no eyes, just the skin that had been peeled from their bodies and formed around plaster skulls.

Bastion's arm ushered me back. He'd reverted to survival mode, and this time it wasn't for himself. I took a final look at the faces. My heart twisted at the thought of how many undead still might've had their emotions and memories while being dissected. That could've been us.

Bastion took my hand into his, our fingers intertwined with one another as he led us out of the room.

We rushed through two more areas before hearing the shrill screams drawing closer. There was only one way to go—we had to follow. A deep hum sang its way across the halls until the lights flickered. The humming sound dipped in tone before falling silent. Light declined to darkness, the power now off aside from red flashing beacons every several feet.

As we entered the next room, we were confronted again with a choice between two doors. One was made of solid wood and sanded smooth to the touch. The other had glossy, white paint with a round window at face-level.

A plea for help scratched at my ears from the opposite side of the white door. More screams followed. My curiosity reeled me toward the window like a hooked fish. I needed to see what had been so important, so devastating, that it'd interrupted their twisted games. They didn't seem the type to leave the undead without supervision. I moved in at an angle, inching my head toward the glass until just one eye peered out. There was nothing—only a dark, empty hallway. I was sure I'd heard someone. Bastion had too by the way he held his stare on the door. The way he readied his footing in case someone approached.

Just as I was about to turn away, the silhouette of someone turned into the hall. They limped in our direction, almost buckling a leg on their approach. Her face came into view from the red, blinking light that cast a dim glow through the small window. She looked to be in her thirties, a long face and short hair cut straight at the shoulders. I was confident I'd seen her face in the crowd during our death match. I'd memorized every one of the sneering, anxious, excited bastards who watched our downfall. A *thud* sounded on the other side of the door as her body collided with the surface. She smacked against it in panic, her face twisted in fear. Confusion struck me first. I didn't understand what would stir everyone to this extent. They didn't seem to fear the undead—we'd been more of a joke to them.

A wail echoed across the hallway—the sound you'd expect from someone undergoing painful torture. But I'd heard it before. A slender silhouette followed. It closed the ground between them faster than humanly possible. The red, blinking glow shone just enough to reveal its claw-like fingers and barred teeth. It screeched before adjusting its head back into the shadows—a ravanger. Here, inside of their walls. The woman reached out for salvation, her eyes meeting mine for a speck in time.

Bastion's hand shot out, gripping the door handle with both hands. Beneath his hold, the handle shook as the woman pleaded for passage. Her fate was sealed. We both knew it. Opening the door would welcome the end for us. I'm not sure what came over me, but I grew intrigued. I wanted to see what would happen next.

Curiosity killed the cat. A saying my mom would tell me as a child. I never understood it until now.

At that moment, I felt like the cat.

The handle ceased all movement. Silence followed.

In a sudden burst of noise, the ravanger croaked. A hoarse and ghoulish rattle that leaked through the door and held me in place. Blood sprayed across the window. Through the splatter, I watched the woman's torso arch back. A clawed hand pushed straight through her abdomen. The arm retracted just as fast as it'd first struck. Teeth shone against the darkness as the ravanger followed the woman to the ground. It planted its face against her exposed belly and chewed.

A firm push moved me from the window. Bastion hurried to the wall and shoved a nearby shelf in front of the door. I looked up, my awareness of the situation back in full effect. Once the ravanger devoured the woman, the door barricade wouldn't hold it off for long. The severity of our predicament sank in as my mind processed a solution. I'd seen enough ravangers to know that they hunt in packs—there had to be more.

I heard the woman on the other side, screaming in pain as she was being eaten alive. It was haunting. As sick as it was to think about, her cries meant our chance for survival. It was borrowed time we could use to get away. A part of me still sympathized with how awful it must be to remain alert while your body's consumed right before your eyes.

Her screams had silenced by the time we'd reached the opposite door. Though the villagers seemed occupied by the attack, that also meant they were on high-alert, prepared to shoot down any movement they couldn't identify. Danger surrounded us.

After passing through what looked to be a common

recreation room, we arrived in a hallway that opened up to the outside. The sky was like endless emptiness, drowned in darkness. Floodlights cast a bright glow in front of the building, providing circles of protection.

We'd be safe from the ravangers in the light, but we might as well paint a target on our heads for the living to see. A smaller building was at the edge of the light's reach. If we made it out there, we'd be able to use the walls for concealment. We might be able to move around the backside and slip into the forest. The people wouldn't be bold enough to follow us out there at night—at least, I'd hoped not. With so many bodies running around, the ravangers would pursue them first—fresh, juicy meat. We'd have to be cautious and move as fast as possible. Just because there was a distraction, it didn't put us in the clear.

Gunshots fired, followed by waves of shouting and cries for help. The noise must've alerted dozens of ravangers. It sounded like a massacre. It wasn't my sweetest thought, but I felt karma had come back to bite them in the ass. The world out here was abrasive, and it'd hardened me.

I took Bastion's hand and readied my footing. More gunshots to the right, we needed to go. I pushed off the ball of my foot, moving quicker than I had earlier in the day. I shifted one leg in front of the other, as fast as possible. Our shadows stretched across the concrete like freakish ghouls. We were halfway to the other building when the ear-shattering thunder of an assault rifle sounded. The ground near my feet sprayed up small bits of concrete.

They're aiming for us! No, this can't happen now, not when we're so close!

Another round shot. A deep, tearing pressure in my calf left me with worry. I knew at least one bullet had struck. The low grunt from Bastion told me he'd been wounded too. Thank god our assailant had horrible aim. One shot to the back of our heads, and it'd all be over.

Don't look back. Keep going.

I pushed myself harder than ever. Do or die.

Our assailant pulled the trigger again; a loud, lingering crack echoed against the buildings—another bullet to the arm.

If we didn't make it to the wall soon, there were only two logical scenarios. One: the attacker would run out of ammo before finishing us. Two: he lands a shot to the brain, and we're finished.

A thought crossed my mind. *Would their bullets kill us?* It hadn't occurred to me until that moment. I had no idea if the outside world shared similar technology to Nialus. Our scientists had created bullets that triggered the release of a chemical which would shut down the entire nervous system. The brain would cease to function. An image of Lace filled my head. They killed her easy enough, granted it was at close range. Most of her head had been blown to bits. My stomach churned. I wasn't sure if it was because of the sorrow I felt for my deceased friend or the hunger that continued to rise. *Food. Hunger.* Beneath my tongue, saliva pooled.

Bad timing. Hold your damn focus, Oshin!

My left foot shifted forward, but before it reached the concrete Bastion's hand pulled me back into place.

What are you doing?! My eyes screamed.

He looked to the front, then over a shoulder behind us. As if on cue, I did the same—and yet again, I was the curious cat who couldn't resist knowing what's around her.

Shit.

Someone stood near our destination. Their scent filled my nose, despite the distance between us. They stepped into the light, their stare focused on me from behind small slits in a cloth head wrap. Their appearance hidden from sight, but that didn't bother me. What *did* was the gun aimed in our direction.

Death stood to our front and our backs. We were pinned down in the center. My hand clamped down onto Bastion, who tried his best to position his body between me and the danger. Sweet Bastion, he was only following his heart. But, we both knew that without cover, we were screwed.

Another gunshot cracked like a wild storm, reverberating in our ears. I wanted to pinch my eyes shut.

One second. Two seconds. My heart punched at my insides.

Did they miss?

Something fell heavy against the ground. I turned my attention behind us to where the other assailant had stood. Now, a crumpled mound of flesh lay with a crimson circle soaked into their shirt.

"Hurry!" the other person called out while waving us in their direction.

A familiar voice; it was Raven. Raven the betrayer. Raven the savage. Raven, who was our only hope.

Bastion tightened his hold on me with one arm. My eyes trailed to his other hand, where I saw the scalpel held within tightened knuckles. I didn't realize he still had that thing. Remind me why I thought it was a good idea to give an unstable, distraught man a weapon? This was bad.

Bastion, don't. We need to get out of here.

Despite my feelings about Raven, I thought that if she'd wanted us dead, she would've done it when she had a clear opportunity. Even if this were all part of a trap to lure us back for another cruel match, we'd at least be buying ourselves more time to escape. Fighting now, while standing in the middle of a spotlight and at mercy to her impeccable aim would be like calling the Grim Reaper to our side.

Bastion took the first step. Good. He must've come to

the same conclusion as me.

"Put some effort in; we need to go now!" Raven urged.

She lowered her weapon as we approached, sighing in relief.

"Okay, we've gotta-" Her body hit the ground before she could finish.

Bastion—no!

He was on top of her before I'd had any time to convince him otherwise.

"Are you stupid? I'm the only way you're making it out of here," Raven forced her words through gritted teeth.

Bastion pushed his weight down, forcing her arms to her sides. His jaw widened, teeth bared.

I hated Raven and would've loved to see her endure what we'd gone through. To bid farewell to everything she held close and welcome the bridge between life and death. But if there was a chance for her to help us, we needed her. My feet pushed forward until my hands collided with his ribcage. I shoved him in a single, sharp motion that sent his body tumbling to the ground. He returned to his feet with immense speed that took me by surprise. Before the next breath escaped my lungs, he was standing at my toes. His eyes held wide with a combination of anger and confusion. He thought I'd betrayed him. I felt his rage radiating outward. My hand reached out to his, only to catch air as he withdrew.

I needed him to see that my loyalty was still between the two of us. We would make it out *together*. I reached again only to have it redirected by his palm. His fingers trembled as spiraling emotions consumed him. The next thing I saw was his back as he turned and walked away.

So, that's it then, Bastion? You're just going to leave after all we've been through?

"We've gotta go," Raven spoke with urgency. "If he'll let his emotions cloud his judgment, we're better off if he goes on his way. He'll end up getting us both eaten by the phase two's." She checked our surroundings. "If Pa' finds me, it'll be even worse."

I couldn't care less about what her reasonings were. There was no way I'd give up on Bastion. He had many opportunities to leave me on my own, yet every time he was right there when I needed him.

"Please," Raven's voice softened, "let me make things right."

I scoffed. It didn't concern me if Raven's pa' ripped limb from limb off her body. But, what kind of father would want to harm their child?

"Please," she reinforced the word while extending a hand.

There was no trust between us, and I didn't care much for the thought of having her around. Outside of my city walls, it was a world where survival was built on loyalty—in which she appeared to have none.

If she wanted to make things right, she'd be able to spare a few extra seconds. I needed to convince the person she'd hurt the worst. A firm stare and a gesture toward Bastion let her know my intentions.

She shifted and steadied her rifle.

"Make it quick," she said with a nod.

Bastion hadn't gone far. He stood with his back to us, staring outward. I couldn't tell if he was lost in thought or had just given up.

The dangers that surrounded us, the things that used to terrify me, now seemed obsolete. My focus, my priority, was Bastion. The gunshots and screams all faded into the distance, consumed by the sound of leaves crunching beneath my feet as I approached. I positioned myself in front of him and took hold of each of his arms, giving him no option but to face me. Through the milky white of his eyes, I saw his pupils shift in my direction. He remained still.

We don't have time for this.

My body took control and, in a moment that lacked

better judgment, I lifted a hand. The night air swept against my palm before it met the side of Bastion's face with a clap.

Why did I hit him? Of all the ways I could have coaxed him back, I chose that? Dammit, the stress of this situation is testing me.

Maybe it was in a moment of frustration. Not being able to speak grew more difficult to tolerate. Perhaps it was my heightened adrenaline from everything that led to this point. Regardless, what I'd done didn't deserve an excuse. A wave of guilt swept through me.

My body locked up, reverting to the timid and insecure girl I was before this journey began. My hand froze on his cheek. I waited for his reaction.

I might've just lost the only friend I have out here.

Instead of the usual growl I'd grown accustomed to when Bastion was upset, he placed his hand over mine. His expression softened. In the following seconds, he swept me forward and into his arms. He tightened his embrace.

I exhaled, relieved to where my mind felt invigorated.

It'll be okay. I'm sorry.

That was the moment everything changed. Hearing the faint beat of Bastion's heart, knowing he hadn't had the time to grieve his loss. And yet, he still attempted to hang on. I had a strong notion it wasn't just for himself. I decided that I was willing to fight for life. Somehow, I'd get us back to Nialus before time ran out. It was our only hope of being saved. There has to be an experimental cure after all these years. White coats worked around the clock for the cause. They had to be close, if not already there. Even if things didn't work out, we'd be no worse off than now. I had to try.

The rhythmic sound of gunfire flooded my head. It cracked like two stones slammed together by force. We spun around to see the body of a ravanger, mangled from the number of bullet holes. Its face had deep, oozing craters, and the damage had erased most of its features.

"Time's up. They're coming!" Raven called out from our side, her weapon readied.

Another round released as a second ravanger lunged through the trees.

I looked at Bastion. *Please, let's go.*

His hand met with mine. Our fingers lacing together with a firm squeeze.

I turned to Raven with a nod.

"Follow me. Stay close, I'm not slowing down on your account, and not turning back," Raven said while keeping the butt of her rifle secured against her shoulder. Her left hand glued in place to steady for the next shot.

We took the outer perimeter of the camp. The night was shrouded with the sound of death, allowing us to move across the scattered debris without notice. Trees lurched over us, their branches like claws waiting to tear us apart. How could Raven navigate through this? There were no landmarks or identifying features. Her lack of hesitation in the direction we were heading showed that she had a destination in mind.

Please don't be far.

Paranoia wore on me as the wailing of ravangers in the near distance haunted my thoughts. With my goal of getting us back to Nialus in mind, I refused to go down as someone else's feast.

Ravangers. Phase Twos. How did Raven know to call them that? Phase Two was the word I remembered white coats using. I never understood what they were, but I'd heard terrible stories while pretending to play with dolls and eavesdropping on my father's conversations. Stories I now struggled to remember.

I found it odd and unlikely that people who didn't live in the city would share the same terminology. Sure, those who survived out here had guns and basic technology, but they were still primitive in comparison. I wondered if they'd extracted information from our white coats. My thoughts drifted to the doctor from Raven's facility. I was sure he was wearing one of our lab coats. My heart sank, hoping they hadn't forced my people into their sick games.

For once, I was cheering on the ravangers. Good riddance to this town and all of its people. It was bittersweet knowing they might fall to the undead after having used us for heartless entertainment. Those who survived would understand the sorrow of losing the people they cared for. As cruel as I might seem, there was a sense of satisfaction in hearing their downfall.

We walked through the night for what had to be miles. It seemed as though I had endless endurance. My legs felt little pain, though my stomach growled in hunger. If not for my growing desire to feed, I could've walked for hours more. Raven, on the other hand, was wearing down. Her steps had become staggered, and her breathing was heavy.

"It's just past these trees," she muttered through each breath.

She led us forward until coming to a trench. We stopped at the edge, just before it dipped down. Wooden planks were in place on the sides of the trench. It looked to be an attempt to reduce the dirt walls from crumbling down into the bottom.

Tell me we didn't walk through the night to sit in a ditch—an open, vulnerable ditch.

"We're here," Raven announced.

You've got to be joking.

Raven steadied her footing and slung her weapon over a shoulder before descending to the bottom.

Yep, it's official. My life is one big joke.

Remaining here at night would be the same as setting up a meat stall and dangling our naked bodies from hooks for the ravangers.

"Well? Come on!" Raven shouted over a shoulder.

She was down on hand and knee, sifting her hands through the leaves that had piled at the lowest point. The sun had just peeked over the horizon and the soft glow of morning washed over the forest. A glimmer of metal reflected between the leaves and Raven chuckled in self-satisfaction.

"I knew I'd remember," she said.

With a single swipe of her arm, she pushed the leaves back to reveal a steel door in the ground.

"Welcome home."

DAY 7

PART 1

The door creaked open as if left untouched for a decade. Nothing but darkness masked the gaping hole inside.

"I need to rest, and we can't be out here wandering, not after what happened. Nowhere is safe for me anymore," Raven said. Her voice was softer than usual.

For the first time since meeting Raven, her face bore the expression of deep sadness.

Why would she just up and leave everyone she knows? Raven was a mystery, but one that intrigued me.

She'd fulfilled her end of getting us away from the carnage. I figured it'd be okay to let her rest for a few hours.

Not that I was trying to lack compassion, but time waits for no one, and we were on the clock. Once she woke, I'd find a way to communicate with her. If she was going to help us, then maybe, just maybe we could find a way back together. I'd get her into Nialus; my city.

When I tried to envision Nialus, I saw the packed dirt walkway of my district. The two-story, narrow building that was my home. But everything else remained shrouded as though a thick fog had rolled in. I had a friend there. She must be so worried about me. There's also a good possibility she assumes me to be dead.

Susie? Sasha? No, Sarah—it was Sarah.

I didn't remember her face, but the sound of her voice trailed through my mind. Deep down, I knew. I was fading from humanity.

Oh, Bastion.

It all made sense why he'd shifted from anger and pain to giving in and leaving with me last night. He forgot too. After losing Lace, a part of him must've let go. To preserve the last of himself, his memory of her dimmed. The thought was frightening. To forget about everything you held dear in life. I wouldn't allow myself to forget Nialus. If I lost that memory, there'd be no hope. Though seeing it was like finding a lighthouse through the storm. There was still a glimmer of light shining through the haze. As long as I could reach it, we'd make it through this.

While lost in thought, my body must've subconsciously continued. When I came to, we were already inside the bunker. A blue couch with big, round buttons was against the far wall. A painting of cheerful sunflowers hung above. In front of the couch was a mahogany coffee table with lions carved out for the legs. The doorframe to the side led to a small room with a bed. Across from the couch, a single counter with one stove burner and a thigh-high refrigerator. A photograph, pinned to the wall caught my attention. Photos were rare, and most people only had a couple taken throughout their lifetime. I drew closer and saw it was a woman. She had long, thick black hair and eyes that matched with Raven's. Her skin was pale and smooth like porcelain. Her well-kept appearance showed that she must've lived somewhere nice—not a crap-hole like where we'd met Raven. I'd also taken notice of the red lip paint she had on. Lip paint was something I'd only ever seen the wealthy wear in Nialus.

"Don't!" Raven said as she pushed her body between me and the picture.

I saw her throat flex as she swallowed.

"No, actually, it's fine. I'm sorry. Just don't touch it," Raven said while falling back onto the couch. "It's my mom," she paused as if waiting for a response. "I never knew her. She died after giving birth. My dad did everything he could to save her, but it just didn't work out. Such is the way of life,

I suppose. That's all I have to make me feel like there's some connection between us. It's hard to remember someone when there were no memories to begin with." She looked to the side, a glassy reflection in her eyes. "Well, anyway, this is my home—or at least it was long ago. My dad gave it to me when I was ten to start my training."

Training?

"It helped me learn to live in isolation; to prepare myself for harvesting without allowing my emotions to get in the way," Raven said with a tinge of resentment in her tone.

Harvesting? And, what kind of garbage father allows their child to live alone in a bunker with the undead and ravangers prowling in every direction?

Thinking of the differences in our upbringing not only made me sympathize her situation but also drew caution. Maybe she was trained from childhood to harvest the undead. Perhaps this was all part of a plan. But then, why would she annihilate an entire town for just two of us? It didn't add up. I still had little trust with her, but letting her know about Nialus and my goal was the only hope I'd have of finding our way back. She grew up in these woods, and with Bastion losing himself, my faith she'd follow through was all I could hope for. Forget waiting until after her nap, I needed to tell her now. Who knows how long I had left before my memory worsened.

Pinching my pointer finger to my thumb, I waved my hand in the air to mimic the motion of writing.

Please have something I can use.

Raven squinted her left eye and tilted her head. Her forehead wrinkled before she pointed a finger in my direction.

"Are you hungry or something?" she asked.

This isn't working.

Raven stood and walked over to a cabinet beneath her small counter. She withdrew a small cloth bag within her palm. Lifting the bag, she brought it to her nose.

"Holy shit, that's awful," she sputtered with a cough. "I don't think you two will mind though, right? I've seen your kind chew through some nasty stuff. Err, no offense," she said while shaking away the smell. "It's not much, just decade-old jerky. But it should hold you over until I'm up. I just need a couple of hours."

Raven didn't bother moving to the bed. She dropped down on the couch and rolled over, turning her back to us. I saw the hilt of a knife from a leather sheath on her belt. Though it was clear she was sharp with a weapon, I didn't understand how someone could be so calm around the undead. Even as I looked down on her shifting into position on the couch, my mouth watered. If we didn't need her; if she hadn't just saved us, I might've been inclined to take a bite out of the meaty part of her thigh.

214

What's wrong with you? I scolded myself for even thinking about something so repulsive.

The conclusion I came to with Raven was that she held onto life, but had been through enough hell to lose the will to care about much. I still didn't grasp why she was helping us; why she'd trigger the fall of her people; or why she'd often glance at me with a perplexed expression.

Not being able to speak or communicate was such a vulnerable feeling. There was nothing more that I could do until after Raven's nap. I approached Bastion, who held his stare on the photograph of her mom. His brows furrowed as if reaching for memories beyond his grasp. I placed a hand on the small of his back and rubbed.

We'll get through this.

Later, I'd think of something. I'd find a way to move us in the right direction. As the memory of my mother faded, I was more determined than ever before.

DAY 7
PART 2

Being underground removed all concept of time. I didn't know how long Raven had been asleep, or how long Bastion and I had stood in silence.

Raven smacked her lips, a puddle of drool beneath her cheek. She groaned and sat upright, stretching her arms above her head. Her eyes flickered open, and she rubbed a sleeve against her face to wipe the mess.

"Thanks for not making me use this," she said while patting the leather hilt of the knife. "You might say I'm a fool for sleeping next to you both. But, something in my gut says

I can trust you. My dad used to tell me that instinct is our best weapon. So, I guess you could say that some listen to logic—I listen to my gut."

Raven slid her legs over the edge of the couch before pushing up with her palms. She made her way across the room, to the same narrow ladder that led us in. Her bare feet curled over a steel bar with each step upward. With the turn of two cranks and a locking mechanism, the heavy hatch creaked open. She held it ajar, just enough to allow a stream of sunlight in. Her head shifted from side-to-side, inspecting the surrounding area of the trench. She paused to listen.

"By the angle of the sunlight, we've got about three hours left before dark. We'll have to scavenge quick and get back here. I said I trusted the two of you, but that all goes out the door if you don't get a better meal soon. I've seen what happens when the undead need to feed, and I'd rather not waste any bullets on plugging your skulls full of lead," Raven said while closing the hatch.

She wasted no time in pulling on her boots. After a quick trip to the bathroom, she slung the strap of her gun over a shoulder.

"I reckon you only have a few days left, at most. I've gotta' think of something soon, or you'll have to go on your own way within the next day. To be honest, I'm not looking forward to going back to life in solitude. No matter how many years you live it, you don't get used to the loneliness. So, let's figure something out," Raven cracked a smile.

I wanted to tell her I'd come up with an idea, but this game of communication wasn't working out in my favor. I could always try to draw in the dirt. That wasn't a bad idea.

As Raven's hand wrapped around the ladder, it was as though our minds were in sync. Our fate was weighing on her too. I thought about what it must've been like to live alone for so long. Then, to destroy the only life she'd had with people to help us. She must've had a deep resentment toward them. Something I figured didn't fester on the day we arrived. It had to have been something she'd tolerated each day, waiting for a reason to get out. No one goes to those lengths for anyone they've just met.

"You know," Raven's words broke the silence, "I might have a plan." The inflection in her voice was strange; there was a sense of hesitation as she spoke. "My father— my *real* father, not the man you met who was told to take on the role—he works on things; tests things. There may be something he can do. He's worked on your kind before."

And? What happened to them?

The way she spoke made me uneasy. And, that her father wasn't here protecting his daughter. The same man who sent his own child out in a dangerous world to live alone. A cruel kick in the ass to toughen up. Not to mention he had someone else pretending to be her dad. It seemed unsettling.

But, until I could devise a plan to get us back to Nialus without getting shot, Raven's idea seemed like our next best option. Her father sounded accustomed to being out here with the undead. Maybe he knew something we didn't. Perhaps the people beyond the walls of Nialus were closer to breaking ground with a cure than I thought.

"We can leave to meet with him tomorrow. Crazy as it sounds, I haven't seen him in a while. The most interaction we've had in the past year has been through two-way radios. Anyway, we've gotta' get food," Raven said before shoving her palm up against the door.

Before climbing out, she reached to press a small, green button. The soft hum of the generator fell to silence, and the only light now shone in from the hole above.

Once we were up on the surface again, Raven secured the door shut and concealed it with leaves. The toe of her boot kicked at the dirt, spraying grains of sand across the reflective metal.

"There's a small town nearby. I can get us something from there," Raven said while leading the way.

The sun hadn't shifted much by the time we'd reached our destination. Through a break in the trees, there was a clearing ahead.

"This is as far as the two of you go. Unless you care to become a warning totem like the rest," Raven said while securing an empty backpack over her shoulders.

Warning totem?

"I won't take long. This is one of our allied territories. Even if any of the others made it through last night, I don't think they'd have come this way. There's other resources closer. Stay here, and I'll be back before you know it," her voice was firm.

As she left, Bastion put a hand on my shoulder. Was I that easy to read? My curiosity was swirling out of control. I wanted to see what the town looked like, even if from afar. Were they all like Raven's former home? What if it was like Nialus? It would just be a quick peek. Then, we could eat and plot out our plans to meet with Raven's father the following day. No harm there, right?

A tingling spasm ran through me at the thought of finding a cure. My lips bent into a smile as I envisioned Bastion returning to Nialus with me. He'd be able to get a job, build a life. Never be alone. I thought about Bastion strolling side-by-side with me, the others envious of our bond. Though I assumed he was a couple years older than me, he might still be permitted to join me on my last year of schooling. Or, maybe he'd already graduated. There were so many things I looked forward to learning about him.

My knee buckled at the pressure of Bastion's shin. The forest scenery returned to sight. Images of Bastion and I faded away. I shot a stern look at him; one he couldn't mistake for anything other than frustration. Air pushed past my lips, I needed to loosen up. Being a total bitch wouldn't help coax him into letting me satisfy my curiosity about the town. These might be my last sane days.

I'd seen nothing beyond the city walls until the past few days. This was something I needed, selfish as it was. The door had opened to a new world. I wouldn't let the hours slip by staring at tree bark. I'd learned my lesson about close encounters. This time, we'd play it safe at a distance.

I pressed a finger into Bastion's shoulder, then to the direction where Raven had gone. His head shook from side-to-side before I retracted my arm.

Oh, come on. I paused. *Curiosity killed the cat.* I heard my mom's voice again. *To Hell with the cat.* I was going to see what the world looked like before rotting back into the earth. I would try my damnedest to save Bastion and me. There was still a chance for the worst to happen, but we weren't going down without a fight.

Mmmmmrrruuhhhh, my voice sounded like a wounded animal. So much for my attempt to pout.

Three short puffs of air left Bastion's throat, and I

knew he was laughing at me. With a shake of his head, he took hold of my hand. A sudden shift in his mood. He gave me a firm stare and brought his fingers to his eyes. He then pointed at me, then his head, and followed up by sliding his finger across his throat.

Just a quick look from afar. Don't be stupid. Use my head or else we'll end up deader than we already are. Got it. I was getting good at this.

I curled my fingers and erected my thumb straight up. Excitement tickled at my insides. Bastion wore his nerves on his sleeves. He crept forward as if we were preparing an ambush, hugging against each tree within reach. We took a route to the right of where Raven had gone. The territory seemed foreign to Bastion, and I imagined that he'd never traveled too far from his old home. Despite his lack of familiarity, being out in the wild had left him with a superior ability to navigate. He took caution and paused to listen before moving forward at each break between the trees. We wove around a few clusters of brush before the town walls came into view. Gray concrete with shoddy masonry work. We were elevated on the hillside, and I could see over the walls. My sight wasn't sharp, but I made out shapes and movement.

A flood of sounds filled my ears. I'd been so focused on our approach I had paid little attention until now. That was an aspect I needed to work on. I relied too much on Bastion's senses and it often left me feeling too secure. I'd let my guard down—big no-no out here.

Bastion pushed my shoulder, bringing us both to a lowered position. My joints were so stiff; like a rubber band pulled to its limits. We had to endure though. If we got caught, it was on me—this was my idea. I'd drug Bastion along to satisfy my curiosity. A little discomfort was worth the concealment.

After adjusting myself into a tolerable position, I looked ahead. For a moment, I thought I might have to pull my jaw up from the ground. It was awful. Pure anguish surrounded the town's walls. Undead of all ages were attached to chains on tall, steel poles. A small figure, a child who couldn't have been more than five, stood on the closest side to us. He bore his weight on the chain, his arms outstretched. We were close enough to where I made out some of his features. It wasn't something I was grateful for at that moment. One of his eyes was missing, and the left side of his torso looked to be chewed clean to the bone. My heart ached at the sight.

How can people live within the walls knowing this is just outside?

I didn't want to see anymore. My attention diverted back to the town—the reason we'd come to this point. Houses were fuzzy, but I could tell that the roofs were made of a thatched material. It looked like something out of an old *National Geographic* magazine my mom had inherited from Grandma. There were also mobile homes lined up. I spotted some of the inhabitants, though their fine details were a blur. They moved to and from different tasks. The one thing I found odd was that most of the people appeared small, child-like. Something about this place didn't feel right. Near one side of the town, I made out a fenced pen packed full of small animals; rabbits perhaps. Two child-like residents dumped bins of food on top of the animals. A frenzy took place as the little creatures jumped over one another. In one swift motion, one citizen reached out and took hold of the animal's scruff, dangling it before them. A pointed object was in their other hand. I understood what was about to happen, but I didn't care to watch. We all had to feed, and I was hungry enough as it was. The distance didn't stop my mouth from pooling with saliva. I knew if I saw the blood, my senses would arouse and there might be no controlling the urge to eat.

Bastion tapped my arm and tilted his chin up to direct my attention to our left. Raven was leaving the town. We stood. A soft rustle sounded nearby, leaves brushing against one another. We both stiffened.

Did someone see us?

I held my breath until my body rejected it from my lungs. This only caused me to suck a large amount of air back in, defeating the purpose of trying to remain silent. Though the undead wailed in our surroundings, in my mind each breath I took sounded like a wild storm swirling with force from my throat.

Maybe it was just a bird. Something felt off. Like a warm current of air in the dead of winter.

We needed to get back before Raven noticed we'd ventured off. I didn't want to lose our only potential lead toward a cure.

After a moment of silence passed, Bastion took the first steps in the direction we'd come.

Just a bird, I thought. Relief swept over me.

We made it back within seconds of Raven. To our advantage, there had been concealment from the forest. As Raven approached, I noticed her bag bulged at the seams.

"We made out, big time," Raven said while slinging her bag onto the ground.

An eruption of mouthwatering scents infiltrated my nostrils. My fingers twitched, and I fought to control myself. My body was taking control.

Raven, get back. Please. I was losing myself.

My feet shuffled forward, beyond my power. It was like riding in a machine you had no control over. I was a trapped soul within a shell of flesh.

Bastion stood at my side, his fists curled so tight that his knuckles bulged. He was trying to resist to the point of biting his lower lip until it bled.

We both knew that if we lost control, Raven might

become the side dish in our feast. A vibrating purr rumbled in my throat.

Stop, stop, stop!

I was a marionette; my hunger, the puppeteer. Before my mind had caught up with my instinct, I was down on my knees. My hands ravaging the backpack. Bastion knelt at my side, a fistful of raw meat in his grip.

Raven leaped back, keeping her distance, but never leaving us.

She watched as I ravaged the tender meat with my teeth. Flavor burst with every bite, and it slid down my throat in chunks. The feeling I got while feasting was a rush that couldn't be described. It was like being in love combined with a powerful adrenaline rush all at once. Explosive.

The last piece of meat was at the bottom of the now-torn bag. Bastion and I reached for it, our hands scratching at one another to tear it from the other's grip. Blood oozed from the pink meat, causing it to slip from his fingers. I shoved it into my mouth, crushing my teeth down to claim the reward before he had the chance to pull it back into possession.

The food was gone, and I huffed on all fours. My palate savored every bit of flavor until my saliva washed it all away.

What in the hell was that? My mind screamed, mortified. *That wasn't me. That couldn't have been me.* I was regaining consciousness over myself. It was the most terrifying experience I'd had yet. At least when we were in danger of other humans, I was still in control of my actions. Able to make my own decisions. Whatever had happened just then was surreal, like living a nightmare.

Raven emerged from behind a thick tree. Her eyes bulged from her face. "Tomorrow will be the last day. We have to contact my father, or that's it. I thought you still had control," her voice drifted.

My eyes met with hers, and I tried my best to convey that there was still some humanity left within me. To not lose hope just yet.

Raven let out a forced cough before crossing her arms against her chest. "I can't even imagine what it must be like," she spoke to herself. "Anyway, no one from my old home made it out this far. That was a huge relief. They handed over the food without question. I can see now you both needed it. I'm not sure how well tonight would've gone over with us all in the same house together. Speaking of which, I'll be in my room—with the door locked." She reached into her pocket and retrieved a clear bag of dried fruit. "Glad I held onto this." Her eyes met the shredded bag. "I'm lucky, to be honest. If anyone here had been radio notified of what went down last night, I wouldn't be standing here now. Stupid kids."

Kids. So that is what I saw. But where are the adults?

Raven pulled her bag of fruit open and reached a hand inside. Faster than my eyes registered what was happening, a glint of steel twinkled through the air. The tip of a blade struck with precision at the center of Raven's hand.

She howled in pain. A gritty yell followed as she looked down at the damage. "Dammit!" she called out while shifting to scan our surroundings.

There was no one. Nothing but an eerie stillness. I sniffed the air but only detected Raven and the blood-soaked bag on the ground. Had it not been for the swiftness of the attack, I'd have thought the scent of meat had attracted other undead.

Raven raised her wounded hand, the knife still embedded deep. She tightened her jaw and rolled her shoulders to let the strap of the gun fall to her elbow. Before she could take hold of the weapon, the bush to our side shook as a creature dove toward Raven. Its face resembled leather, paper-like and dry. Two recessed eyes looked ahead. Its body was covered in an ankle-length coat, made of sewn patches of skin. Within each of its blood-coated hands was a knife, about a foot long.

Raven was pinned to the ground before she'd even noticed the attack was coming.

The assault on Raven had distracted Bastion and me long enough for two more individuals to ambush us from behind. I hadn't even heard them approach. Whoever, no, *whatever* these things were showed incredible stealth and speed. Knives pressed to our throats and pointed at our backs. Any movement forward or back was self-execution.

My first instinct was to caution Bastion. *Don't try anything stupid. We don't have a clue what they are. Or, maybe you do?* I felt so small. So out of place. I understood nothing of the world. I'd always been bottom of the barrel, last in line. The poverty-stricken pity party who had it so bad. Little did I know that I was living the life of a king in comparison. Safety, food, a soft bed. So much taken for granted. Damn, I'd had it good.

"So, one of Unit Four strays out alone. Lucky day for us," a smooth, male voice said. Still keeping Raven pinned against the ground. His leathery face shifted to where Bastion and I stood. "Well, almost alone. What's Unit Four doing with a set of roamers? Curious. They aren't bound, which means there's a relationship here."

I don't know if I was more confused by everything going on, or shocked that he, no, *it* could speak.

Bastion grunted and pressed forward until the blade at his throat dug into his skin. The wound from our previous incident at the 'death-match' split open. Our bodies didn't heal as they did when we were among the living. If you got an injury, it stayed with you until the end. We were sliced up and filled with bullet holes.

"Whoa there. Take the tantrum down before my friend behind you has the privilege of piercing through your diseased brain," his tone was serious. "I've wanted a new coat."

I stared at his attire. Jagged pieces of skin sewn together with thick, black thread. A variety of skin tones and textures.

The man-thing stood, his mud-covered boot pushed down against Raven's chest. Her gun many feet away, leaving her helpless to his sheer force.

"Since your mind doesn't appear gone yet, answer me something. Were you with her unit? Do you carry out the same plan?" the man-thing said.

He didn't have to be looking in our direction to know that his words were meant for Bastion and me. In near unison, we both shook our heads.

Same plan? Who was the real Raven? It was clear she wasn't just a farm-hand. She knew her way around weapons, had a father who held some significance and was part of a special unit. I wondered if anything she'd told us had been only false hope.

The man-thing hummed, spinning the handle of his knife within his fingers. "Very interesting. The puzzle pieces scatter farther. I enjoy a good mystery." He continued to roll his wrist, the blade twirling hypnotically. "Tell me this then; do you have any idea what she does?"

Our heads shifted to each side.

Not a clue. Would you just tell us? I swear, if everything she's told us up to this point was a hoax—a ploy to lure us into another sick game, I'll take my chances with the man to my back and finish Raven myself.

"You devious thing, you," he spoke down to Raven.

"It's not like that!" Raven groaned while forcing the words out. "I'm done with unit four."

The man-thing dug the tip of his boot harder against Raven.

"I don't recall asking you for input. You'll speak only when spoken to," he said.

The man-thing seemed to have a purpose. This wasn't a random ambush by petty thieves. Whatever this guy was, he'd shown no fear. Every action was executed with precise motion. He seemed to know an awful lot about Raven. If her unit had been the bad guys, were these the good ones? Or, did good no longer exist out here? No. That can't be true. Bastion was rough on the edges, but he's a great person. Lace was too.

"The darkness this one has wrapped around her soul is thick," the man-thing said while looking down at Raven. "I was planning to kill the three of you. But the situation seems to have many layers. I like to stay current on what's going on so close to home, so you'll be coming with me. I'm sure we can scratch through the surface of lies with a bit of persuasion."

He flicked his wrist to the side, his pointer finger extended. "Karlo, show them a little insight to what their *friend* here has been involved with."

The thing behind me shifted, retracting his blade enough to guide me to our right. Until that moment, my captor had been still. Despite having held a knife up to my neck for the duration of our encounter, his arm never wavered. I hadn't seen what they looked like. For all I knew, the thing at my back could be another mutated variation of the undead. Multiple footsteps sounded just behind us. Shuffled feet. Bastion and his captor were heading to the same destination. I recognized the path. It was the same way Bastion and I had taken to inspect the town. I thought about resisting capture and fighting, but there was something about these three that intimidated me. An unsettled feeling about how they moved, how they struck. A part of me also craved answers.

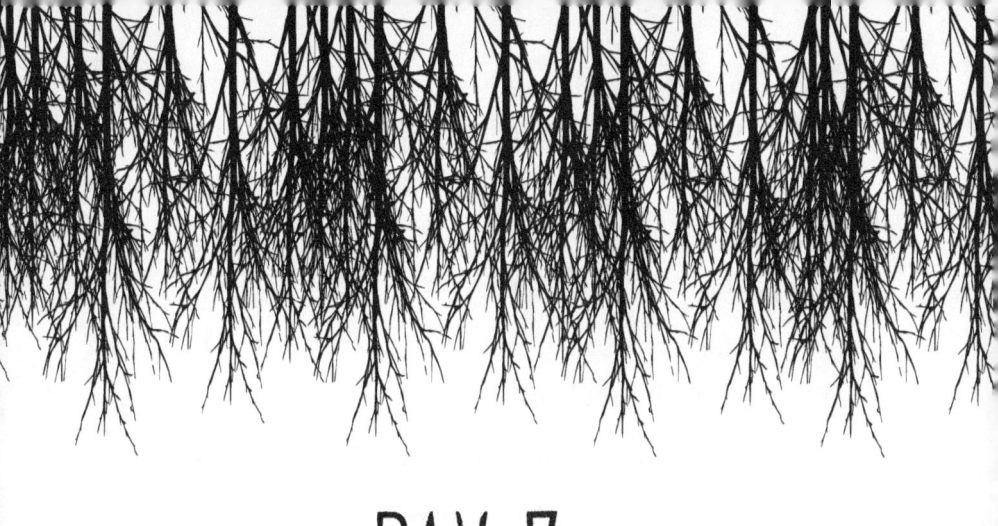

DAY 7
PART 3

The town came into view. This time, we were closer. A large rock formation gave concealment. I saw an open field that spanned between buildings within the walls. To one side, a child held a tool they raked against the ground. To the other, a dirt path. Little green clusters I assumed to be weeds scattered the walkway. It couldn't have been used often.

I didn't understand the reason we were being shown something that appeared to be of little significance. We'd already seen children in the town. It wasn't like anything out of the ordinary was happening.

No sooner had I ran a series of questions through my

233

mind, Raven's voice moaned. My shoulder shifted to see the man-thing approach, his hand tightened around a thick lock of Raven's hair. She fell hard to her knees, the knife still buried in her hand. Tears stained her cheeks.

"Make one sound, and I twist it," the man-thing said while tracing the handle of the knife.

I didn't know how to feel. If Raven was part of something terrible, or still affiliated with Unit Four, then maybe this was how things were meant to be. But, regardless of everything, I had a hard time seeing her as an awful person. She was either a victim of circumstance, or the world's best con artist.

"You've picked quite the day to visit. Especially when you throw claims of no longer having a connection with your unit. You'd think if that were the case, you would've avoided this place like a disease," The man-creature spoke in a casual tone.

The deep hum of a horn eclipsed all other noise. Sound-waves traveled with such intensity it trembled beneath my feet. The child I'd seen raking the ground threw the tool to the floor and scurried their little legs toward the dirt path. There seemed a sense of urgency in the way they moved. Many others soon arrived. Though my vision made each body look like a fuzzy silhouette of color, I saw there were at least a few dozen people.

A stillness swept across the open field. I didn't see any further movement. In a sudden, sharp jolt, a man's voice boomed through speakers. A group of individuals—adults by the look of their girth and height—marched in unison. Damn these failing eyes. I wanted to capture every detail so I could better understand what was happening. All I made out was the black clothing they each wore. It looked like they were carrying weapons, but the path was too far for me to tell with certainty. Behind the group of potential soldiers walked a handful of individuals. They held no formation like the people in black and had clothing similar to the children I'd seen. Brown-toned and resembling a potato sack with the same colored pants. At the rear, more dark-suited people marched. Their knees rose with each timed step.

The children lined on each side of the path burst into cheer. I heard their excited squeals over the moans from the surrounding undead. I wondered what type of celebration they were having. More than that, it didn't make sense why our attackers felt the need to show this to us.

As if right on cue, the man-thing tipped his chin, and the individual's behind Bastion and me brought the knives back to our throats. They guided us back into the forest, out of sight.

Raven's feet stumbled over one another as firm hands shoved her against a nearby tree, her cheek smashed against the bark. The skin of her hand was no longer visible, now masked by a coat of blood.

"I'm sure that seemed like a warm celebration. Happy town, happy kids," the man-thing spoke with a sharp inflection in his tone. He laughed. It was one of those laughs you hear from your parents when they're trying to reel back their anger.

Wait. Is his mouth missing?

I noticed for the first time. It was as if the man-thing's voice came from beneath his skin.

"Ms. Unit Four here knows a great deal about this place. The group she works with comes here to visit the little ones every couple of months." The man-thing looked to Raven. "Want to tell them why?" he asked while tapping his boot against Raven's.

"Don't listen to him! I only did what they told me. It was the way things had to be, they would've killed me if I disobeyed. I'm not that person anymore," Raven pleaded while looking at me with widened eyes.

Why does she care so much about what I think?

The man-thing *tsked*. "This is only one thing of many. The secrets Ms. Unit Four tried to bury will soon resurface. You can't wish away what you've done. Your aura smells foul with sin. I wouldn't be surprised if you were escorting these two undead to see a bit of fun under the knife."

What? My brain couldn't keep up with everything.

Unit Four, the town, the celebration. Too much. *Maybe we're fools to have followed Raven. She'd betrayed us once. She betrayed her own people. It's also possible she's working for someone above them—someone worse. But she seemed so sincere.* Nothing made sense.

"We call this place, Mill Six. There's eight total we know of. I'm sure you've noticed the lack of adults, aside from the shadow soldiers. They visit once each year. There are a few guards, but you won't see them often. Your friend here is the footwork between their annual visit," the man-thing said, speaking to Bastion and me. "Once a year they come, and you just *happen* to show up on the same day? I intend to find out why."

"Do you have no ears on your deformed head? I said I'm not with them anymore," Raven shot back.

There was her fearless spirit. Though, I might've been mistaking fearless for stupid.

"There's no denying that you've got a backbone. At least, until we rip it out," the man-thing curled his middle finger to his thumb and flicked the handle of the knife.

Before the cry of pain left Raven's lips, he shoved a wad of cloth over her mouth.

"I'm sure you love to be the center of attention with the tales you twist, but we can't risk drawing notice," the man-thing cleared his throat before continuing. "I know from this perspective you must all see us as the ones in the wrong. But we're fighting for the right side."

I'd bet that both sides of war share the same perspective, I thought. His words gave me no reassurance.

The man-thing turned his head to face Bastion and me. "If you're really not with Unit Four, or the others involved with them, then you must not understand what's happening. Let me enlighten you. We call this Mill Six because it's just that—a mill. But I'm not talking flour or goods. It's people. A people-mill." For the first time since arriving, his broad shoulders dropped. "The ones you see being escorted between the horde of shadow soldiers are making their way toward the largest building at the far side of the town. Residents call it *Steel Haven*. The exterior walls shine like metal, and they believe it to be their salvation. The place where they'll move up in the world. To travel on to the big, white-walled city to live a life of luxury for their hard work. A place where they'll reunite with their families." The man-thing laughed. "They couldn't be more wrong. The reason you only see children here is because that's all there is left once the shadow soldiers go. Every year on this exact day, they come to harvest anyone eighteen years of age. They're brought to Steel Haven—the last place they'll remember before their minds and body are broken. I'll call Steel Haven for what it is, a breeding house.

"When the children become of age, they're brought there to mate. Once the woman has been inseminated, they take the male away. The woman then lives in a cell for almost three years. Until her child reaches the age of two. On the child's second birthday, there's no celebration. Instead, they pull the toddler from their mother's arms. The toddler remains in town, sent to be raised by the other children until the cycle repeats itself. They take the mother, never to return. On the occasion, they may hold the woman to repeat the process a second time. It keeps the population flourishing for their needs. They're bodies, used to birth flesh. Property of evil. Both parents are experimented on; tortured."

The man-thing fumbled with one of his knives, still holding his body to Raven's. He continued, "Once I had knowledge of what was going on in Mill Six, I came back with a group. My brother included. We intended to get inside and convince the children to leave with us. My father warned us time again to stay far from its walls. He promised we'd find another way to make a difference. But each year that passed, we knew more would die." The man-thing dropped his voice. "Things didn't go as we'd hoped. The children's minds were lost. They'd been fed lies for so long. Unbeknownst to my father, we'd come back each year. Every time at night, and only after scouting the youngest of children who still hadn't been corrupted with false dreams. We saved a few. But at a great cost to my family," his voice trailed for a moment before he regained composure. "The older kids look after the little ones. It was difficult to find them alone, but we'd managed small windows of opportunity. You'd think it wouldn't be such a challenge, they're all just kids, right? That's so far from the case. The older children are the most vicious, willing to defend the town until the end. Hellbent on proving their worth to make it into the next stage of wealth and happiness. To them, *we* are the monsters. They're trained from such an early age with one goal—one lie. Work hard and earn your place where the shadow soldiers come from. The promised city of Nialus."

I almost stumbled back into my captor's knife at the man-thing's words. His story was chilling; horrific. But, why did he just say the name of *my* city? Were the shadow soldiers *our* dark guard regiment? *No, no, no . . . Impossible.*

The last thing I remember at that moment is the pressure from the syringe at my neck. Then everything faded to darkness.

DAY 7
PART 4

The room was dark, aside from two dull bulbs that lit each side. Rock walls, rough and natural. Unsmoothed by tools. Through the shadows, a single entrance no more than two bodies wide.

"Get these off of me! I've done nothing to any of you," Raven fought with a tangle of chains that restrained her wrists together.

Her hair stood out at the sides, wild and painted with dirt. The red ribbon she'd kept tied at the front, now unraveling at the bottom. At the knee, her pants had been torn. The crosshairs of scraped skin were red and swollen.

I still wanted to know what Raven's affiliation was with everything. Did she have it in her to lead children into an early death?

Bastion sat at a short distance to my right. He was just coming to after whatever the human-like *things* injected us with had worn off. He hadn't been bound like Raven, which only added to my uncertainty with what the intent was. His stare shifted across the room, and I noticed the black collar around his neck.

We can't catch a break.

My arm rose, fingers curling around a flexible material that circled my neck. There were no bindings attached to the collar. Aside from our new piece of jewelry, there was no other sign we were being restrained to the room.

I wondered if the thing on my neck was a tracking device. It was possible that our captors were using us to lead them back to Raven's home or the town they associated with Unit Four. Thoughts raced. *Maybe they only want Raven. But is it really this easy for us to up and walk?* I doubted that they'd bring us all the way here, just to let us leave. It was too easy. There had to be an ulterior motive.

Bastion had discovered his freedom from chains and rose to his feet. He approached my side, his arms pulling me into a firm embrace. His chin rested on my head. I didn't need to feel his warmth for my heart to find comfort. His touch alone gave me hope. I imagined what his voice would sound like if he could speak. His gentle words of reassurance to let me know that everything would work out. Another light squeeze before he took a step back. He held his palm wide and gestured for me to stay where I was. His feet shuffled across the room, slow and steady as he made way for the opening. His stance dropped, and he listened.

Raven had since stopped her demands and silence settled in the room. I heard every paced breath as it blew past my blistered lips; smelled no one aside from Raven.

With no warning, a loud buzzing sound cut through the silence. A steady hum followed. Bastion's spine bent back into an arch. His fingers curled and body tremored. As the buzzing dulled, Bastion fell limp to the ground.

The collar. They were never planning to let us leave.

My fingers reached to my neck. Electrocution. We had defied death, but we were far from immortal.

"You're awake. Fantastic, I don't do well with the unknown. It's time for answers," the man-thing said.

I hadn't heard him approach, nor identified any scent. He'd arrived without so much as the sound of his boot touching the rock beneath. I still couldn't figure out how he traveled in silence.

The man-thing entered the room. An entourage of others following in his wake. Six in total. Their movements were ghostlike, without a sound. Each one that came had similar features: leathery skin, sunken eyes, and a coat of flesh-patches.

"Are you ready to talk now? I want to know what your intentions were at Mill Six. You can also explain why you're traveling with two roamers," the man-thing looked to Raven as he spoke.

"I have nothing more to say to you. If you didn't listen the first time, then maybe you need to sew bigger ears onto that massively gross head of yours. I want no part of that life anymore, so let me out of these damned chains so I can go on my way," Raven said with a tone of regained confidence in her voice.

Yep. Brave, or stupid. Their reaction was about to determine which.

"If I trusted each one of your crew we've encountered, my comrades and I wouldn't be alive today. This isn't the first tall tale we've listened to. Lying comes easy to the wicked." The man-thing's hands rose to his jawline. He pinched down on his leathery cheeks and pulled up.

My upper lip rose in distaste. The man-thing's skin shifted and moved toward his scalp. It peeled from his head like papier-mâché. Blue eyes, more vibrant than a clear summer sky looked toward us. Blonde hair fell just beyond his shoulders, framing his soft, yet masculine features.

The three of us stood in astonishment. How had we been so unobservant to not notice our captors wore a disguise? A sick realization hit me: he'd been wearing a hardened composition of rotted skin, left to dry.

"We've had to adapt to survive," the man I'd once considered a *thing* spoke; this time his lips visible.

He paused for a few seconds as if awaiting our reaction. None of us moved, nor made a sound. He'd caught us off-guard with the big reveal.

"The roamers can't detect our presence like this. It conceals the scent of the living. Some might call us scavengers. We walk amongst the dead." He handed his mask to one of the others.

Raven straightened her posture. It was if she'd gotten her second wind with the knowledge of our captors being humans. Not some sort of evolved super-being.

I had to admit that I was relieved. Humans were dangerous; deadly. There was no doubt about that. But humans could be killed. Before knowing what we were up against, I lacked that clarity.

"I know who you are," Raven said. "You're known as The Faceless. They used to talk of your group after you'd murdered two men from Unit Four. You speak as if you're righteous, but you're nothing more than murderers too. Monsters, just like them." She spat at the man's boot.

Before her saliva fell, one of the individuals behind the man sprang forward. They were so swift they'd brought a knife to Raven's throat before I'd even noticed it was drawn.

"Halt!" the man called out. "Put it down," he commanded to his comrade.

The attacker listened and returned their weapon to a hardened leather strap. Their fingers rose, lifting the skin-mask from their head. Short, black hair fell upon a fair complexion. Chin length at the front, short and layered in the back. One side shaved. She was Asian, fierce and battle-worn in appearance. A thick scar ran down the left side of her face.

"With due respect, General, I can't allow someone to enter our home and speak to you in such a manner," she said while resting her hand over the knife.

"It's not your call to make, Isa," the man we now identified as their general replied. "I still need information. You can't extract that from a corpse."

"She doesn't need her fingers to speak," Isa shot back.

A sharp stare from the general silenced Isa.

Their intentions were becoming clear. The general was a figure of authority to them and planned to get answers from Raven at any cost. I had a bad feeling we were part of that—nothing more than dispensable undead. I wondered how he'd gained such prestige with the others. He looked so young. Not much older than Bastion. This world hardened people from such an early age. Nialus was the land of luxury. My heart sank as I remembered Mill Six. Nialus, the *promised kingdom*. The seed planted to lure unknowing children to their death. But what role did Nialus really play in all of this?

There was still a possibility that the shadow soldiers weren't the dark guard regiment. That they used Nialus as a cover with no real connection to it. I had a hard time believing that my city would have any involvement with such extremes. Things were routine there. Sure, it wasn't perfect, and I'd seem some unusual things in the past, but it was home. A thriving community where they looked out for the children. There were no ulterior motives for us. We went to school and trained for our future jobs. Life was so simple. At least, I thought it was. I couldn't recall what the city looked like. Just pieces of memories that would flash in my mind. I knew I'd gone to school, but didn't remember what I'd studied, or who my teacher was. I missed home but had no idea what I did there in my daily routine. Frustration grew.

The general approached Raven. "You might think we're horrible, but you're aware of what your people have done. You see what they continue to do. So, call us what you will. Condemn us for our actions. But someone has to bear this burden—someone has to make hard choices for the salvation of the innocent. My shoulders hold these weights. I may die trying to help better this world, but I assure you, I'm taking them down with me," he spoke in a near whisper, but sharp enough for the room to hear. "So then," he clapped his hands, "shall we begin?"

The general cared not for honor with his motives. It wasn't like those samurai books where a code was in place. He was a 'get the job done' kind of guy. He was smart. Why give your rival an opportunity if it leaves you with a fifty percent chance of dying? What honor is there in leaving the threat alive? If you're going in intending to harm or kill, you get it done. Away with the bullshit formalities.

Yes, I plan to kill you. But let me offer you a fair opportunity to kill me first. Stupid.

It was crazy. If anyone had met me just days before this, they'd be talking to a different person. I used to be so kind—soft. Not that there was anything wrong with being a nice person. I still was in my core. But hardened. I saw through the fluff. No more getting walked on; no more being sweet to where it blends into stupidity. If the world thought it would destroy me, it couldn't have been more wrong. Pandora's box had been opened.

DAY 7
PART 5

The woman he had called Isa stepped toward Bastion. Her eyes met the general's, and she gave a silent nod. Thin fingers reached where her dagger rest. She slid it from its sheath.

Don't fucking touch him. Adrenaline flooded into my bloodstream. My heart, a bass drum behind my breast. We'd been through too much. Treated like animals. No more, not again.

A gritty, deep moan sounded from Bastion. He pushed up off the ground with the palm of his hand. His feet planted, stance tall.

"Oh, this won't be a fight. Though, I admire your drive. I'm not giving you the opportunity to infect one of us. We're doing things my way," the general spoke. A hand waved to signal one of his lackeys.

A burly figure took a single step forward. Tall, with broad shoulders. They kept their skin mask on, concealing all features aside from dark, deep-set eyes. A controller rest within fat, curled fingers. Their thumb shifted, gliding over a bright orange button. The finger trembled as if waiting with eager anticipation for something spectacular to come. It came down heavy, mashing the button until it was flush with the rest of the controller.

Bastion's body tremored. Waves of electricity racing through every limb until he buckled to the ground.

I shifted my stance. This needed to stop. I had to do something. Anything.

The general clicked his tongue and shook his head at me. "Your brain hasn't deteriorated yet. The moment you didn't dive at me in hunger when we met, I realized you were still there." He pressed his pointer finger to the side of his head. "You know better than to move. One step and you'll be in the same predicament as your boyfriend."

Boyfriend? The word caught me off-guard, but I rebounded. We weren't to that point. No formalities or titles between us. *But, I swear to God that I'll shred the shit out of you if you hurt him.*

"Now," the general continued, "you three can see how this is going down. I'm in no mood for resistance. Too many have suffered at the hands of her people." His stare was on Raven again. "So, I'll ask you one more time: Why were you at Mill Six. And, why are you accompanied by two roamers? I've seen a lot of things, but never the living and undead together without consequence. You should be dead. Your body at the bottom of their bellies. I want to know what Unit Four is up to."

"Why are we running in circles? My unit fell. Because of me. In case you missed that for the hundredth time—I said, it's because of *me*," Raven emphasized the last word louder. "I'm not sure why you can't get that through your head, Goldilocks. As for these two, I'm-" Raven's words cut short as the general raised his hand.

Laughter. Not from his mouth, but rising through his throat. His head shook. Disappointment smothering his face. He retracted his arm, taking a deep breath. "Okay, so you're going to keep this charade going. I asked for just one thing— answers. And yet, you continue to feed me lies. I do recognize you. I never forget. I saw you with your people; two years ago. There you were, a good, loyal little dog amongst them. I watched as your group invaded a small community over the hilltop. I watched as you stood without morality. Your people took a young child, torn from her parent's embrace. She'd just been bitten but hadn't turned. Her parents, still clean. No marks, no infection." He pointed his index and middle finger together. Aimed it at Raven's forehead. "They shot the mother and father, square between the eyes. I've always wondered *why*. Why would you need to silence grieving parents?

"You and your people took the child. Handled her like an animal. Muzzled her face, shoved her around as though you were tossing a ball back and forth. I want you to understand that I'm very aware of what your people do with the undead. The child left this world in agony. One can only hope she'd already turned before they began." He retracted his fingers, relaxing his stance. "My comrades had separated to scavenge for goods. It was just Isa and me. We were no match for the well-armed group you were with. Had it been any different, I assure you, you wouldn't be here today." The general pinched the skin between the bridge of his nose. "I'm rambling now. Let's finish why we're all gathered here." He looked to the petite, yet fearless woman. "Isa. You're up."

Her dagger spun a full three-sixty over the back of her hand. It stopped with the tip of the blade pointing straight down. Her fingers clamped on the handle. The weapon was steady and still. With a single, swift motion she fell to a knee. She was precise, calculated. The dagger now within an inch of Bastion's bicep.

His movement was slow. The effects of electrocution still lingered.

"Let's be real. No one in their right mind travels with roamers. And no roamer will have enough restraint to not tear your flesh from the bone. Their hunger tempts their senses to the point of no control. So, that leaves me with the conclusion that these two must mean something to you. You wouldn't risk so much otherwise. Family? Perhaps dear childhood friends? Last chance to confess the truth." The general had lost his witty gleam. His forehead creased and corners of his lips bent toward the ground.

"Son of a bitch!" Raven pulled on the chains as she shouted. "How can I tell you anything different when it's all been the truth? What more do you want from me? You expect me to fabricate a lie to satisfy your stupid revenge-bent mind. Fine. I can feed you with lies if that's what you want. Damned idiot. You're just going to kill me anyway."

The general remained quiet. He nodded to Isa. It was a nod with finality. Firm. The kind you understood meant something terrible was about to happen.

Isa's hand pushed down with such intensity that the blade was buried before I'd seen it reach his skin. One inch. Two. It sunk in until clearing through his arm and reaching the floor.

I knew he didn't feel the pain, but my heart wasn't able to stand the sight. There was no way I'd stay idle while this bitch mutilated him. Adrenaline rose. A surge of energy shot through me. My breath was rapid and sharp. Everything around me slowed. It was as if the world had stopped. Motion suspended. I heard even the slightest sounds. Every breath, every shift of the foot. My heart, thumping at an accelerated rate. My mind had perfect clarity of the actions happening in my surroundings.

Isa withdrew her dagger. Her narrow eyes met the general's.

"It's the only way. One of these two roamers means something to her. I'm sure of it. She'll talk when we find out who it is. Proceed," the general said.

Isa followed his command. Her dagger shifted over Bastion's eye. Two hands gripped the handle. The blade ready to pierce with precision.

She's going to kill him. My muscles tightened. Fingers curled until tendons bulged. *No, bitch. Not today.* Oxygen was flooding my lungs. My chest rose. *This ends now. But not with Bastion's life.*

I pushed off of my right foot, toes bending up against the rock beneath. My right leg hadn't left the floor before I felt the current of electricity travel through me. For a moment, I lost all control. My muscles spasmed. Deep vibrations rumbled in my throat. It shook my skin like a violent storm. My teeth parted, and I cried out; eyes locking onto the one who held the controller in his hand.

You can't stop me, bastard.

Something surged deep within me. A sensation, unlike anything I'd ever experienced. A phoenix bursting from the flame. My head tingled. Not from the electricity, but because of something inside. A part of me that was emerging from darkness. My muscles burned as if they were expanding, tearing apart. It didn't hurt, and fueled me with incredible energy. My clouded vision was now crisp. Sharp. Every fine detail was visible, down to the tiny hairs on the fat thumb that crunched down on the orange button.

Electric currents intensified. The man was cranking the volts.

Now or never. Turn off the controller, save Bastion.

My body tightened, muscles throbbing.

The dagger crept toward Bastion. Time slowed. Or maybe I had sped up. I wasn't sure. My legs trembled; not from the electricity that fought to hold me in place. But from the overwhelming amount of adrenaline that had circulated its way through me. My veins flooded. A river of energy. I pushed off once again. This time, he could crank the controller, and I wouldn't let it stop me.

Go ahead, turn it up, asshole. It's over.

Before his pointer finger had time to spin a dial and increase the volts, my hands shot forward. My mind tunneled on one thought: saving us.

I erected my fingers, palms flat and stiff. Both hands

plunged through the man's leathered clothing, right into his torso. My arms twisted, hands clamping down on what I assumed to be his ribcage.

Ba-dum, ba-dum, ba-dum. My heart drummed. The sound filled my head. They knew me as a monster. But a monster who cared for another. And when you have someone worth saving—someone worth living for—it can give you the strength to do unimaginable things.

My arms parted with incredible force, his rib bones still clamped in curled fingers. Blood fanned out, raining down in every direction.

What was that?

My strength took me aback. My feet shuffled in the opposite direction of the man. I watched as two halves of his torso fell limp at his sides. His head had torn at the neck; eyes devoid of life, but still open. Looking right at me. It was haunting. But I didn't care. He was a threat. *Was*, now gone. One less worry. The man's lifeless body buckled at the knees. He hit the ground with a thud that echoed off the walls.

A commotion behind me jolted my senses. Bastion hadn't let the situation blind his survival skills. Though still shaken, he seized the opportunity from the distraction and rolled out from beneath Isa. At first, Bastion's intentions were unclear. He moved toward me and dropped to a knee. His hand slid beneath the bloody corpse. We had mere seconds before our captors responded. Bastion pulled his arm back, a handgun within his grip. Even with visual clarity, I hadn't noticed it.

His arm slung to the right. The shot rang in my ears.

Isa yelped. Her body shifted back from the force of the bullet. The entry oozed blood at her shoulder.

Nicely done, Bastion. Let's get the hell out of here.

Two steps forward and the barrel of Bastion's gun was met with the general's blade. The general showed no fear. He stood in the path of Bastion's weapon. Eyes narrowed, jaw tightened.

Does he really want to test us right now? I readied my footing in preparation. My body still throbbed from the rush of killing Mr. Button Cruncher.

"Halt!" an old voice bellowed from behind the general.

The general's blade fell to his side. Feet stepped back. His jaw remained tight.

"Have you not seen what they've done to Alex?" The general questioned in his defense. "Let me finish the two undead. We don't need them to get information. The risk is too high to keep them here."

An elderly man pushed past the general's lackeys. His eyes wandered across the room. From us to the destruction that'd been caused. Unlike the others, he wore cloth, not skin.

Loose, black pants and a matching top. No shoes protected his dirt-covered feet. His long hair hung to his waist. White as the moonlight.

"What happened to Alex is the reason we must keep them alive," the old man replied, calm and composed.

"Father, I can handle this," the general shot back. Trying to maintain authority.

So, they're related. I hoped they didn't share the same mentality.

"Silence, boy!" The old man took a step in our direction. His feet moved silent as he closed the space between us.

Bastion had no hesitation. His gun rose to prepare for firing.

"Put that thing down. There's no further need for such violence between us." The old man waved a hand. A gesture for Bastion to lower the weapon. He showed no worry or fear in our presence. He was numb to the carnage.

What is with the people out here? Before all of this, if I'd witnessed what just happened; hell, if I'd been within twenty feet of the undead, I'd have pissed my pants. It wasn't the most ladylike thing I'd thought of, but it was true.

I wondered what kind of hellish past the elder must've had to be so stone-cold at the sight of death.

"I won't harm you."

The old man was now standing before us.

"You've no reason to trust me after the actions of my reckless son, but I greet you as a friend," the old man said, his eyes gentle and comforting.

Friend? He can't be serious. In my thoughts, I questioned his sanity. I wanted to trust him. He seemed convincing. But we'd been through enough hell to know how deceitful people can be.

"You're different from the rest," the old man continued. He was looking at me. "Judging by the condition of your companion's skin deterioration," he gestured to Bastion, "he's quite special too. Remarkable, in fact."

We held a hard stare on one another for an uncomfortable minute that ticked by. It seemed like hours had passed in those sixty seconds.

The old man cleared his throat and smiled as if satisfied by whatever he'd been thinking about.

"I'd like to prove my assumptions. But you must trust me. You've no reason to—but it's the only way I can show you what you *really* are." The old man extended his arm, nodding his head for me to take hold.

I couldn't move. After all the crap we'd endured, I found myself torn. Not to mention how stiff my body felt. Adrenaline dump. None the less, curiosity chiseled at my brain. The old man had me intrigued. I wanted answers. But, did I trust the old man? Not one bit.

As if he sensed my hesitation, he smiled. The kind of smile a father gives his child. Warm reassurance.

"The boy can come too. I'll even allow him to hold on to the gun until you're both comfortable enough. Though I hope they'll be no more bloodshed tonight."

I shot a look at Raven. She'd been silent ever since my outburst. My rage. I glanced at my hands. Fingers still masked by the blood of the man I'd murdered. I shook any remorse. He had it coming. Cruel bastard. Thoughts went back to Raven. If what the general had told us was right, she deserved to stay chained until she rotted. But the general had proven that he had no concern for us. We were disposable pawns. So, who's to say that his words weren't meant to manipulate the situation? I couldn't bring myself to just leave her. We owed her nothing, but she might've been our only lifeline to find a cure. I tipped my chin in her direction.

"Ah, yes, yes. She can join us. Though her bindings must remain on for now. Her people have done horrific things, and the risk would be far too great until we understand where her loyalty lies."

I nodded. *Please let this be the right decision.* I needed to understand what the old man meant about Bastion and me. If there was something different about us, then what and *why*?

"It's settled. Pay no mind to my son. Not he, nor his friends will cause you harm. Follow me."

The last sight before we left the room was the daunting glare coming from the general. A stare that told us, '*this isn't over yet.*'

DAY 7
PART 6

W_e entered a room that appeared far more civilized than the first. A set of plush, brown couches framed a wooden coffee table. Ivory-colored cloth adorned the stone walls. It made me feel less like we were sitting in a cave, which we were, and more like I was somewhere sophisticated. Someone had paid great attention to detail. From artificial silk flowers in each corner to little knick-knacks in a china cabinet.

My energy was depleted. Eyes flickered, and knees tried to buckle. Bastion took notice and clung to my arm with his left hand. The right still gripping the stock of his gun.

"Please, take a seat. Your body is coming down from the strain it just endured," a man's voice said from behind us. "If my theory is correct, you've just withstood three times the amount of adrenaline that a living human can produce." He shook his head, "Forgive me, I've yet to introduce myself. I'm the doctor here."

I'd guess the man was about fifty judging by his features. Gray stubble, white brows, shaved hair at the sides, bald on top. He dressed much like the general's father. Blue shirt and dark jeans. My vision was returning to its previous state, and I was losing the ability to see fine details, but I felt an odd sense of familiarity.

The doctor looked at me for a moment, then to Raven. Back to me again.

"Unbelievable," he whispered just loud enough for us to hear.

"Is it what you were hoping for, Doctor?" the old man at my side questioned.

"I believe so. I'm heading back to my lab to check on a few things. While I'm gone, explain the situation to them," the doctor stated. "I'll be taking the Unit Four girl with me." He gestured toward Raven, who'd been so quiet I'd forgotten she was there. "I assure you, she'll be just fine. I only wish to talk."

The look of hesitation on Raven's face made me uneasy.

With a heavy sigh, the doctor approached Raven. "Right. I'd almost forgotten this." He withdrew something round from his pocket. The object was positioned so that only Raven saw.

Her eyes widened, and she nodded without a word.

With no further exchange, the doctor left with Raven. Chains still strung from her wrists.

"Yes," the old man muttered to himself. Lost in thought. He paused a moment before clapping his hands together. "Well then, I'd like you both to remain seated on the couch."

The old man snapped his fingers, and another member of the Faceless Ones appeared. A calf-length coat of skin draped over his body. I wondered how many corpses they had used to make it. An axe hung at his side. A warrior.

Without an exchange of words, the warrior placed a long, black lightbulb into the old man's hands.

"You have no reason to believe a single word I say. But, if it's answers you seek, I'll need your right arm," the old man said while holding the palm of his hand up.

A memory flickered. The old man's soothing demeanor reminded me of the doctors back in Nialus. A tactic they'd use on kids to ease them into getting pricked by a painful injection.

I remembered feeling betrayed, even after the memory washed back into the fog. Mom was right. As always. I'm a curious cat. I wanted answers. No, I needed answers.

Mom. Her warmth. Her embrace. All fading. *Hazel eyes. Mom has hazel eyes. But, why can't I see her face? Oh, God. What's her name? Not 'Mom,' but her real name. Caitlyn? Catrina? Calinda?* My memories slipped through the cracks of broken thoughts. *That's it. Here goes nothing. Time to place my trust in a random old guy whose son tried to kill us less than an hour ago. The story of my life.*

My arm shot out. Our eyes met, and the old man nodded.

"As I said, no physical harm will come to you. If the doctor is correct, I want to show you something that might help piece things together. For all of us."

The old man snapped a switch at the base of the long, dark bulb. A low hum, followed by a deep purple glow. I'd never seen anything like it. The light colors on our clothing lit up as if enchanted by magic. My blouse glowing like the moon on a clear night.

His thick brows, dark in contrast to the white of his hair, pressed against the skin between. Wrinkles deepened like ravines. With a gentle twist, he rotated my forearm.

"Be damned for doubt," the old man whispered. "He

was right."

I writhed beneath his grip at the sight of my arm. Until this moment, I'd known about my odd birthmark. Three black dots that formed a triangle if traced. Nothing unusual. It was ordinary—like me. Or, so I'd thought. What shone beneath the dots shook me. Mind spiraled, doubt stirred. A numeric code glowed: 179. My veins also shone through my skin. White like luminescent worms.

One-seventy-nine. Who am I? What am I? What does this mean? I wanted my mom. I wanted to run into her calming embrace and unleash a sea of tears. Falling to the disease had hardened me. But I still held onto my emotions. Sorrow, joy, anger. And at that moment, I was like a child who needed someone to rub my hair, kiss my forehead, and tell me everything was okay. At the core of me, my soul flickered. I was still me—for now, I still held a piece of humanity. But for how long?

Bastion's hand fell onto mine. He squeezed.

I'm here, his eyes spoke for him. *I'm here.*

"Calm down, please," the old man's voice was firm, yet still gentle. "I need to process all of this." He looked to Bastion. "Your arm now."

I squeezed Bastion's hand in return, hoping to encourage him to follow instruction. My thirst for answers outweighed my increasing hunger. The satisfaction of our

266

previous meal was wearing off. We didn't have a lot of time.

The firm grip of the old man's fingers met Bastion's wrist. The light hovered over Bastion's arm. No numbers. But his veins glowed brighter than the stars.

"Everything he said, all true," the old man muttered to himself. His tone and body language revealed a sense of disbelief. Astonishment. Excitement.

He waved the bulb across his own arm as if he needed to double-check that what he saw was accurate. No glowing veins.

"You two are the first I've seen. I've doubted the doctor's words for years, but now I see his truths."

Stop speaking in riddles and tell us what's going on. You promised me answers! I shifted, growing impatient. He was old, but living. His life might go on for many more years. We were lucky to have many more hours.

"Bring in Charley," the old man spoke to one of the others.

The rattling of chains echoed against the stone walls. Closer. Louder. Animalistic growling, untamed and desperate to feed. I knew the sound well at this point. Charley was no longer among the living.

My eyes held fixated on the entrance of the room, waiting to understand the purpose of what was happening. Charley was coming.

The four Faceless who stood guard in our room took a step to the side. Attached to a long pole was a metal collar that adorned the neck of an undead man. Charley. He wore sweat pants, old and filthy. Across the lower part of his face, a leather strap that concealed his mouth. I still heard the muffled snarls and tapping of teeth. He smelled what I did, fresh, juicy meat.

My mouth filled with saliva at the thought. Teeth sinking into soft tissue. Blood pooling against my lips, seeping into the corners of my mouth.

What is wrong with you? Stop! I scolded myself for once again giving in to the persistent aching in my gut.

They brought Charley within feet of us. His face became more defined. The poor soul only had one clouded eye. Where his other should be, a hollow hole filled with darkness. The skin on his cheeks stretched so tight it followed the shape of his skull.

The old man took a thick, padded glove and slid it onto his left hand. He then reached out to take Charley's arm. Two of his fingers were missing. Clean cuts.

What did they do to you?

My heart sank at the sight of Charley. He was pitiful looking. Despite how ravenous he'd become, I knew that at some point he'd kept his memories. At one time, he was like me. Whatever had mutilated him, I hoped it'd happened after his mind was lost. If this was at the hand of the Faceless Ones, then they were just as bad as Unit Four. They were far from righteous. Was there no goodness left in the world? Had it all died along with the plague? Was Nialus the last beacon of light left in a world shrouded in darkness? Or had all light been snuffed by duplicity?

I scooted forward on the couch. My feet planted on the floor. If their true intentions were to harm Bastion or me, it wouldn't be without a fight.

"Please," the old man spoke before I'd finish adjusting myself. There was a sense of desperation in his tone.

I paused.

"I'm aware that Charley's first impression doesn't help build trust. But the two of you and Charley are alike in some ways. Both between a state of life and death. And yet, you're also very different. Different to where I hold a sense of bitterness. Resentment toward the hands of fate. However, I'm a rational man. I understand that none of this is your fault. You see, Charley is my son."

DAY 7
PART 7

The old man held his grip on Charley's right arm. Another Faceless guard kept his left in place. Charley continued to snap his jaws. His face shifted from side to side. The leather strip across his mouth the only thing between teeth and flesh.

"Allow me to show you something," the old man said. He didn't seem bothered by the noise.

He brought the bright purple bulb to Charley's arm. Nothing. It was the same thing we'd seen when the old man had done it to himself. No veins glowing, no numbers.

"As I said—the same, and yet different. The two of you have been introduced to their plan. You're a part of it.

By the reaction you both had at the sight of your arms, I'm confident to say you knew nothing about this. In fact, I'm sure they don't realize where you are at this moment." He looked at me. "There's no way they'd allow you to roam so far from supervision otherwise. We'd have already been bombarded with dozens of soldiers. Him, however," eyes turned to Bastion, "he might have a tracer embedded. Though I doubt they'll be retrieving him soon. They're most likely still collecting data."

Bastion and I exchanged the same look of confusion. I wouldn't have believed a word from the old man had it not been for what I'd seen beneath my skin.

"You may find our ways unrefined. Our lifestyle, outdated. But I assure you we just want the evils of this world put to rest. People have been through so much for so long now. We desire an end to this corruption. Restoring peace is necessary. Or, as close to unity as possible while those who defy death still walk. I mean no offense to either of you. I'm sure you can understand my outlook.

"Let me tell you about something that happened long ago. My personal experience and how it's led me to this point." The old man released his hold on Charley's arm. He patted him on the shoulder before waving to the man at his left. Without an exchange of words, Charley was escorted back to wherever he'd come from.

"I'm aware that Corrin, my oldest son, has told you

about Mill Six. But I share far more history with that God forsaken place. Have you ever seen a six-year-old try to flee for their life? All they want is to find safety in someone they can trust. Someone who will comfort and protect them. They desire a place to recover from the trauma of having their mother torn away. A mother who would become fodder for a cause that would make most grown men sick at the mere thought. Most children at Mill Six have fallen victim to the lies fed to them as they grow. Others are alert. Aware of the truth. Encountering someone trustworthy was as rare as innocence in this world. The ones who know the truth, the ones who take heed to the whispers of what happened to their parents; they bear a significant burden. Day and night, they're forced to play along. Behave like good little slaves and obey. If the others, even their closest peers realize there is doubt, they'll become an example.

"Those who pay their dues and work hard get to leave for the great city. The same line is told time and time again. Those who disobey, those who question the system, well, the great city has no room for such people. They'll bind anyone who falls out of line to a stake and starve them for two days. Then, everyone gathers for the finale. A bullet is too good for those who show any resistance. It'd be a death too quick to strike fear in the hearts of those who watched.

"No, the soldiers in black, the enforcers, they want to ensure we understand to behave. They use hammers, starting at the child's legs. The enforcers strike with such force you can hear the bones cracking. They work their way up; a slow and torturous endeavor. Ribs, arms, fingers. Hammered so brutally that the body resembles soft mud that can't support itself upright. By the time they reach the child's skull, most have already passed out from the pain. With a final blow, they're gone.

"Most of the older teenagers cheer at the sight. Their loyalty lay with a false promise. They're so far brainwashed that they find the event to be a victory. Justice served. The younger children cower in fear. After what they've witnessed, they know to never doubt the system in place." The old man swallowed so hard that I saw the lump in his throat shift. He looked to the side. It was evident that the subject was difficult for him to re-visit. He took a moment to recollect himself and then continued.

"I know all of this because I've been there. Born and raised within the walls of deceit. A member of Mill Six. Or, as they call it, Apollo."

Apollo. The Greek God. God of healing, truth, light. I remember when mom used to read me books about the Olympians. She'd memorized their names, their stories. It surprised me that I still remembered. A memory that flickered. It seemed like a sick joke to name such a place after Apollo.

The old man intertwined his fingers. "I bore the burden. The burden of knowing things were not as they seemed. We were spoon-fed lies. Day after day, I kept my thoughts to myself. When trusting the wrong person meant a gruesome death to follow, I learned to keep my mouth shut. But, as time passed, I grew restless. My *big day* drew closer, I was almost of age. I'd end up getting hauled off like the rest, never to return.

"You might wonder how I discovered it all. When I was eight, a boy who slept within my quarters told us of the horrors within. He'd been assigned food delivery to the enforcers. Children aren't permitted beyond a certain point in the building where they reside. But he'd slipped down the halls without notice. I guess they'd grown so accustomed to us falling in line that security wasn't a top priority. We had no weapons, they did. It was a simple equation of who would win, should we rebel. The boy came back with tales of what he'd seen. Our peers locked in small, cage-like rooms. Voices talking about how they would soon be hauled off for experiments. Medical terminology he didn't understand. The boy should've known to keep quiet. Most of the others in our quarters saw him as mad. Thought he'd made it all up. But my gut told me otherwise. The itch I'd had for so long. The unease that always made my stomach flutter when the shadow guards would pass. It all made sense. I knew the boy spoke the truth.

"By morning, the boy had disappeared. The next time I saw him, his body hung lifeless from the pole. Another example made. He'd tried to warn us, to save us. I wouldn't let his bravery die with him. I was as good as dead anyway once I reached eighteen.

"For over a year, I examined the younger children. I'd listen to them speak, watch how they'd interact. I'd take careful steps to converse with them in ways that would provide me with answers, without leading on what I knew. You could tell the ones who were already too far gone from those who still had doubt in their minds. Once I was confident, I set out to talk with the few who shared my belief. Thirteen in total. It wasn't a lot, but I understood the importance of being cautious. Speaking to those with a corrupted mind meant . . . Well, you know.

"On a storm-shrouded night, the rain poured without relief. Thunder bellowed from the heavens. It was the opportune time to escape without drawing as much attention. We wouldn't be able to hear the undead, but it was a tradeoff we were willing to take. Humans were calculated, skilled. The undead, become mindless. Driven by hunger. It makes them far more predictable. You two are a rarity. It's a sad world we live in when our fellow humans are more feared than the living dead. Anyway, at that time of the year, few adults remained in town. Those who stayed were unseen, holed up in the building of no return. If we didn't act then, another chance might never come.

"We all met as planned. Each child clung to a single

sack. Enough rations to last a day or two, but light enough to carry a considerable distance from that hell-hole. I was in charge, the one responsible for them. We slipped past the gatehouse, unnoticed by two teenagers who stood guard. Everything was going well—too well. Out into the open field we went. The part I'd dreaded most since there was little concealment. We were almost to our freedom. We'd made it past the walls, but had to be swift to stay out of sight. I looked back over a shoulder to take a head count. I wanted to make sure we'd all gotten out okay before leading the group into the forest. Twelve. There were only twelve of us. Someone was missing. My eyes shifted to the gate where one child stood. They gripped their little sack and, through the rain, I saw that they were sobbing. I took only but a second to notice the two men behind him. Anger washed over me. We'd been betrayed. I knew it was because of the young boy's fear, but I couldn't help but hate him at that moment. We were so close.

"I spun on my heels and shouted for the others to run. There were no other options. The sound of rapid-fire echoed through my brain. My feet slid across the wet grass, racing toward the trees ahead. To my side, two little ones kept up. *Come on, we can do this!* I kept repeating it in my head. Another round of ammunition fired. The child to my right reached out for me. He'd barely grazed my arm when the bullet penetrated his small body. The enforcers show no mercy. None. They didn't care if you're five or fifty years old. The essence of a child's precious life means nothing. Every person in that town is bred to be dispensable. Out of the thirteen of us that started our escape, I made it out with one. *One* child."

The old man lowered himself to a knee. He was close but remained at enough distance to react if Bastion or I should make a move.

"I know I ramble, but all I've told you is important. You need to understand. Especially since you're connected," the old man spoke with eyes locked to mine.

"My son, Charley, lost his life when returning to Mill Six against my orders. He was a foolish boy, but one with a big heart and more compassion than most men have in their lifetime. He and his brother attempted to rescue more of the youngsters from that place. They created an elaborate plan to make it in and retrieve some of the children who'd been recently parted from their mothers. Their minds still filled with innocence and able to be saved. They thought they had a fool-proof plan. But, as you've seen, nothing went as planned. My eldest, Corrin, the one you were earlier acquainted with, he blames himself. Since that day he's worked a barrier around his heart. Rightfully so, I suppose. They both knew better than to meddle. I warned them time again of the dangers.

"I lost Charley three years ago. Yet, here he is. We've seen some of the undead decompose to bones, but I've discovered that feeding seems to preserve the body. You also have to pay mind to the maggots. Can't let them infest the flesh. I'm a logical man. I realize my Charley is gone. He's not like you. His mind went within the first forty-eight hours of infection. It sounds insane, even cruel and selfish, but I can't bring myself to finish his existence. So, I keep him in his room, well fed.

"But I'm rambling again. My purpose in all of this is to let you see how special the two of you are. And, to understand where I come from and why I'm so passionate about everything. You're a beacon of hope. You're fading, I can see that, but you've held onto your humanity for longer than any other I've come across. Your cells and genetic code are different. Altered. I believe it all traces back to the promised city. Nialus."

My insides ached. There it was again. Nialus. Confirmation I'd picked up the breadcrumbs and my assumptions were correct. The men I'd made out at Mill Six, the dark guard regiment. But, why? That wasn't the way of my people. We were just an ordinary society, getting by in a fallen world. We helped people—helped work toward a cure. A way to end this plague of death. Right?

The old man then did something unexpected. He reached out with no fear or hesitation and took my hand.

"We need you. Young lady, the *world* needs you." His pale eyes weaved into my soul as he spoke. "You have an opportunity to get help. The only ones with the technology

278

to cure you are *your* people. Judging by the numeric code on your arm, they're not yet done with you. This works in your favor and ours."

At that moment, I wasn't sure if I wanted to return. A city layered in secrets. Unspoken horrors. My hopes and dreams shattered. What was the intention behind labeling me without my knowledge? Mutating my DNA to react with the disease. Was everyone in Nialus like this? Or was I singled out? Another experiment for them to toy with. I tried to remain optimistic. Maybe there was good behind this. What if they injected all the students, intending to make us more resilient to the virus? To protect us.

Since the day I'd wandered out and into the woods, it seemed like every answer was met with more questions.

"I'm going to retire for the night, but I'd like for you to speak with the doctor. Then, you can decide if you'd like to join our cause. The choice is yours, but know that it may be the last opportunity you have before the disease takes you. You have a chance to do something incredible. Not only for yourself but for those of us left out here with nothing more than hope. All we want is a future where humanity is united. It's time we take back our earth from the undead anomalies." The old man stood. A soft popping from his joints as his legs straightened. "Until tomorrow, I bid you both a good night. Should you remain here until morning, you'll have food supplied to hold over your appetite. And please, consider all

I've said."

He turned to the door. The group of guards parted to each side to allow passage. On his exit, Bastion reached over and clutched my hand. We'd taken in an abundance of information. Almost too much. I found it difficult to process the situation in its entirety. And, there was still this doctor. My hand squeezed down on Bastion's. He was my rock. No way I would've gotten through everything alone. He was the reason for each breath I still took. We'd grown to understand one another without a voice. Like times before, I knew he was assuring me we'd get through this; the same way we'd gotten through everything else. Not even death kept us down. We were anomalies. Resilient. Special.

Those last hints of humanity in his stare cut away any reservations. I was ready to hear what the doctor had to say. For the same reasons I'd followed Raven, if he could help us, I had to at least listen.

DAY 7
PART 8

We sat for another round of awkward minutes. Us silent. The guards staring. They looked like statues with their masks on. Expressionless and still. They seemed more inhuman than us by appearance. Every so often I'd catch one of them shift their footing when we'd move. It was subtle, but I found it to be an entertaining way to kill time and suppress my anxiety. I caught Bastion repositioning his arms a few times just to get a response.

Never lose those qualities, Bastion. You can be childish. Dumb. Stubborn. It sometimes drives me mad. But it also makes you incredible. I need you to hold on to the man you are.

A part of me felt as if we were tethered to the earth, unable to die. I knew that our bodies were only a shell. Our minds could be lost. Without memories, without emotion, I'd consider that death in itself.

An echo of sound stirred within the dark hallway, just outside of our room. Two people in conversation. Raven was one, but I wasn't familiar with the other. The cluster of guards once again side-stepped.

"I thank you for your patience," the doctor said while taking full strides across the room.

As if we had a choice.

Raven drew closer to me. She didn't appear to have any new wounds, aside from red welts where the chains had been. Her mentality seemed different though. Color had washed from her face. Her expression reminded me of my own when I'd heard the news of my father passing. Lost. Hopeless. Her eyes looked glazed. Every time she caught my stare, she'd turn a cheek.

She's avoiding me.

"Do you mind if I have a better look at the two of you?" the doctor spoke without waiting on a response as he inched closer.

A rhetorical question. Why bother asking.

He unrolled a white cloth on the nearby table. Various tools I recognized from routine medical checkups.

How long had it been since I'd seen a doctor? I couldn't recall. I had to prompt myself to retrace memories. It was beginning to seem like trying to solve a labyrinth. One recollection only led to another dead end. I wasn't able to envision my past without it being chopped into small segments. It was similar to reading a book with pages torn out. You only got pieces of the story.

The doctor's eyes drew close to mine. I'd be lying if I said the thought of biting his nose right off of his face didn't cross my mind. He felt so familiar.

He brought a long, metal tool between us. A light shone through a small hole.

"I want you to follow the light with your eyes," the doctor said.

I did as he requested. My eyes moving with the yellow beam. Side-to-side. He then did the same to Bastion. Next, a reflex test. No response. He checked our hearts—still beating. Took a sample of blood. No pain there. And last, he braved looking into our mouths with the longest tongue depressor I'd ever seen. It was a smart idea. I don't think I'd have been able to control myself from tearing off a finger if they'd come close enough.

"I'll have a look at these samples tonight. They may

prove valuable to understanding what makes the two of you so unique. You especially, my dear." The doctor patted my head as if I were a young child.

I'd watch that arm if I were you, Doc. My mouth pooled with saliva. There was only so much more I could withstand. I'd hit a point where my body needed to feed more frequently to stay sane.

"We'll get you fed soon. I just need to go over a couple of things," the doctor stated. He took several steps back.

It must've been evident to the others we were growing restless. What did they expect when inviting two undead to sit for a discussion? A tea party?

"I'll cut through the bullshit and give it to you straight. You deserve as much," the doctor stated.

The sharpness in his words caught me off-guard.

"I doubt you recognize me, Oshin, but I remember you."

My body stood upright before my mind had caught up to the action. *What did he just say?* Two guards were at my side with weapons raised before I filtered my thoughts.

"At ease, men. It's okay. I expected this would be a shock to her. The reaction is normal," the doctor said. His attention directed back to me. "I wasn't sure at first. And please understand that this is just as much of a surprise to us all. It's unheard of to see someone so young make it past the city wall. I worked with your father long ago. You were just a child, but I remember the markings on your arm well. Your father and I were on the same team for years, working endless hours in the lab hoping to find a better life for everyone. Only later did I find out just how far some of the others would go. I left. I never said goodbye to your father, nor the others. It was during routine scouting out here when I went. I'm sure they'd long assumed me dead.

"I'm not a perfect man, and I've taken part in things that will forever haunt my mind. But I've spent years trying to make it right again. We need to end the cycle before it grows beyond reach. An unstoppable force that will level the earth. It shouldn't be this way. Life is too valuable. The soil we walk upon, the sun we stand beneath. Resources we can use to build a unified existence. To take back our planet. Rid it of disease. But I need you."

There were truths in his words, and then there was the unknown. He knew me. That much was clear. But everything beyond that was something I had to decide if I wanted to believe. If lies could build a city, it'd be more magnificent than Nialus.

"You're more important than you realize. A message needs to be sent. I believe that there's still a chance for us to resolve things without war. The men here are ready to fight. They've hidden in the shadows for decades, silenced while watching horrors unfold. I want to avoid that. To seek peace between what's out here, and behind the city walls. I'm willing to offer them something they've been trying to accomplish since my departure. I was on the verge of finding a cure. It wouldn't eliminate the virus, but it might suppress the effects long enough for the body to fight it. At least, this was the end goal. I was close though. Had the other scientists continued working on my formula, I'm sure it would've been a success. But, at the time, I couldn't trust them not to use it for ill causes.

"There's a way to get what we both want. I can't go back there myself right now. No, it'd raise too many questions and put the people here at risk. But you can go back. You're a citizen of Nialus. You have a family and friends there, I'm sure. I'd even bet they'd recognize you, despite your current condition. By now, word has spread about your disappearance. Surveillance has shown every step you took before leaving into the forest. And there are the markings on your arm. They'd want to bring you back to the laboratory to analyze your cells. You're not dispensable the like rest out here. That's why it has to be you.

"A small team of scientists leaves the city twice a month to gather samples. As luck would have it, tomorrow they will be in the forest. They'll have guards present, but they won't shoot you. Not when you're one of them. I have something for you to wear so they'll know you're not a typical roamer. I mean it when I say that this is your last hope for a cure before the chemical imbalance in your brain is irreparable. The level of decay to your body will no longer allow the ability to regenerate new cell growth. It's now or never."

The doctor walked across the room to retrieve something. I looked to Raven, staring hard.

"This is important. Listen to the doctor," was all Raven said. Her chin tilted down, stare back to the floor.

When the doc returned, he held a small vial in his hand.

"This is what can unify us. This is what we can use to barter for peace. It's a sample of my life's work. I'm confident that once they see what it can do, they'll rely on my knowledge to recreate it. That's our opportunity to negotiate change. If we can reduce the risk of the undead, there won't be a need for places like Mill Six. They'll no longer need to experiment on children. I just need the chance to convince them of this. To find a lawful way to ensure it stops. Otherwise, the carnage to both sides could be detrimental. The human population doesn't have an opportunity to thrive and grow outside of those walls. But we can do this—I'm certain. You and I."

A chance to return. A cure. Peace. Was this all too good to be true? The plan seemed so simple. I knew that in reality, we didn't have a choice. If I'd declined the doctor's idea, we'd be useless. Disposable. But, just like all other times, I had to try. The facts were that I was desperate and out of other options. But, what about Bastion? I wouldn't leave him behind to die. Sure, I might get cured and go on living. But the guilt I'd bear would weigh me to the ground. We were a set. If I go, he goes.

I turned to look at him. *Bastion, my friend. My . . .* Okay Oshin, focus.

"I can see you care for him," the doctor said, taking notice to my actions. "You must understand that it'd be a great risk bringing him. A selfish risk. *You*, they'll take. But, your friend here . . . Well, there's no guarantee they won't shoot him on sight. He's genetically modified, which may prove of interest to them. But the guards won't know this when you first encounter them. Even if I label him, there won't be any assurance he'll make it."

Bastion clamped down on my hand, lifting it so that the doctor saw our intertwined fingers.

We're together. A set.

DAY 8
PART 1

Eight days. Eight long days filled with hardships most people couldn't imagine. I never thought I'd make it this long. My anticipation for what was to come made the minutes drag by. Guards had rotated out for the night shift, and they'd fed our endless appetite every hour until morning. But now, more people than I had expected roamed the halls. It was noisy and hard to think. No one stopped to look at us. They passed by without a glance. My nerves were sky high. This was it. Under an hour to go before the trek back to Nialus began. The doctor knew the approximate location where the white coats would be. Just past the walls, in the nearby forest.

I pat Bastion's shoulder. *Ready for this?*

He didn't acknowledge me. His stare held forward, expression left without emotion.

Bastion? I nudged a hand against his back.

He turned for just a moment, but it was as though I was a stranger. His eyes resumed ahead.

Bastion! I tapped harder.

No response.

Oh, God. No . . . Bastion, I can't lose you now. I felt sick. Not physically, but my emotions were in a knot. He was leaving me. We didn't have a lot of time left. My biggest fear for him was becoming a reality. If his mind was too far gone, not even the white coats in Nialus could bring him back. Or, if he lost control and tried to attack the white coats, he'd get shot on sight. The other night, I'd shown an inner power that extended past the physical limits of any human. I was fast, but not stop-a-bullet fast. Bastion wouldn't stand a chance. We needed to leave. Now.

"Good morning!" the doctor said with enthusiasm when entering the room.

In a moment of panic, I stepped closer to the doctor, ignoring the guards as they readied their weapons. I pointed at Bastion. Sharp, undistinguishable sounds burst past my lips.

Please help him, please. With each passing second,

the reality of the situation hung heavier.

"Oh dear. This isn't good at all." The doctor shook his head. His hands never leaving a small box that rested in his palms. "Young man, nod if you can understand me."

No response from him yet again.

"I didn't expect his brain to deteriorate before we'd reached our destination. I know it's not what you wanted, but it may be in the best interest for both of you if you went alone. If you remain here, you'll die. If he follows you, he'll die. There's no subtle way to put it."

If he's lost his mind, then he's already dead.

A firm hand clamped down on my arm.

Bastion?

His jaw was tight, and eyes revealed an internal struggle. His head tipped to nod.

He nodded! Did you see that? He nodded! We're losing him, but he's not gone yet. Motivation swept through me. I was ready.

"This is beyond surprising," the doctor sounded astonished. "He's fighting with everything he's got right now. His frontal and temporal cerebrum lobes seem to be stimulated. It might not last for long and will come and go in waves until he fades. His survival instinct will soon drive him to feed. The same thing happened to Charley, but not like this. When it was time, Charley's memories flickered for mere minutes before he was gone. This young man appears as though he's trying to hold on until completing our mission. I must be upfront with you though. It's my medical opinion that the odds of him making it to our destination while he's still himself are slim. You need to be prepared for the worst. If you allow your emotions to override our plan in the presence of the guards, you'll both end up as maggot food. You're too close. Don't cloud your judgment when there are so many out here depending on your success." It wasn't a request.

Sure, whatever, let's just please get going.

I was hanging off the edge of existence. When hope is all you have left, you hold on. You don't let go. Letting go means giving into the void. Darkness and death. So, I held onto the hope that we'd make it. Both of us.

Bastion acknowledged nothing that'd been said. He was lost again. Lost, but not gone.

"The others are gathering now. Some of the Faceless will accompany us until we arrive. They'll be present, just in case things don't go as planned, but out of sight." The doctor set down the box he'd been holding and opened the lid. "This is the vial you'll be taking. A larger and more perfected version of what I'd showed you last night." He placed it into a leather satchel, stuffed with cotton. "I need you to take the utmost care with this. It cannot break. I've already left instructions inside. Under no circumstances are you to open the vial. If the contents spill, everything we're trying to accomplish will be over. We have one shot—*one*. Once you've made it to the inside, all you need to do is hand this pouch over to them. They'll have all of the instruction needed to take it from there. This is the most important step to saving everyone. No matter what happens in there, you cannot forget to give them the vial. The deaths of dozens of children will be on your hands."

I couldn't believe he put that on me. Asshole. I didn't start this. If this was his way of pushing me into accomplishing the task, it was a crappy way of going about it. Deep breaths. *I'm not doing this for him*, I told myself. *Don't get agitated now. We're almost home.*

A low, guttural growl filled the void where silence had been. The doctor took one look at Bastion and sped his momentum.

Bastion took a step back to increase the space between them. My stomach fluttered. I wondered what went through a person's mind as they transitioned to the mindless. Would Bastion become a ravanger? He'd turn on me too. Me against him. Would I have it in me to kill him? I didn't want to dwell on it any longer. *Positive thoughts, Oshin.*

The doctor draped a silver-colored chain necklace around each of our necks. The guards stood nearby. Weighing down at the bottom of the chain was a bright orange square. A numeric code on each. He followed up with a white band around each of our wrists. Words too tiny to read had been written in dried ink.

"We feed them and then depart," the doctor instructed to the guards. "Ready the others. It's time."

DAY 8
PART 2

Crisp morning air filled my nose. A symphony of scents surrounded us, but no fresh meat. Those accompanying us on the journey, the doctor included, were each wearing a suit of weathered skin. Their hands and shoes painted with blood, but not of the living. It was old and looked brown and had no scent I could pick up on. It was impressive how the Faceless had adapted to the dangers of the undead. They'd survived. Just like I would do for Bastion and me.

The sun peeked just enough to cast a soft pink and yellow glow across the sky. In the distance, deep gray storm clouds loomed. Our pace was slow. No matter how fast I wanted to hurry and get to our destination, my feet wouldn't keep up. Shuffled steps slid across spongy soil, covered in morning dew. Bastion and I had been roped together. Torso to torso. He had given little indication that he understood what was happening, and continued to follow in my wake. If he went ravanger on me, there'd be no escaping. Me against him.

Ugh, stop thinking about it and fucking focus! I had to keep my mind sharp for what was to come. We still didn't know how the dark guard regiment would react to our arrival.

It was a long and tedious trek through the forest. We'd passed an old town, long abandoned. Houses, some in ruin. Concrete blocks were broken down and consumed by grass, vines, and fuzzy moss. It's funny how nature took back the earth. The destruction humans had caused in past generations was almost reversed. Trees towered high across the lands, greenery flourishing in every direction. The undead decaying and returning to the soil. Humanity hung on though. Less in numbers, but always fighting for a chance.

Thunder rolled from behind. Long and low, like a thousand stones falling from the sky. Flashes of light echoed above, but I didn't stop to see how close the storm was from engaging us. It wouldn't be much longer, that much I knew. The wind had caught up to us and sifted through the leaves. The trees reached their branches in the direction we walked.

Slack in the rope tensed, and resistance pulled from where it was wrapped around my belly.

Keep up, Bastion. We can't have much farther to go.

Just a little longer, please. For us.

A quick glance back. Bastion was still moving, but slower than before. His feet didn't break from the ground and instead slid across the surface. Any obstacle, even as small as a fallen branch caused him to pause. His brain working in overdrive to process a way over.

The first drop of rain fell to my forehead. Another. Then another. Movement stopped.

"This is where we part ways, for now," the doctor whispered. Or, maybe it was hard to hear him over the storm. "We'll be near, but concealed. It's no longer safe for us. Just ahead, you'll find shelter from the rain. Stand under the wide branches and wait. I hadn't expected such weather. We can only hope they still pass through on their way back to Nialus. Or, that they even came out to collect with a storm approaching. It was a chance we needed to take. I wish you luck, my dear." He patted the pouch that hung around my neck. "It all rests with you."

I looked down to where the vial was. By the time I straightened my neck, the others were already gone. I hadn't even heard them take their first step. The doctor was the last, and I watched as he slipped past two narrow tree trunks into the forest.

A drop of rain hit my bracelet, the ink beneath the water now clouded and misshapen.

Move. Move! I tucked my arm against my shirt and worked my legs as fast as possible while tugging Bastion behind. If his label washed away, there'd be nothing left to save him.

The large branches were in sight. Bent and low. The ground still dry beneath.

We made it, Bastion! I could almost reach out and touch our destination. *We're going to-*

My inner voice fell silent at the sound of the first shot. *Behind us.* I turned, feet sticking to the mud like wet cement. Bastion's pant leg was saturated with a mixture of water and blood. His orange label smeared with black lines where rain had fallen. Another shot. The mud sprayed near his feet.

A group of regiment guards poured out from between the trees. White coats right behind in suits that covered every inch of skin. The regiment men held their weapons at ready. They shouted commands at one another, but the sharp crack of thunder made it unclear. Two white coats ran in my direction. One held his arm outright, pointing at me. More words followed that I didn't make out. The rope tightened, pulling me to my knees from the sudden jolt. They'd surrounded Bastion.

I cried out. Pitchy moans that no one could understand. But maybe they might read my desperation. Maybe, they'd already recognized me. *Please read Bastion's label.*

My arms were pulled behind my back with such force I thought they'd tear from my shoulders. The tension in the rope was gone. Severed threads now dragging on the ground. I saw Bastion in the mud, face down without movement. A regiment guard's boot on his back, gun aimed at his skull.

Come help us, damned cowards! My thoughts screamed, anger rising toward the Faceless who I knew were watching from concealment.

The white coat at my side lifted the lid of a foam case. From inside, he withdrew a syringe. His fingers slid to a blue cap, revealing the longest needle I'd ever seen. I jolted and thrust my body to each side. Nothing was going as I'd hoped. There was no warm reunion or a gentle approach to seeing me alive. Nothing was as the doctor had made it seem. Though that might've just been my interpretation all along. And Bastion, he didn't have much longer by the look of it. The regiment guard's finger shivered against the trigger. The barrel moved closer to the back of Bastion's head.

No! Please, no!

I felt the pressure of the needle entering near the base of my spine. Within seconds, my body became paralyzed. My vision fell black. I was alone in the darkness.

DAY 11
PART 1

A siren blared in the distance. Commotion stirring in every direction.

A woman's voice crackled over the intercom, "Please follow protocol forty-seven. Do not engage the infected without proper reinforcement. The virus is highly contagious and transferrable by contact. Remain calm and make your way to the research office for further instruction and escort." The messaged repeated in a loop.

Light filtered through my closed eyelids, alerting my senses. The metal was cold against the bare skin of my back. A chill ran down my spine, hair pricked on my arms and at the base of my neck. Every muscle in my body ached, my joints stiff.

"Ugh," I groaned, rubbing my forehead. It throbbed straight through to the back of my skull. "What's going on?"

My hand shot to my throat. A voice. *My* voice. Eyes fluttered open. The brightness of the lamp above my face caused me to wince in discomfort. Despite the chill of the table beneath me, the bulb of the lamp emitted enough warmth to leave my forehead damp. I ran my fingers down along my body. Was I alive? If so, where were all the doctors?

Eyes shifted and scanned the room. A wheeled cart with a tray on top. Medical tools aligned in a row. A chart on the wall:

Patient: Oshin Fletcher, Age: 17, Under treatment for Virus 071-G. Prep for metamorphosis to strain 077-X

I plugged my ears. The damned woman's voice on the intercom wouldn't allow for a single thought to solidify in my mind.

"Metamorphosis," I said to myself. "Where am I?"

My fingers left my ears, tracing down my cheeks. Soft. Not rough like a callus. The wounds I'd endured were stitched shut. The skin around it tender. I felt disoriented; confused. Nothing made sense. My memories were coming back. The last thing I remembered was the rain. Wait, no, the trees. A forest. I was there with the white coats and dark guard regiment. They were supposed to rescue us. *Us . . .*

"Bastion!" My heart kicked up a gear as my adrenal glands became stimulated. The adrenaline caused me to shiver. "Hello?" I called out. My instinct told me to stay quiet, and I pinched my lips shut. The word *metamorphosis* playing in my mind louder than that damned woman on the speaker. Something about this place made me uneasy. It wasn't the lab I'd remembered on visits to see my father. I needed to find Bastion. If Bastion ever made it here. Wherever *here* was. My eyes glassed over. "Not the time for that," I whispered to myself.

Both of my arms had multiple IV needles inserted with tubes that intertwined in a tangled mess. Bags hung from metal hooks, each with liquid inside and a numeric code stamped near the top.

Oh God, please don't let any of these have to do with whatever metamorphosis shit they were planning, I thought.

I wanted to use my voice. I wanted to scream at the top of my lungs and jump for joy because I hadn't fallen into a mindless void. That my body appeared cured on the surface. But everything seemed so odd; any celebration would have to wait. The intercom, the siren, the lack of doctors. And the chart. Then, there was Bastion. Right, back on track. The doctors might return at any second, and I didn't think they'd be bringing a welcoming committee.

My left hand trembled as I hovered over my veins. Without knowing what was in the drip bags, I was hesitant to remove the IVs. What if it was the only thing keeping me this way? Would I die without them? Or revert to the monster I once was?

I curled my fingers, tightening my fist until my nails dug into my palm. *Steady. Focus. You're not leaving this room with these damned things in your arms.* It felt like I was part of an action book I'd once read, where the main character had to diffuse a bomb. I was the bomb, and without knowing the effects of the fluids, the result could be horrific.

"Please follow protocol forty-seven. Do not engage the infected without-"

Shut up, shut up, shut up! I pinched my eyes closed, trying to drown out the surrounding ambiance. *Okay, on the count of three. One. Two.*

The sound of metal scattering on the ground jolted me upright. It was outside of my room, but close.

Times up. Three. I opened my eyes and pulled back on the IV. Having done nothing like this before, it tore at my skin. Stung like hell. *It's like a band-aid, just pull them out fast so you can get the hell out of this room.*

Seven more times, the needle slid from my vein and out of my skin. Had I not endured what I did in the past days, I'd have passed out at the first attempt. Speaking of days, I had no idea how long I'd been here. It seemed like only a nap since the forest, but judging by the IVs and the chart, it was likely longer. I lifted my hospital gown to ensure there were no more needles or other devices. A few sticky squares were across my chest and belly in various areas. And there was a rectangular hole right beneath my ass. I looked down into the hole to find my bodily waste sitting at the bottom of a clear plastic tray. It didn't appear to have been cleaned for a couple of days. My stomach churned as I inhaled, causing me to gag. My thighs were damp from my urine. I looked away, scared to cough in case it'd draw attention.

I curled my toes. Legs tingled. My fingers pushed against my skin, massaging my calves. I had to be careful of the bullet holes, now stitched together in a puffy line of skin. Once the numbness had worn away, I swung my legs off the edge of the metal table. I paced myself, lowering to the ground with enough time to ensure I'd be able to hold my weight up. My legs wobbled, and it took a moment to release my grip from the edge. Dizziness blurred my vision for a few seconds, and my head continued to pound.

You can do this. You have to. Before taking my first steps, I grabbed a drill from the metal tray. The fact that there even was a drill made me even more uneasy. Worries aside, even without electricity, I could use it as a weapon to puncture through the skin if the need arose.

My feet inched toward the door, and I saw a light

304

through the frosted window. It flickered and hummed. My back met the wall, and I took a moment to process everything. Unless this was Hell, I was confident they'd brought me back from the disease. I felt very much alive.

For the first time, I sat and listened to the message from the woman on the intercom. Was this the same place where they'd taken the people of Mill Six? Was it a research facility? Or, was the message a warning because something terrible had happened? There had been no one monitoring me or entering my room during the entire process of removing my IVs. It didn't sit right.

There was a chance Bastion had been placed in a room somewhere here too. If he were, I'd find him. We're together; a set. The reality still sat in my mind that there's always a chance for the worst. He might not have made it. I remembered the stories from the Faceless; they may have used Bastion to run experiments on. What if I found him, only to see he was no longer himself anymore? They were possibilities, but ones I would risk for a chance they'd saved him.

My fingers wrapped around the door handle. I stopped to listen. Aside from the flickering light on the other side of my room, the wretched woman's voice, and the distant siren, there was nothing else. It wasn't what one would expect from a hospital, research facility, or wherever the hell I was. There should be people moving about, talking or tending to patients.

Something to show there was life out there.

I pulled the door in, just enough to allow a sliver of sight. My breath stopped short, and I withdrew my fingers from the handle. A narrow hall stretched into darkness. Blood streaked along the floor. Handprints smudged across the walls.

You can't stay in here, I urged myself. After everything I'd assessed, I wasn't about to call out for help. It was like being back out in the forest. You didn't know who to trust. I was on my own until finding Bastion. *If* I'd ever find him.

DAY 11
PART 2

My hand met with the door, this time pushing it wide enough for my exit. The air in the hallway was chilling. The tile cold to the touch beneath my feet. Each step forward was slow and steady. I was mindful to my surroundings, listening for any hint of movement.

The first two rooms I came to were empty. Everything tidy and in its place. Undisturbed. I'd made it to the third room, still not a soul in sight. A quick listen. No voices. I pushed the door open.

"Oh my God," the words passed my lips, and I froze in place.

At the center of the room, a man was strapped to a metal table. Limb restraints held his arms and legs in place. His torso was split open like a butterfly fillet, and medical tools were still clamped to his organs. His jaw hung open. I saw that some of his teeth had broken from biting down on a rod that was strapped to his mouth. He must've been alive when they did this to him. *Why?* How could this have been going on without anyone ever knowing?

Warm breath hit the back of my neck. I stepped forward and spun around to face a set of teeth that snapped down where I had just stood. A nurse in blue scrubs with her hair pulled into a bun. Her left cheek was gone, her teeth exposed. She stepped toward me, arms extended. The full force of her body weight hit me, sending us both tumbling to the ground. She rolled to my side, snarling and grasping at my hospital gown.

Not again. Not this time. I shoved my fist as hard as possible into the nurse's breast. There was little space between us, but it was all the opportunity I needed to scurry upright. I grabbed the drill I'd dropped in the fall and moved across the room. The undead nurse was between me and the exit. There might be more of them just outside. If I didn't leave fast, I'd end up trapped. Misfortune seemed to follow me. A shadow that crept behind my every move. A darkness that I couldn't detach.

I thought about jumping over the nurse, but then I'd

risk her clawing at my skin. They'd brought me back, but there was no confirmation I was immune. She was getting up. Faster than expected. There went that option. I squeezed the drill, prepared to push the bit deep into her skull if she got too close. I was no longer afraid of the undead—I'd been one. But I was fearful of death, and fear is a great motivator to do incredible things.

The nurse was on her feet. Her wrist must've broken on the fall. A large bulge protruded just below the joint. It didn't seem to affect her at all. I knew all too well she didn't feel the pain. Just hunger. And the bitch was ready to feed.

My hand steadied on the drill. The nurse staggered toward me. Closer. Closer. My eyes burned from holding them open. And then, she turned. Without another concern for my presence, she buried her face into the open torso of the man on the table.

I didn't stay to watch her devour him, rest his soul, he'd bought me time, and for that I was grateful. My feet met with the cold hallway floor. I held the drill at ready in one hand, pulled the door shut with the other. It was clear. For now. If that damned intercom would just shut up, I could hear when anyone approached. Then again, it also had the benefit of concealing my movement from any of the staff. Though, I'm sure at that moment I was the least of their concerns. The nurse I'd encountered was gone to the disease. It made me wonder how long ago everything happened. How long

I'd been laying on that table. It couldn't have been for many days. The man she feasted on hadn't decomposed yet. And my drip bags still had fluids. Nothing made sense.

Door five. Another pause to listen. A steady, flat piercing noise, but otherwise no voices. I opened it enough to scan the room. Another body laying on a metal table. My hand pressed on the door, swinging it wide enough to allow passage. I stepped inside and looked to the person who laid in silence. My knees buckled, and I pushed against the wall to stop from hitting the floor. A moment to recompose.

"Bastion?" I whispered with relief in my tone.

My feet swept across the room to the table. It was him. My companion, my friend, my love. Days of bottled emotions rushed to the top, pouring from my soul. My eyes pooled, tears rolled down my cheeks. He looked so different, and yet still so familiar. My finger met his cheek. So soft, so warm. There was a slight stubble across his upper lip, but hardly noticeable. His hair fell just over his eyebrows. Dark and no longer matted with filth. His full lips rest without expression. I thought of his awkward smile. I rubbed my eyes against my gown. As the tears brushed away, I noticed the chart on the far wall.

**Patient: Bastion Grey, Age: 19, Under treatment
for Virus 071. Prep for organ harvest.**

"Bastion, please. It's me, Oshin," I said in desperation.

The steady noise continued screaming in my ears. A heart monitor with a wire that snuck beneath his hospital gown, to his chest. Flatline. *No* . . .

"I won't accept this Bastion. I won't. You can't be gone."

At that moment, the world around me fell silent. I threw my arms over Bastion's chest and buried my face against him. Heavy sobs with intermittent draws of deep breaths. I lifted my tear-stained face, bringing my forehead to his.

"We were supposed to make it through this together, stupid," I caught my breath through staggered words. "I did this. I brought you here. It's on me."

A sudden realization hit me. Bastion's body felt warm. The dead are cold to the touch. Movement startled me, and I looked up. Red flashing letters piqued my attention: Warning: Lead Wire Disconnected.

Another nudge from beneath my arms. Before I assessed the situation, a hand met the back of my head. I went to pull back, but it pushed me forward; firm, with fingers that gripped my hair. Bastion's lips met mine. Warm breath. His mouth parted, and he kissed me hard. Deep and passionate. A moment I hadn't realized I'd longed for. I wanted to give myself to him and embrace the feeling between us, but the shock of it all took me by such surprise I withdrew. My face twisted in confusion.

"But, what? Why? How?" I sputtered nonsense, unable to piece my words together.

"I'm sorry," he said, his voice deep and alluring.

I grazed a finger against my lips. My god, his eyes were beautiful. *Focus.* "No, I'm sorry. I thought you were dead," I paused, "Wait. If you aren't dead, then why in the hell didn't you say anything sooner?" I turned a cheek to wipe the remaining tears from the corners of my eyes.

"I'm sorry Oshin, it wasn't my intention. I woke up just before you got in here. The voice," he pointed to the ceiling, "I realized something was wrong. And then there's *that*." He gestured to the chart. "I was about to come to look for you when I heard something outside of my room. So, I pretended to still be out cold." He opened his left hand to reveal a scalpel. "I was waiting for the doctor to come in. Even when you called my name, I couldn't be sure at first. Hell, I had no idea what you'd sound like. But after I felt you, I knew." He moved his free hand to my cheek. "I don't have any idea what happened here, but I'm glad for it. I don't think either of us would have made it much longer otherwise. At least, I wouldn't have with the plans they had for me." His eyes shifted back to the chart. "We need to get out of here. If we can find a way out, maybe we can make it back to the woods. We'll tell the others what happened."

He leaned in once more, kissing my cheek. This time, I didn't pull away. My arms slid around to his back, holding him tight against my body.

"I'm so glad you're okay," I whispered into his ear.

"If death couldn't keep us apart, there's nothing while I'm alive that'll stop me from being with you," he replied. "We'd better get out of here though while we still can."

I nodded, disheartened that all of my hopes for us to live a happy life within the walls of my city had been shattered. The Faceless were right all along. There was a dark secret here. Maybe the Faceless would have another plan. A plan—the vial! My hand met the space against my chest. I knew it wouldn't be there, but the void where it'd once hung was a cold reminder. They must've declined the offer for a cure. Or took the sample to recreate it themselves. The doctor with the Faceless Ones said it was near impossible though. That it'd require more time and knowledge than anyone else here would have. But time might not have been a factor for them. Why give in to the request of rebels when it came at the cost of losing all of your test subjects. I should've known how stupid the idea was. But we were alive. Both of us. And as long as our hearts beat, we had a chance to get out of this mess.

Thoughts flashed to my mom and Sarah. If they didn't know about any of this, and my heart told me they didn't, then they might be in danger too.

Bastion had already removed his IVs and was standing

near the door, his arm extended and hand open, waiting for mine. I made a promise to myself that once we made it out, I'd warn my mom. I missed her so much.

Bastion stepped into the hall first. His scalpel, my drill. We were alert after I'd told him about my encounter with the nurse. Slow and steady steps down the hallway. The darkness closing in where lights had stopped working. A black hole without sight. We had to proceed. I grazed my knuckles along the wall to search for any doors. We'd opened a few to find more corpses or vacancies, but nothing to indicate an exit. Just ahead, a sliver of light. It came from a crack between blinds in a window. A small, red dot blinked just above a doorframe.

A camera. We're being watched, I thought.

"We need to keep moving," I whispered to Bastion.

We took each step with caution to avoid making any noise as we passed.

The sound of a desk drawer closing drew our attention. Footsteps. It moved closer to the door. Something heavy slid across the floor, and the handle turned.

Bastion pushed me against the wall and positioned his body in front of mine. He held the scalpel at his side with the blade pointing out.

The door creaked in, exposing a flood of light into the dark hallway.

"Are you sure?" A woman from inside questioned.

"You doubt I'd recognize her? Of course, I'm certain," a man's voice snapped back.

In the door, he stood. Thin, tall, in his early fifties. Brown hair, wire-framed glasses, white coat.

"What?" The word came out gritty and hoarse. I'd hardly recognized my voice.

The blood must've stopped circulating to my brain altogether because, at that moment, I thought I'd fall to the ground at any second. My head spun, and fingers quivered so badly that I dropped the drill. The breath left my mouth in rapid bursts. I gripped the back of Bastion's hospital gown, unsure if my legs would support my weight much longer. My lips trembled. I was staring death in the face.

". . .Dad?"

DAY 11
PART 3

They brought us into a break room. Food supplies and an area to cook. A woman over by the stove stared at me with dark eyes that looked as though she'd crawled up from the pits of Hell. I sat in an uncomfortable plastic chair, my elbows on a smooth, round table. The man sat across from me—my father, Max Fletcher.

"Sweetheart, I know this must come as a shock, but I need you to breathe and listen to me," he spoke in a calm and collected tone.

His hand reached to mine. I retracted and sat upright. Maybe I was in a state of shock, but I couldn't believe that this man was my dad. The person who had died when I was eight. The person who had left mom and me to fend for ourselves and live in near poverty. I'd grown up watching my mom slave hours away at the greenhouse, taking on side jobs in the market just to make ends meet and bring food to the table. That same mother who I'd caught crying on many occasions over her husband's passing. And yet, here he was. Older, gray in the hair, but very much alive.

"Are you . . . really my dad?" I looked up but deflected his stare.

You'd think discovering a parent wasn't dead would bring boundless joy to your heart, but this was far from how I felt. I was a spectrum of emotions, all woven and tangled.

"I am. It's me, Daddy," he replied as if things were the same as when he left.

"How?" It was the only word that came to mind.

"I never wanted to leave you, Sweetheart. I *had* to. But I've always thought about my little girl. One day, I'd planned to come to you. To let you see the truth. I'm so sorry." His hand reached out again, waiting at the center of the table for mine.

There was something that didn't sit right with me. This man, my father, lacked the emotion one would expect from a parent who's just reunited with their child after nine years apart. His demeanor seemed too calm. Maybe he was going through the same shock I did. So many emotions thrown at you all at once to where you can't separate them. Then again, he was a scientist here. A scientist in the place where I was scheduled for metamorphosis and Bastion's organs were to be harvested.

"How could you leave me in that room? And what were you planning to do with me?" I blurted before taking the time to weigh my words.

This situation wasn't close to warm and fuzzy. I was no longer the gullible girl I'd been. Trust wasn't given, it was earned. And this man, my father, had abandoned me. Now, years later, he left me in a room. He must have known I was in there.

"The room was secure. I'd never leave you in harm's way. As I'm sure you've seen, something terrible has happened. We've had an outbreak. And, my dear, you brought it here. Though, I'm sure you're aware of that," his fingers tapped the table as he spoke.

"You knew I had the disease when I came in. Why didn't your staff take better precautions? It's not like I snuck myself in here. They brought me back!" I was frustrated. How could he accuse me of everything happening? Shouldn't he be wrapping me in his arms and telling me how happy he is to see I'm okay?

"No, Sweetheart, the formula—the vial. It was clever,

though I'm not sure why you would collaborate with such terrorists. Nialus has always provided everything you've needed."

"What are you talking about?" I snapped back, irritated.

"Okay, we'll just say you had no idea you'd brought an active virus in with you. And that you were oblivious to the fact that once it opened, a well-thought chemical compound would combine, causing an airborne reaction." He tapped harder, thick sarcasm in his voice. "The pathogens infected my colleagues from the inside. By the time the results from testing the contents came back, it'd already spread inside their bodies. They'd interacted with others. We didn't realize it would enter the body through droplet transmission. When the contents in the vial combined, they never stood a chance. Anything before this that we've tested has required some form of physical contact. I've never seen anything like it. An evolution of the virus. More resilient with delayed symptoms and the ability to spread with only a sneeze. It took around sixteen hours before symptoms appeared. Fortunately for me, Ariella here was fast on her toes to administer a vaccination we'd had in trial. There's no guarantee, but we're still here. So that speaks for itself. Research at a price. It seems fortune has smiled on you though. Despite having one of our resident physicians in your presence, post-infection, you made it through. Your cells are fascinating." He retracted his hand

and rest on his elbow. "Whether you knew about it or not, the damage caused is catastrophic. Many lives were lost. And, here we are. Trapped until help arrives."

This wasn't the father I remembered. He was kind; loving. Bastion was leaning forward from across the room, giving us our space to reunite, but observing. He must've had the same unease I did. The dark-eyed woman in a white lab coat, who I assumed to be Ariella, had been at the counter stirring a drink for far longer than necessary. She'd never taken her eyes off of me. The whole room felt the tension in our conversation.

My father pinched the skin at the bridge of his nose. "Look, I'm sorry. I didn't mean to make accusations. I believe you didn't know about this."

Had the Faceless filled me with lies? Was there never a cure in the vial? Or, was my father a master manipulator? The answer might be *yes* to all three. While I had the opportunity, I needed to find out more about our circumstances.

"Then, why was I left in the medical room? And what about him?" I waved a hand toward Bastion.

Maybe I was opening a door I should've kept closed. Perhaps, playing ignorant would have bought me more time to find out what my father's intentions were. I had a hard time with words. Maybe that's why Bastion stuck around me before. Silence is golden, they say.

"It was just a precaution until help arrived. You were both going to be transported to safety once we had a full evacuation plan." He smiled. "You are far too important, Baby Bear."

Baby Bear. I hadn't been called that since I was a child. It was strange. Like talking to someone I'd never met. My father was a ghost in my heart, and the person before me was nothing like him, despite the attempts at nostalgia.

"I saw the chart in my room." I'd mustered the will to look him in the eye. There was no brushing things under the rug at this point. I wanted to make a statement.

"Ah, yes," he replied as though there was nothing wrong, a hint of excitement gleaming from behind the frame of his glasses. "Once we're settled and safe, I'll need your cooperation and trust. There're a few tests I'd like to run to ensure you're free from the virus. That's all the chart was to imply. Your safety is my top concern."

Oh, how I wanted to believe him. How I wanted to dash around the table and throw myself into his loving embrace. My Daddy. His Baby Bear. To catch up on time for every year we'd lost together. But, I couldn't. He'd left things out of his story. A puzzle with missing pieces would never be complete—and thus, was the same with our relationship. Incomplete. Broken.

"After this is at an end, we'll never have to be away

from each other again," my father added. "This is what I've been waiting for m-"

The sound of gunfire tore through his words.

My father stood at attention, he looked to Ariella. They nodded to one another, and she dropped the spoon against the counter. She hurried over to a white bag and dug around inside.

A bang on the door. Once. Twice. By the third strike, the door hung ajar. By the next, it swung open, the doorframe fractured. Three individuals entered without hesitation. The first person held a handgun in one hand, a small black case in the other. The people at her rear held blades. Each wore a gas mask and concealed their hands with gloves. I recognized them. Behind the concealment, it was Raven and The Faceless Ones.

"When is enough, enough?" Raven shouted from within the mask.

"What are you doing here? You weren't supposed to arrive with the delivery for another six months. And, who are they?" Dad had stepped forward. A serious tone in his voice.

"I know everything." Raven flung the case at my father.

It snapped open on impact with the floor, revealing an electronic device.

"It's over. I'm done doing this shit just because you're

my dad. You've held me prisoner for too long," Raven said. The gun rest in her shaking hand.

Wait. Hold on. Dad? It felt as though the air had been sucker punched from my gut.

"Yeah, that's right, Oshin. This is good ol' dad. The one I told you all about. Who would've thought he had another child? That I had a sister. I knew you looked familiar when we met. He'd been watching you for years. Want to tell her about it?" She steadied her grip and took a step forward, the barrel of the weapon threatening his existence.

"Let's not allow things to get out of hand. I can explain everything. There are valid reasons," Dad's voice wavered, and he shot a look toward Ariella.

I went to shout, to warn the others, but Ariella moved fast. She plunged a large syringe needle into the arm of one of the Faceless. He quivered and contorted, spasming his way to the floor. Her expression was twisted with the hellbent intention to kill. She lifted another syringe, needle readied to strike the other man.

This time, he was aware. Alert. I'd never seen anyone move so fast. It was like a dance, beautifully choreographed. His feet stepped in a perfect, circular formation. His blade readied at his side. With a single thrust, it pierced her belly. His hand pulled up, the blade with it. Within a matter of seconds, in the time I took to draw breath, he'd split Ariella up to her throat.

Through the commotion, Bastion had rushed to my side. He stood between my father and me.

I heard Raven's heavy breathing through her mask. "Last chance, Dad," her voice shook, but she maintained her stance. Finger at the trigger.

"Okay, okay. Raven, just put the gun down Sweetie," he held his hands at level with his face. When he realized that Raven wasn't about to give in to his request, he continued. "Yes, I have another daughter. Oshin is your younger sister, as you've discovered. By the current scenario, I assume you expect more insight as to why I never told you."

Silence.

"Right." Dad cleared his throat. "Oshin, I would ease you into this, but since we're clearly strapped for time, under the circumstances, I'll tell you." He looked at me. "I liked your mother, she was a good woman, but very naive. She never questioned any of the falsified tales I'd told, or even doubted my death. Truth be told, I never loved her the way she'd believed."

Never loved her? I had to control the urge to slap the shit out of him. I needed to hear what he had to say. He had a lot of nerve to speak that way about the woman who mourned his fake death for years.

"I needed her though," Dad continued. "She was

strong and healthy. Her ancestry lacked any fatal disease, and she was in her prime years, making her an ideal candidate for mating. Our combined genetics, our child, would be the perfect blend for a trial study I'd been working on. Nothing that would've hurt you. And, it wasn't as though the situation was a complete loss for her. When she discovered she was pregnant with you, she glowed like the stars. However, my calculations must've been off, because when the time came for her to give birth, it was a tragedy. You were born without breath. I couldn't understand how something like that happened. At first, I saw failure. But you were my child, and this was an opportunity to test something that had failed so many times before. I'd tried a variety of things in the past, using re-created variations of Ophiocordyceps fungi and parasites. But never the new concoction I'd completed. I'd built upon each previous failure to perfect my work. You were my first human subject with it. I'd tweaked things to allow for cell regeneration. To reboot the body's system while removing the ill effects I'd seen with previous studies using parasites. With you, there was a chance. I risked injecting you with the more evolved and modified version of Gen-twenty-seven-two. As I've said before, you're far too important to me. You were never meant to be alive. But I gave you that gift. I created something incredible. The ability to bring someone back without the disease.

"One hundred seventy-nine. That's who you really

are—it's your identity. The first case of success. I'd gone through a hundred and seventy-eight patients before you. All failures. All still dead, crazed, or part of the Phase Two program."

Phase Two . . . Ravangers. Failed experiments.

"I've watched you grow. Once you were a healthy child, I knew I could resume working here while keeping an eye on you at a distance. I needed a way out before your mother, or any other commoner drew suspicions about my intentions. You were my masterpiece. I was waiting until your eighteenth birthday when your body would have completed its growth. Your body would be matured, an adult.

"I'd never expected you to leave the city. I thought you far too wise for that. To my utter disappointment, you'd lost the tracer implant the first day. We found it in the undead's gut who'd bitten you. The stroke of ill luck left me discouraged, but I had a hunch you wouldn't stray too far from home."

I looked down at the skin graft near my ankle. Still healing, but otherwise free from any sign I'd been bitten.

My father uncrossed his legs and leaned into the table. "I sent a recovery team out to find you, but it proved fruitless. I'll admit that at first it fueled me with anger and resentment toward your actions. But you've returned, and that's what matters most. You're so special Oshin. Which is why I need you. You're destined to become something extravagant. My finest accomplishment and a milestone in scientific history. You'll be the first Phase Three. A human that's capable of incredible feats. Someone worthy of executing tasks that no normal man could dare try. Then, we can be together again. You can have your daddy back."

I was speechless. Floored. How does one respond to finding out they were only another experiment to their father? A lab rat who shouldn't have been alive to begin with. I wasn't sure if I'd be able to unravel the reasons he was that way. A cold and calculated human being with no love in his heart for his wife or child. Selfish intentions and evil desires. The person I remembered as my dad was an illusion, someone shrouded in a facade. The man before me, well, I hated him.

He reached out to touch my knee. I pushed back with the ball of my feet, the chair beneath me sliding to distance us.

"Don't you see all that our lab has done for Nialus? We have no fame or glory. Commoners live each day unaware of all we risk to ensure the city's safety. The Phase Twos, the experiments, the endless hours we work. All to ensure we live without threat," Dad said.

"The ravangers—phase two's, they're a huge threat. People out there are suffering because of you. You don't give a crap about life. You care about your own accomplishments," I spat out, shaking from the anger that swelled within me.

"A necessary sacrifice!" My dad's voice rose. "We don't have any idea what happened to other parts of the world. There could be unimaginable horrors beyond our territory. Years ago, we would send teams out to research beyond our area. They never returned. What we do keeps the land beyond our city from an unexpected attack. The diseased are our first line of defense. A lesser threat than what might be out there. We know how to kill the undead. What we don't know is what's out there after we lost communication so many decades ago. The disease started as a catastrophic phenomenon. But we've used it to our advantage. I will sacrifice anyone on the other side of these walls to make sure it stays that way. The success of this city is my life's work. Don't you see? We're not all equal—just as it should be. The people out there, they're disposable. Flesh for a higher purpose.

"Therefore, metamorphosis is essential. You must allow me to complete the process. You would evolve into something wondrous. The first Phase Three; a person who extends beyond humanity. You wouldn't have to worry about difficult decisions or bear moral concern. I'll reconstruct your brain pathways, and maintain control over some aspects of your function. Don't you see? We would be a team. Me at the helm of decisions and you executing tasks to protect Nialus. We'd be an unstoppable force."

"You're a piece of shit," Raven said, taking a step forward.

I'd almost forgotten about my gun-wielding sister during my father's speech. Sister. The word ran through my mind. Family.

"You left something else out," I said to him, no longer taking caution with my words in fear of disrupting our reunion. "If Raven is older than me, then why was she never around? How did I go through seventeen years with no knowledge of her existence? And, the bunker. How could you do that to her?" I felt a sudden need to defend her. My sister. She wasn't perfect, but she'd been hurt as bad—if not, worse—by this man.

"The case, *Dad*," Raven didn't wait for his reply. She had her own questions. "The tablet had everything. Your logs, your journal, your lies. You told me that mom died from childbirth. That she'd passed away after labor."

I knew by the way her breath stuttered that she was crying.

"False information," she added. The gun fired twice with a deafening pop. The first bullet ricocheted off the floor and landed somewhere in the kitchen area, the other drove through our father's foot.

He howled in pain, falling back into the chair. "Dammit, child! What have you done? Without me, you'll have nowhere to go, no way to survive. I'll give you a final chance to put the damned gun down and talk this through.

The evacuation team will be here soon. None of you are going anywhere without me."

"What happened to Mom?" Raven aimed the barrel at his leg. "I want to hear the truth from your mouth. This isn't a request. The evac team can move your cold corpse from here for all I care."

"Fine. You were the last one I thought to betray me. But, so be it, I'll tell you what happened. I want you to understand that I had a good reason for my actions," Dad spoke through his teeth and adjusted his foot to an elevated position. "As you know, your mother, Kathleen, worked alongside me for years. She had volunteered to test an experimental treatment we'd worked on. Before the treatment's completion, we were alone in the office one night. Certain *tensions* rose, and we ended up sleeping together. This happened on multiple occasions. Mind you, I was married to Oshin's mother at the time as I'd already planned to have a child with her. I get that this doesn't shine any favor my way, and under any other circumstances, I'd approach it more subtlety. But you've seen things I can no longer conceal. Please, just put the gun down now."

"*What* did you do to my mother," Raven pushed.

She wasn't asking. She already knew the truth. But she needed to hear it straight from the piece of crap. It was her way of getting closure. Though every word he spoke made me loathe him more.

"Kathleen discovered she was with child. Our child. I couldn't have that kind of reputation. I'm a revered scientist who was married and wasn't about to give up on my work. There were plans in the making. I . . ." his voice drifted.

Raven closed more space between them. Two hands on the gun's grip.

"No! Let me finish." Dad held his arms up, his fingers spread wide. "As her pregnancy drew near the nine-month mark, Kathleen gave me an ultimatum. She told me that once our baby came, I needed to end things with Oshin's mother or she'd bring the truth forward. She didn't want to raise you alone, or in secret. That wasn't an option for me. I'd invested too much already into finding an ideal mate. Your mother didn't have the genetic qualities I was looking for. You wouldn't have been compatible with my goals. So, I led her to believe that I'd go along with her plan once you were born. The day after she gave birth, she was willing to continue forward with the treatment we'd planned. She was dedicated, I'll say that much.

"Instead of the experimental serum, I injected her with poison. I assure you she passed quickly and with minimal pain. Then, there was still the issue of you to work around. The last thing I needed was a child to care for while working in the lab. But, regardless of how things came to be, you were still mine. So, I made sure you'd be taken care of. I set you up with a place of your own when you were able, assigned

331

someone to take the role as your father, and gave you jobs to ensure you were a useful asset. It was all going as planned; our secret had died with her. Well, until today," he smirked, lacking any form of empathy after all he'd done.

The next shot fired so fast, so loud that I had to cup my ears to dull the ringing.

Dad had fallen out of the chair and onto the ground. He hugged his leg, tucked up against his chest. Blood oozed from an opening in his shin. His khaki-colored pants soaking up the deep red color.

"We're done here," Raven said, her voice flat. "Oshin, it's time to go. There's no evacuation team coming for him."

I nodded. Even if there was help on the way, I couldn't stomach being in his presence any longer. Hell, I just might've finished him myself.

A low, hissing growl came from behind. Standing in the doorway, an undead man. White lab coat saturated in blood from several bullet holes. Whoever had attempted to kill this man had the world's worst aim. Not one shot to the head. They knew better. But I suppose in a state of panic, and with lack of weapon training, it's possible to miss the target. For scientists with the highest intellect in Nialus, you'd think learning to handle a gun would've been top of the list considering they worked with the undead. Dumbasses.

The Faceless readied his weapon as the undead

staggered into the room.

"Wait!" Raven called out. "Leave it be."

The Faceless nodded, and they moved to the side.

For a moment, the undead white coat sniffed the air in all directions. So much variety. But Dad was easy prey.

Bastion gripped my wrist and tugged me to where Raven stood. I tipped my chin, ready to depart.

Dad threw his arm into the air, reaching out at us as we passed. "Stop, please! Oshin, Raven, have some sense. It's me, your father. Together we can accomplish great things! You can't leave me like this, I'll die."

Just before reaching the busted doorframe, I turned to face him. An intense, hard stare I hoped haunted him until his last breath.

"You've been dead to me for years, *Dad*."

His screams echoed down the dark hallway as we left.

DAY 11
PART 4

We emerged into the open air. Bastion and I had been in a lab base buried beneath the surface. It was just beyond the central district of town, hidden from sight. All of these years, I'd never known it existed. Right beneath our feet, deceit, torture, corruption. Down there, they had everything they needed to survive. To remain in concealment, their experiments unknown to civilians. Raven informed me that there was another entrance into the lab from just beyond the walls. Camouflaged to the naked eye. She'd been there many times before though, running errands for our father.

We'd both been used. Two children, each with a different purpose. One, an experiment. The other, a pawn. Neither truly loved. But unlike Raven, I had a home. I had a mother.

Mom. I needed to get to her as soon as possible. To let her see that I was okay. Whether I'd tell her the full story about dad was undecided. But she needed to at least know about Raven. I had no doubt in my mind she'd take Raven in as her own. Sure, Mom had her moments, but she was one of the gentlest souls I'd ever met. Kind and caring. She always put others before herself. And yet, it made her happy.

I looked around but saw no one. We needed to be cautious. White coats worked under the authority of Sheriff Banner. I knew there was a good reason I'd never trusted the bastard. The mayor might be in on it all too. We all obeyed anything Sheriff Banner said. He'd somehow weaseled his way into having ultimate control over what went on within our walls. The mayor had always seemed to be a nice fellow, but was about six shy of a dozen. Had the brains of a house plant. His father had been the previous mayor, so when it came time for elections, he knew all the right things to say. Rehearsed scripts he'd been told to recite time again. Not a soul ran against him. Even Banner cheered him on. But why wouldn't he? He had the mayor wrapped around his pinky.

Things were quiet. *Too quiet.* There were always

people coming or going from jobs.

Raven slung the strap from her backpack off and rummaged around inside.

"Here. It's all I could grab with enough time to make it in to rescue you. But it'll cover your asses from hanging out the backside of your gowns." She handed Bastion and me a lab coat.

"Thanks," I said, appreciative for what she'd done. "I need to find my mom. She has to see that I'm alive."

Raven nodded. "We'll take you to her, just show us the way. Dad never allowed me into the city, aside from the lab. So, I'll rely on your guidance this time. I wouldn't recommend sticking around though if I were you. What we just did . . . It won't go unnoticed. They'll look for answers. A girl who returns from the dead at the same time tragedy strikes won't sit well in your favor. You'll be putting your mom in danger too. We don't have long before dark. Say what you need to, then, we'll need to go."

"What *we* just did?" I snapped back as I pushed my arm through the coat sleeve. "I had no idea this would happen. That *doctor* said it was a cure. That we would negotiate peace, not launch a full-on terrorist attack!"

"He lied. I know. But you have to understand the reasoning behind it. These people were beyond negotiations. They've terrorized anyone and everyone outside of these walls. I've seen it with my own eyes. I've been a part of it. Things had to be set right, or it would never end. It's been decades of torture, decades of death for their experiments. They've unleashed monsters, unlike anything out there before. Phase Twos, faster than the undead with a hunger twice as big. They've made the world unsafe not only from the diseased but from the living. We had an opportunity to end it. And I knew that you might not go along with the plan if you were aware. The doctor remembered who you were. He was aware of all that dad had done. Some died, yes, but you don't understand how many more you've saved."

My eyes dropped to the ground. I saw the truth in Raven's words, but because of what they did, I bore the weight of mountains on my shoulders. I'd killed so many people. In the back of my mind, I understood that it wasn't solely my fault. Raven was right, if I had known, I might've declined. Thinking back, I'm not sure how I would've handled such a burden. But it was done. Maybe the people of Nialus would sleep a little safer without horrors happening beneath their feet. The people beyond our walls would. The cost of peace.

I said nothing to Raven and began my approach toward home.

We rounded one of the white coats office headquarters and began our cross through the market. An eerie silence surrounded us. Not a soul in sight. The booths looked ravaged. Wilted vegetables sprawled on the ground; meat torn from the hanging hooks of the butchers.

"Stop," Raven spoke through her mask, her raspy breaths slowing. "There's someone over there."

At first, I saw no one. Then, a shadow drifted behind a stack of boxes. On the opposite side of the market, just beyond the seamstress stall were people standing in a tight cluster. I wondered if the town had gathered in alert for what we'd just done to the underground lab. Word spread fast in Nialus.

Two people in gas masks and two wearing lab coats in hospital gowns wouldn't make for an unsuspicious entrance. But I needed to know what was going on. We crept low, circling around to get a better view. We couldn't have been more than fifteen feet away when the bodies turned. Pallid skin, hazy eyes, and teeth that snapped at our scent.

"Run," I commanded in a sharp whisper. "Run!" I took Bastion by the arm and pushed off.

The gathering of undead were pushing over one another in our direction. Dozens, possibly more than a hundred emerged from every side entrance and from behind the shops. At our backs, the market became eclipsed with the diseased. They continued to pour in from every alley and nearby building.

"There," I pointed to a home at our right.

I gripped the handle, relieved to find it unlocked. We rushed inside and slammed the door shut with a click. It wouldn't hold for long, but it'd give us a minute to catch our breath and come up with a plan. Raven closed the blinds and pushed a nearby armchair against the door. Bastion made his way to the kitchen, taking a knife into possession.

"What the hell happened? I thought we only infected the lab bunker?" Bastion spoke up, shaken by what we'd encountered.

"I-I don't know, I'm sorry! It was only supposed to spread through the lab. The doctor must've not realized how long it'd be before the effects of the disease would show. Not everyone in the lab was like Dad. Some had families they went home to each night. I think they were already carrying the virus and didn't realize it when they came into the city. It was designed to spread fast, and by the look of things, that's just what happened. But people didn't find out until it was too late." Raven gripped my shoulder and pulled me to face her. "Oshin, you have to believe that I didn't know this would happen."

"Nor did I," The Faceless man who had been silent until this moment, spoke. "We've long been rivals with the scientists and shadow guards of your city, but we understood many were innocent. People who lived without knowledge of what went on. The doctor wanted to restore peace. He didn't want so much carnage. Please accept my most sincere apologies." He fell to a knee with his blade drawn before him. "I will do all I can to right this tragedy."

How does one even respond to that? I couldn't excuse all that had happened. Neither of my two companions intended this, but my entire world had crumbled. My home destroyed. All I wanted was to reach my mom and get her to safety. There'd be time to process my thoughts on the whole situation later.

Heavy banging on the door shook our already heightened nerves. Through the blinds, silhouettes of the undead in the masses stood. Their hands clapping against the fragile barrier of glass.

"We can't stay here any longer," I told the others. "They'll get in soon, and the last thing we need is to find ourselves trapped and barricaded upstairs. The back window is our best bet. We can slip out and into the back alley. My house is two districts down."

The others nodded in agreement. Bastion slipped the knife into his coat pocket and gripped the window. He raised the glass, pausing every couple of seconds to listen for movement in the back alley.

We weren't alone.

Thud.

Something heavy against wood. Close.

Thud.

There it was again. Closer.

The hissing of hunger. Another series of heavy steps. I looked up to see a woman near the top of the stairs. Her beige dress with embroidered music notes flowing from curvy hips. Mrs. Katz, one of the elementary teachers. Her eyes had already become tainted with dust and airborne particles. Now grayed over and soulless. Sunken cheeks took the place of a once plump smile. She was gone to the disease.

At the sight of us, Mrs. Katz increased her pace. She staggered down another step before losing her footing. Her body tumbled down the stairs, bones crunching as she reached near the bottom. A moment of silence before she twitched. Her arm reached out, hand clawing down against the wood floor to lift herself upright. Her head bobbed at the side, neck broken.

"Go, go!" I pushed Raven toward the window. Mrs. Katz at my heels.

No sooner had I turned to run, Bastion leaped between my former teacher and me. He pulled the kitchen knife from his pocket, placed an outstretched arm against her chest, and buried the blade into her skull.

Her knees slammed against the ground, her torso toppling to the side. No further movement.

Rest in peace. I'm so sorry . . .

I took one last glance over a shoulder before I climbed out of the window.

DAY 11
PART 5

The back alley was deserted for as far as I could see. We made haste across the city, toward the gray district. With every step closer, my worry grew. We hadn't encountered a single living person. The virus had plagued Nialus. Mom was clever though, and I had faith she'd barricaded the house and hid. There weren't many people in close quarters at the greenhouse. She often worked in solitude while tending to the plants. There was still hope she'd avoided contact. Still a chance she'd never come across someone who'd been infected.

Just ahead, I saw the backside of my home. Brown, like the others nearby, but with a bright yellow plastic sun in my bedroom window. It was a decoration I'd had since I was a baby. Mom had bought it in the market, and over the years I'd grown attached to the thing. It lifted my spirits, even during the worst of storms. Right then, it left a lump in my throat. I thought about my mom singing *You Are My Sunshine* at bedtime when I was younger. I wanted to hear her voice again.

"Hey," Raven whispered and extended an arm out to block my path. "I just saw somethin' move up ahead. It went between the houses, and moved pretty fast."

Given there were only about two feet of space between each home, I couldn't see it being a large person. They'd moved so fast that by the time we'd stepped forward to look, they were gone. Maybe it was a survivor. The sun was descending, but not enough for the ravangers to come out. And even if it was night, unless the walls had fallen, there was no way they'd get in. I wondered if Dad's one hundred and seventy-eight failures were the only ravangers. Or, if there were more out there. With all the testing and experiments they'd done over the years, it wouldn't surprise me if there were mutations that stretched beyond our imagination. What if the thing Raven saw was one of them?

We closed in on my house, my eyes sharp and mind alert. Now that we were here, my anxiety soared. This was the moment I'd longed for. To be home. To see mom again. But what if things weren't as I'd hoped? No. I wouldn't allow my fear of the unknown to stop me from reaching her. There was no turning back.

Bastion and I exchanged a nod. He pressed his fingers against the window and pushed up. It wouldn't budge. Locked from the inside. I remembered mom hammering two fat nails above the bottom window panel. She'd told me it'd help keep the window sealed tighter in the winter months. We could break it, but it might draw attention.

"Wait here," Bastion said as he slipped between the houses. He had to walk sideways to maintain speed and stealth through the narrow gap.

We watched as he peered out. Looked each way, then disappeared from sight. Before my heart had time to give out on me from worry, he reappeared and crept back to where we stood.

His voice dropped to a hushed whisper. "There's around five of them to our right, near the porch with the rocking chair."

"Mr. Peprin. He was one of the oldest in our district. When he wasn't rocking in his chair, greeting the neighbors, he was walking the market with a smile. I doubt he made it through this," I replied, my heart filled with sorrow.

"I know you're hurting. Trust me, I know. But we need

to get to your mom, and this may be our last chance before the roamers realize we're here. We haven't even come up with a plan on getting the hell out of here." Bastion's hand rest on my shoulder. "If we hurry, we can make it inside your house before they catch the direction of our scent. Just be quiet and don't draw attention. I checked the door, and it's unlocked. I opened it enough to see there's no barricade. Now, let's go get your mom."

No barricade. My eyes burned from not closing them for so long. I rubbed my lids, hands shaking. There was still a chance she'd moved upstairs. Deep breath. Time to move.

We hurried to the front door. The group of undead swaying, walking without purpose down the path. A creak from the wood of my front porch made us freeze in place. The undead tipped their noses to the sky. Their bodies turning.

"Get in!" Raven said in a sharp whisper.

We poured in through the front door, then closed it as gently as possible.

With my hands on my knees, I took a second to catch my breath. I wasn't all that winded; it was the deep gutted worry that made it hard to move. A scrambled mess of emotions that weighed me down.

Glass shattered nearby, rattling the silence. The sound set me upright and stiff. It came from the kitchen.

The Faceless stood at my side, readied for a potential

ambush. We moved past our small dining table, a dirty plate left in mom's usual spot. The kitchen came to view, a woman with her back to us, hunched over.

"Oh my God, Mom." My heart soared higher than birds in the sky. "Mom, I'm back! It's Oshin!"

I'd gotten two steps forward before my peripheral vision caught sight of a dark object rushing at me. We hit the floor before anyone realized what was happening. The Faceless drew his sword to our intruder's neck.

"Oshin, I knew it was you," the voice was so familiar.

I turned my cheek to see golden locks pulled back into a bun. Deep blue eyes and black-rimmed glasses that had fallen askew on the bridge of her nose.

"Sarah?"

The Faceless One retracted his weapon on the realization that she wasn't a threat.

She buried her face against me, her eyes welling with tears. "I knew you weren't dead! I told them all, but no one believed me. Your mom held onto hope, but I could tell she'd feared the worst. I can't believe you made it back."

An anchor of guilt had been tossed into my belly. My concern had been with one goal in mind. Reaching mom. I hadn't even considered how Sarah got by in this mess. And yet again, I took the role of a terrible best friend as I rolled her off of me.

"I'm so glad you're okay, Sarah, but Mom . . ." I looked over to see she remained in the same position. The far end of the kitchen, hunched over.

"Oshin, no," Sarah said as she moved in my line of sight. Tears ran like streams down her cheeks, dripping from her chin. Her arms outstretched and she pulled me into a hard embrace. "Don't look," she whispered.

"What are you talking about?" I stepped to the side, Sarah's arms still strapped over my shoulders.

Then, I heard it. The light tapping of teeth, the sharp, raspy breath.

"Mom?" I broke free and hurried to where she stood. She wore her favorite pink pajamas.

My hand didn't reach her back before her shoulders twisted, fingers grasping in my direction. Holding her in place, the pole from our clothesline had penetrated her torso. At the sight of me, her body turned, the pole tearing at her gut.

I couldn't see straight. The world dulled and everything around me became a blur. My limbs felt numb, and I thought I might throw up.

"Mom, it's me," my lip quivered at my hushed words.

Her cold fingers wrapped around my wrist, pulling me in. Jaw snapping.

Just take me. Take me. I brought this here. My actions led to Mom's death. A shooting pain spread across my chest. Every breath burned. My energy was depleted. I didn't know how to cope with this. Saying I was devastated would be an understatement. I closed my eyes and envisioned my mom's smile. Her arms rocking me, and soothing voice calming me on the worst of days. Her soft kisses when I'd skin my knee.

I love you so much, Mom.

My body inched closer to her. Step by step. I was ready to go. My friends would be okay. They'd find a way out. This was my home, and I belonged here with her.

Two hands clamped down on my biceps. My body was forced back, away from Mom. Away from her touch. Bastion stood between us, Sarah at his side.

"No. No!" I screamed, my mind no longer rational. No longer aware of our surrounding dangers. I'd become one of those stupid characters you read about and just want to slap the crap out of. But I didn't care. My sorrow consumed me. My heart crumbled to ash.

"Don't let her see," Sarah said to Bastion.

He nodded and pulled me in, cradling my head. My arms thrashed. He took it.

"Let me go!" I pleaded.

The sound of a blade penetrating flesh shot through me like a bullet. I pinched my eyes shut. I lost it. Heavy sobs, tears that soaked Bastion's coat. My world fell. I heard her body hit the floor. It was over. Mom was gone.

DAY 11
PART 6

The door flung inward. Bodies toppling over one another to get inside. I'd been too loud and drew them to us. In one, swift motion, Bastion lifted me up and ran to the back window.

Raven nodded and used her backpack to shatter the glass. No time for playing it safe. She punched out all of the large shards and slipped through.

"Come on!" she called to us.

Bastion passed me through like a rag doll. Raven holding me steady as I met the other side. The others followed, inches from being torn apart.

The undead had our scent. They flung their bodies through the window, landing in a crumpled heap on the ground. It wouldn't be long before they were back up on two feet. Mom was dead, my heart broken to dust. But my friends were still here. My sister. My love. I was grieving worse than words could describe, but I had to snap out of the helpless mentality that almost got us all killed. Emotional pains still seared through me, and my breath stuttered to the point of it being difficult to move. But I mustered the strength—for them.

Sarah said she knew the way out, that there was a bunker just outside of the city where survivors gathered. She told us that there were still many who never showed symptoms. Not yet anyway. The majority were civilians and a handful of guards. No one who held higher authority had arrived. Sarah had seen the sheriff on her first run to search for survivors. The pieces of him. His throat had been chewed straight through to his spine. What goes around comes around. The mayor was still missing, presumed dead. There was no doubt in my mind they'd been part of the corruption. As for Sarah, both of her parents had made it out without falling ill. Time would tell if the virus would die out with the poor souls who'd already fallen victim.

As usual, Sarah talked too much. But I was grateful for the distraction.

We approached the north wall. No guards. Undead

trailing behind, their feet shuffling forward at a steady pace. Just in front of our exit, someone was on their knees. They paid no attention to us, their focus on what was on the ground before them.

I recognized the shirt. White with brown stripes on the sleeves, the surname Coen embroidered on the back. *Codah.* His face lowered, stuttered growls filling the air as he dug into something on the grass. We needed to pass him to make it to the outside.

"Your blade," I held my hand before the Faceless. "Please. These are my people, let me have this."

He paused a moment, looking behind us to ensure we still maintained a distance from the horde before unsheathing it.

I'd been through hell. I lost my mom, the center of my universe. Sorrow crippled me. Through it all, I'd almost gotten my friends killed from my moment of weakness. But I wouldn't allow them to die. All the blood, sweat, and tears from my mom were to raise me strong. To ensure I'd live the best life I could. Who was I to deny her of that by wanting to take my life? I'd been so selfish. Through the pain, a phoenix was reborn, rising from the ash of despair.

As I approached Codah, I saw that his attention was on a body, chewed open at the belly. Blonde wavy hair fanned out across the grass.

Oh, Bethany, you foolish girl. A cold and cruel thought passed my mind: *Karma is a bitch.*

I raised the blade with both hands, fingers wrapped around the grip. "'Till death do you part." I buried the steel deep into his skull. His face falling into the heap of chewed intestines.

We left before the group of undead reached us. With a final glance behind us, I made a promise to my mom. To all of the others who didn't deserve the fate that'd befallen Nialus. When the time was right, I'd return. We'd reclaim the city, restore hope for humanity. This time, in peace. Somehow, I'd make things right.

A tear fell from the corner of my eye as I said goodbye to those who we'd lost.

We were alive. We'd made it.

EPILOGUE
2 YEARS LATER

During the first year after Nialus fell, the survivors regrouped. More fell to the disease, and we had to take shifts to monitor symptoms. If anyone looked to come down with sickness, we quarantined them. Those who we confirmed beyond saving were killed and burned. We had to wait it out— let the disease run its course. It was a difficult time—one I'd helped cause. But the doctor was right about one thing—we became unified through the trials we faced. The bunker gave us what we needed to recover, but we knew that it'd only sustain us for so long. Nialus was our home. Through the course of many months, we fought against the infestation that had claimed our city. Killing our friends and loved ones a

354

second time took its toll on many. But we persevered. We stood strong, despite the emotional and physical hardships. We worked together, in unison for a cause.

I thought about my mom often. They say that time heals wounds, but it never really does. It dulls the pain, numbs it at times. But there are moments when I'm alone, and her memory cuts me from the inside. I still miss her so much.

Bastion and I had to support one another through the difficult times. He'd often wake from nightmares, calling out to Lace. I know he still blames himself for what happened to her. But we made it through, filling the emptiness with love.

At the end of the first year, we'd taken back what was ours. We quarantined, cleaned, and rebuilt. Nialus is now a place of peace; a sanctuary. The children from the mills gained entry into the promised city. A real home. A place to grow old with your family. The Faceless killed the remaining dark guard regiment at each mill. It sounds heartless, but there was no salvation left in their blackened hearts. In time, the Faceless Ones moved out of the caves and joined us. Sarah met a young man from their group and after the first month, they'd become inseparable. Her fascination with the undead led her to a career in the lab. I'd never seen her happier. She deserved it all.

I still didn't trust the doctor, but we needed him. The white coats had fallen, and he'd agreed to teach some of the bright young minds all he knew. A new generation of scientists, this time, with the best interest of humanity in mind. No more cruel experiments or hidden secrets. Raven led the city's law enforcement. Her knowledge of the outside crossed with her witty and strong-willed personality made for a perfect fit. The people respected her, and she was dedicated to keeping our city safe.

We understood there were dangers beyond our walls. Both living and undead. But together, we'd withstand the trials to come.

Some say we begin to die from the moment we're born. For me, I was dead from the start, and again at seventeen. I'd grown to appreciate being here to draw breath. To see the surrounding beauty. How precious and fragile it was. My father was a cruel man, but he'd given me life. I didn't look at myself as someone who was dying a little more each day. I was very much alive, and I savored every minute. Throughout my time in this world, I'd atone for all the destruction I'd played a role in. We'd come a long way, but there's always work to do.

Here we are, two years later. Those who have endured, those who have lost, those who have grown to love again. The human race.

As I stared up at the passing clouds, I couldn't help but reminisce on everything I'd been through. Bastion sat at my side, his fingers tracing from my forehead into my hair. We had a house together, and I fell a little more in love with him each day. We'd pushed each other to get through the hardest times in our lives and came out stronger than ever. He was my breath, and I was his heart. Bastion placed his right hand on my left, playing with the band on my ring finger. We were a family. And one day, we'd plan for a child. A child who would thrive in a better world than we'd known. A child who I'd one day tell the story about how I met their father. A story about the day I died.

THE END

To discover more books in the

Apocalypse Cycle, visit: www.AyaKnight.com

Aya Knight is the bestselling author of
The Chronicles of Kale series.

For more information, visit: www.AyaKnight.com

Join Aya on social media:
Facebook: facebook.com/AyaKnight
Twitter: @AyaKnight
Instagram: @authorayaknight

www.ingramcontent.com/pod-product-compliance
Lightning Source LLC
Chambersburg PA
CBHW020241200626
46816CB00001BA/69